GETTING OLD WILL HAUNT YOU

GETTING OLD WILL HAUNT YOU

Rita Lakin

Severn House

This first world edition published 2018
in Great Britain and 2019 in the USA by
SEVERN HOUSE PUBLISHERS LTD of
Eardley House, 4 Uxbridge Street, London W8 7SY.
Trade paperback edition first published
in Great Britain and the USA 2019 by
SEVERN HOUSE PUBLISHERS LTD.

British Library Cataloguing in Publication Data
A CIP catalogue record for this title is available from the British Library.

ISBN-13: 978-0-7278-8856-3 (cased)
ISBN-13: 978-1-84751-980-1 (trade paper)
ISBN-13: 978-1-4483-0188-1 (e-book)

This is a work of fiction. Names, characters, places and incidents
are either the product of the author's imagination or are used fictitiously.
Except where actual historical events and characters are being described
for the storyline of this novel, all situations in this publication are
fictitious and any resemblance to actual persons, living or dead,
business establishments, events or locales is purely coincidental.

All Severn House titles are printed on acid-free paper.

Severn House Publishers support the Forest Stewardship Council™ [FSC™],
the leading international forest certification organisation. All our titles that
are printed on FSC certified paper carry the FSC logo.

Typeset by Palimpsest Book Production Ltd.,
Falkirk, Stirlingshire, Scotland.
Printed and bound in Great Britain by
TJ International, Padstow, Cornwall.

In memory of the real Gladdy Golds (Gladdy, Evvie and Ida)
Gladys, Ann and Rose, the Banoff girls

ACKNOWLEDGEMENTS

Apologies to the police departments in Key West. There is no Barbara, Gregg or Bud. Fiction characters, fiction.

And thanks to the people at Severn House: Kate, Sara, Carl, Natasha and all the others who are so kind to my books.

And of course, all the fans who are still with me. Thanks again.

PROLOGUE
Death by Marlin. Fish is Winner

R obert Strand, age sixty-one, of Key West, enjoying another fabulous day of fishing on the Gulf of Mexico, always used to say, 'If I gotta die, I wanna die fishing.' Yes, Robert, your wish is about to come true, but with a slight revision – you are going to die *with* the fishes.

Robert is wearing his lucky baseball cap. Even though the white stitching across its top – *The Miami Marlins* – was unraveling. Ditto, his beat-up old sweatshirt with its famous slogan, *I love you, Miami*. His boat is named *Marlin Honey*. That makes it a triple threat – a sure thing. He knows today is going to be his big day, fish-wise.

He leans back, happy with himself. He'd rather fish than do anything else in the whole wide world, with his smokes and an ice-filled bucket of beer cans at his side.

If he ever let himself think about it, and he rarely did, he was a failure as a husband; ask his two ex-wives and they'll sing the same old refrain. Robert is lazy. Sluggish for a lawyer. By now he should have been a judge at least. But instead, when he rarely put his nose to the grindstone, he spent precious time on helping old people. Old, as well as poor. No billable hours in that bunch. King of Pro Bono, they called him behind his back, and not meant as a compliment. He heard it moaned about in both marriages. His legal partners despaired of him, as well.

He was unlike his dear, departed father, the former first partner in his firm. The father was a hotshot, and when he brought his son in, all expected junior to be equally sizzling. Sonny-boy was a bitter disappointment to one and all.

He'd rather fish than work.

Even marital sex was over-rated. What could beat the passion and the thrill of fighting a giant Tarpon or Cobia, or Grouper; the sea was a treasure trove of choices for him. Get one on your line and sometimes it took hours on end, pulling, thrashing, sweating, feeling every muscle, every movement of the body and mind at one with that undersea partner, evenly matched and evenly excited, building up to the climax. Then the awesome release when the fighter was caught and in the boat! Now, that's what you call an orgasm! He giggled; and what one desired after that gratification, was a cigarette and a beer.

He feels a tickle on his line. Shoulders back, arms thrusting out; on instant alert. Something big, feeling like it's a blue, toying with his bait. Easy does it, boy. Take your time old spiky, old blue, sniff it, play with it, twirl yourself around it. Swim away. Swim close. Do your usual dance. Come back because you want it. Crave it. I'm not rushing you. Soon you'll be mine. Make my day!

Robert's only fear was that there might be a shark nearby with the same goal in mind. He has to chuckle. If anyone ever asked him to name someone with whom he'd like to go fishing – anyone, anywhere, past or present – he'd give his one and only perfect answer. He'd want to fish with that great writer, the world-famous sportsman, one of the most important former residents of Key West, Ernest Hemingway.

That amazing guy would bring a machine gun onto his probably 60,000 buck yacht and shoot any shark that dared go near his catch. Rat-a-tat-tat and bye-bye shark. A machine gun! That's a real man's idea of fishing!

Wow! It's happening – a real hit! Killer fish took the bait and it's gonna be gigantic! As Robert excitedly reels him in, fighting all the way, he thinks of the thousands of hours he and his buddies spent in the hot sun and turbulent sea. It's finally paid off. To his amazement, and thrill, the largest blue marlin of his life has pulled on his line. The wondrous blue marlin, among the largest, fastest, most recognizable fish in the world is seconds away from being his. The squid bait had worked!

His big chance has arrived at last. What Robert has waited thirty years of fishing for – the Florida competition with its winning trophy for landing the biggest fish of the year! With one hand clutching his fishing rod with all his strength, the other hand clicked a selfie photo on his iPhone. His proof for posterity.

He captures on his camera a gloriously happy face and the monster marlin's beady eye and spear-like snout as it hangs upside down almost on top of him, ready to pounce. With an immediate 'Send' it went to his four best fishing buddies, who were too busy to fish today. That will show them what they missed by standing him up today. Odd, the guys never miss a fishing date. But never mind. Their loss. He can hardly wait to see those jealous faces when he meets with them later today. Eat your hearts out, guys. But, hey, what? No!!! He screams! This can't be happening. He clutches his gut in pain! Watching his blood spurt wildly as the line holding the marlin snaps. 'No!' he shrieks, but his eyes fog and close. Death had come to take him. Even as his phone accidentally clicks again and falls from his helpless hand onto the deck.

Next to his last dying thoughts were, oh, well, his marlin was probably only a ten-footer, an eight-hundred pounder. That wouldn't win the biggest fish of year contest. The Florida record so far was recorded at fourteen feet, 1,046 pounds.

His final thought. Goodbye, cruel world.

ONE

Guys Going Away. Girls Left Behind

Hello there. I'm Gladdy Gold. Just to catch you up. I live in Lanai Gardens, in Building Q, a pleasant multi-acre retirement residence in Fort Lauderdale, Florida. Off of Oakland Park Boulevard. You'll know you're in the right place because directly across the street from us is this huge hospital, The Florida Medical Center. A place we've been too often. And thankfully come back out. But never mind that.

I'm being specific, in case you want to drop in and visit me. So, if you're in the neighborhood, come on up for coffee and maybe a Danish.

Right now I'm watching a bus loading the men from our entire condominium going on a vacation. And that includes my darling Jack.

I find myself reminiscing.

It's been a fine retired life so far. I, along with my sister Evvie and three best girlfriends, Ida, Sophie and Bella, are in our seventies and eighties, and are relatively well, thank goodness. With the usual aches and pains, of course. No point complaining. Nobody will listen.

I still think of them as my girls, though the politically correct address is 'women'. But we're of the old school. We'd be happy if they'd never invented that Facebook or any of that silly tweeting. Or those special iPhones that do everything but your laundry. The good old days are what we miss, and recollect about and will always cherish.

We are like one big family, though we live in our own private apartments.

We live next door to each other, or one flight down, also across the courtyard. We can see each other out our windows, but that doesn't stop my girls calling me up oh, so many times during the day. Here's a typical situation, which seems we've played like a million times over; say maybe we're going to the movies:

Bella calls Sophie for the fifth time. 'What time is the movie?'

'Sweetie, it's three thirty.'

'Thanks.'

Then Sophie calls Ida, 'We did say three thirty.'

Ida says, (never patient), 'Yes, that's what we did say, fourteen times.'

'Thanks.'

Ida calls Evvie, 'The girls are driving me crazy. Now, even I'm not sure we're going at three thirty.'

Evvie says, (always patient), 'Yes, that was what we agreed on.'

'Thanks.'

Evvie calls me, 'The girls are driving me nuts. If they call me one more time . . .'

Me, 'Don't answer the phone.'

'Thanks.'

And so it goes. We are our lifeline for one another. We call to make certain we are still alive and well. Each day we check in with each other. I sigh. But do we have to do it twenty or more times a day? I guess the answer is yes.

A lot has happened in the last few years. About my immediate family living here. My sister Evvie is it. We only have each other. She is only younger by two years, but I'm still considered the 'big sister', the person in charge. I am her hero, but sometimes I'm not. Hey, you can't be perfect all the time.

Something we never would have imagined has occurred in our twilight years. Both Evvie and I have remarried. I'm a widow no more. I've married a retired ex-cop – a gorgeous hunk. Jack Langford was widowed, too, and we found that happiness was still possible no matter how old you get. Evvie remarried, also, and to everyone's surprise, it was to her first husband, Joe, whom she used to hate and complain bitterly about for fifty years. He looked her up again and, voila! Love at second sight. That's a story and a half.

But let me tell you about our business – *Gladdy Gold and her Associates, Private Eyes*. We girls found out that keeping busy and doing useful things and helping people is a way to stay young. We discovered we were good at something unexpected. We were good at detecting. Much to our chagrin, we started to be aware that so many older people are considered invisible, and therefore ignored by those younger than they are.

So if seniors had problems and they needed representation, it was something there was little of. Who was there to help them? To listen to their problems? Us, we decided. We sent out business cards and handed them out everywhere, even took out an ad or two, and lo and behold, we became detectives.

And we hit the mother lode; we found our niche – senior troubles galore, all over the place. Grandparents fighting their children over money. Grandparents at war with retirement homes. Grandparents with medical situations. Yes, sadly, there is even senior abuse. Believe it or not, senior marriage problems. And, boy, were we busy! Our motto: never trust anybody under seventy-five. That got us lots of clients.

I still giggle when I think about our first case. An eighty-five-year-old woman hired us to find out whether her eighty-seven-year-old husband was cheating on her! Yes, sex among the seniors. I can prove it still exists.

But, sorry, I digress with all those old thoughts and memories. Here we are in the parking lot, waving goodbye to our hubbies, who are climbing into a bus that will take them to the Miami airport. And from there onto a plane to Africa! Our guys are going on a ten-day safari. This is an all-male macho adventure with almost all of the men in Lanai Gardens eagerly making the trip.

In our own Phase Two, my Jack is going. I miss him already. After all, I'm still a newlywed, sort of. Since Evvie's hubby, Joe, is also going, she whispers to me about how much fun we'll have talking behind their backs while they're gone. And happy times, hitting all the bars around town. Party! Party! She promises.

All talk, of course. She's joking. I predict hours of staying home and watching a lot of silly TV.

All of the men are on board the bus, including Sol Spankowitz, who's terrified of everything, especially his new wife, Big Tessie. Even though he's scared stiff about flying, it's his chance to escape her majesty for a little while. Tessie, who is quite overbearing, is somewhat scary at six-foot tall and well over 225 pounds. She's known as *Big* Tessie who has tried every diet on the planet and failed. Why? Because she always quits, unsatisfied, after the first day. We're betting that Sol will have a wonderful time all those miles away, remembering what it used to be like when he was single and could breathe freely.

There's a difference in the saying of goodbyes. To Jack and Joe, Evvie and I are calling out basic advice like, 'Don't get sunburned and have a great time.' From Tessie, Sol is getting, 'Don't get mauled by a tiger and don't eat any African cockroaches and call me every few days.' Poor Sol.

Aha! The only male in the entire condominium staying home is that pesky curmudgeon Hy Binder. His excuse? He's afraid of big animals. And he doesn't like sleeping in tents. Hates eating outdoors. He's got a long list of afraids, hates and don't-likes. Truth is – and he'll never admit it – he's too cheap to pay the price to go, though he can afford it.

Peek-a-boo! There he is crouching behind a palm tree, hiding next to his long-suffering, yet adoring wife, Lola.

My girls and PI partners are here, too, for the sendoff. They should also stay out of sight given the bad mood they've been in these days. They're impossible to be with. There's Ida, she of the usual cranky, negative disposition who today is even crankier. And Sophie and Bella. I always think of them as all in one word, a double scoop of trouble. We refer to them as the Bobbsey Twins. Sophie is all about color co-ordination. Bella is our second-childhood, forgets-everything innocent one. They are inseparable. And just as sulky as Ida nowadays.

It's obvious to me what the group problem is and I'll deal with it. Scarlett O'Hara said all problems should be put off 'til tomorrow, and I agree. I'll think about it tomorrow.

So Evvie and I are last-minute waving to our husbands who are looking at us from their bus windows. 'Have a great trip, we adore you,' we call out. We get lots of 'I adore you,' back. Lots of 'we'll miss you's,' of course. Smiling as they wave back to us. They look so cute in their pith helmets.

'Where ever did they find pith helmets?' I ask Evvie.

Her answer, 'I have no idea, but they are endearing.'

With last air-kisses, off they go. I hope Jack packed his iPhone, so maybe there'll be WiFi and we can stay in touch.

The bus has barely blown its farewell exhaust at us, when in a matter of moments Hy appears at our side. Chipper as usual and just as offensive. Rubbing his hands gleefully, something he does when he's up to no good, he addresses the five of us. 'Well, with all the guys abandoning us, I guess I'm gonna be one of the girls for a while. What fun. We can all hang out together and have a hot time in the old town.'

Ida whispers loud enough for our cliché-maven neighbor to hear it, 'Fat chance.'

Bella, who is usually confused, asks, 'How can he be a girl?'

Evvie, with hands on her hips, glares. 'Don't think we'll be your harem.'

His big pop eyes pretending honesty, Hy gives us an oily smile. 'Think of me as the leader of the pack. The alpha male.'

'Hah,' Ida grimaces. 'Then go hang out with a pack of hyenas. Not us.'

Bella is triply confused. 'How can he be a girl and a male? And a hyena?' We ignore her malapropos.

Evvie points and pretends excitement. 'Oops. Here comes the mailman. Sorry, Hy. We gotta run.'

And off we race, as best we can, aggravating our arthritic legs. To our mailboxes. A ho-hum daily event mostly useless, since we usually don't get much. Once in a while some flyers from restaurants, with free dinner coupons. Politicians asking for money. Frequently scary pamphlets with the latest drugs for the elderly; which we ignore. We especially scowl at the usual warnings of side effects: suicide or death. Sure puts us off.

But at this moment the mail is a great excuse to escape that annoying Hy. And one more reason.

Recently, there has been something odd showing up in my mailbox, which has drawn a lot of interest from the girls.

They crowd enthusiastically around me, waiting expectantly. I turn my key, as they hold their combined breaths.

Evvie asks, 'Do you think there'll be another one today?'

'I hope not.'

Sophie hugs Bella in her excitement. 'Hurry up. Open your mailbox.'

Ida pretends her typical indifference.

I open the box, and yes, it's there. All by its lonesome. Another plain white envelope, stamped and addressed to me, postmarked from Key West. I say envelope, not 'mail'. The girls watch me eagerly as I tear it open. Sure enough, another plain white sheet of paper is enclosed. And, yet again, with no writing on it. Not one single word.

This is the fifth of these non-letters I've gotten this month. It must be some kind of prank. But who is sending them?

We have hashed it over and over again; everyone has an opinion.

Ida. 'Some dumb kids.'

Sophie. 'A mystery advertisement.'

Evvie. 'I haven't got a clue.'

Bella giggles. 'Gladdy, you have a secret admirer. Sending you secret love letters. So secret, you can't even read them.'

Leave it to Bella to put a romantic spin on it.

TWO

Bored, I am Bored. Deliver Me

Tomorrow is here and it's time to deal with my problem. The girls are bored. Very bored. Some people, when they are tired of something, look to other things to keep them involved. Go to a movie. Overeat. Buy a new outfit. Read a book. Eat too much candy. A new craze, child-like coloring books for adults. And don't color out of the lines.

Not my trio; nothing interests them, so they mope. Not so much, Evvie. She just keeps her moodiness to herself. Just my triple pests. They are vocal.

We take our daily morning walk around the perimeter of our condos, and what do I hear, loud and clear:

Sophie, 'This is so dreary. I feel gosh-darn pokey.'

Ida, 'We see the same old trees and grass every day. Is there anything duller than watching grass grow?'

Bella won't be left out, 'And the same old, old people.' She always adds a coda. 'We need new old people. But where would we get them?'

Including Evvie, 'Yawn. Yawn.'

Here's a new wrinkle. We see Hy creeping up on us. And there's Lola, known for her jealousy and insecurity, playing the spy, Mata Hari, or maybe The Shadow, hiding behind a bush to see what her seemingly nefarious husband is up to. She adores him, but she doesn't trust him. How did he get away from her; she micro-manages his every moment. Ha Ha, as if any of us would be interested in spending time with him! And why is he picking us, anyway; go bother some other residents.

Hy thinks it's playtime for Bonzo and we're not having any. We are passing the bathrooms adjoining the pool, so in order to escape him, we hurry into the Ladies Room and hide.

We wait long enough until we think he's given up and gone home. We peek. Oops. Hy is still standing there, Lola is still lurking. Back in we go, we need to linger in the bathroom some more.

Finally, after a count to ten, he's gone. And so is Lola. We exit, and as we stroll around, the girls are once again wailing their favorite *kvetchings*.

Sophie, 'Dull. Dull. Everything is so dull.'

Ida, 'Same old, same old.'

Bella, 'Old, very old.'

Etcetera.

We go out one afternoon to play Bingo, which is the group's absolutely favorite pastime in the entire world. I always have to fairly drag them home after a regular four-hour exhausting, numbing session at the Bingo Palace. Now I get:

Ida, 'This game is rigged. Nobody can lose as often as we do. It's not fair.'

Bella, 'That Lolly Finster wins twice and we don't win once. It's not fair.'

Sophie, 'I was on three times. And that woman who sits next to me, who never shuts up and always gets the number I need, she gets to yell Bingo! It's not fair.'

And Evvie. 'They called my favorite number three, but do I win on it? No!'

They can't wait to leave.

And who should show up just as we're heading out the door? His arms filled with bingo game packs. His pocket bulging with marking daubers of many different colors. A big grin on his face. Eager to join us. You know who. Hy, the guy.

We wave goodbye at him. Evvie calls it. 'Sorry, we're done. Early day today. Bye.'

We pass him and walk out on him, leaving him with colored

ink on his face. And is that suspicious Lola hiding behind a lamp pole, still in spy mode? Yes she is.

And the beat goes on.

And what about shopping? Mention a trip to a mall, any shopping mall, their favorite way to spend time, with spending little amounts of money. Today we take off, slowly for them, to a local mini-mall. I would have taken them to their favorite Sawgrass Mills mall but that has 300 stores. We would have been there all day and I would have to drag them out of there at closing. So, I keep them local. Hoping for only three grueling hours of waiting. However, surprisingly, I get the call to leave after one half hour.

Sophie, 'I can't find anything I like. Let's go home.'

Ida, 'The salesgirls are just plain rude. Let's go home.'

Bella, 'I saw one thing I like . . .' The other three glare at her. She bends to their will. 'Let's go home.'

Ida again, 'We shoulda gone to Sawmill. More choices.'

I groan. You can't win.

And who should be running to catch up to us? Shopping bags flopping against his flabby hips. Hy, the silly stalker. How did he manage to find us? He must have bloodhound genes in his DNA. Or he followed us. But we smile sweetly and perform a group shrug. Sorry, we're done with our shopping and heading for home. Hy is foiled again. Where's lurking Lola? There she is, cowering in a discount liquor store doorway. Doesn't she ever give up?

We are sitting at an outdoor patio under our favorite palm tree near the pool. Playing cards, a daily happy habit. Not cheerful any more.

Canasta is being played at a fever pitch. Once a friendly game of gossip along with laughing. Gone. This time turned into a real spite and real malice kind of pastime. With beady-eyed mean looks and shouts of malevolence as cards are snapped down on the table.

Ida is furious. 'Cheater!'

Sophie equally angry. 'You're the cheater. Don't you call me names!'

Bella, a teary whisper. 'Please girls, don't fight.'

Ida to Sophie snarky, 'Why don't you just sit on her lap, and save your eyes the trouble of bending over to look!'

Sophie to Bella, (ignoring Ida), 'Don't play the queen, honey bunny. She'll take you down.'

Bella, 'Okay, I won't.'

Ida, grim, 'And you know that she has a queen in her hand, how?'

Evvie groans. '*Oy*, play already! I can't take much more of this. I'm getting a migraine.'

Ida to Sophie and Bella, 'You keep this up and I'm gonna smack both of you!'

Bella, cowering, 'Please don't hit me. I'm old. And fragile.'

Sophie puts her arm around her friend, 'She wouldn't dare. I won't let her.'

With dismay I watch as they slash verbally at one another's throats. Unheard of behavior. This is getting really serious.

Hy, carrying a boxed Jeopardy game, backs off; he doesn't dare come near us with all the screeching and threatening. He tiptoes away.

Where's Lola? I can't spot her anywhere. Has she finally given up, certain her hubby is safe from us dangerous dames? I actually miss her.

Still trying to make them happy, I take my girls out to a new restaurant. Well, new to us. A fancy-shmancy one, Seasons 52 in the Galleria. A reason to get out of shorts and dress up a little. And I offer to treat. This is a huge incentive. They are crazy about going to restaurants. Anything, so as not to cook. Especially great if they don't have to pay. But . . . you guessed it:

Sophie, 'My chicken cacciatore was cold.'

Ida, 'Our waitress was so rude. Her tip will be zilch.'

Bella, 'My veal parm . . . gin . . . parma jain, parma spaghetti was hard.'

Evvie tries to help her out: 'That was veal *parmesan* and *pasta al dente.*'

'Al Who?'

Evvie sighs. 'It's all right. Forget it.'

Dessert is always a restaurant must. Not this night. Unbelievable. They turn down strawberry cheesecake? We go home. The girls are still depressed.

What is their *problem*? Why are they bored? It's obvious why. And it's not because the men have all gone. Except for Evvie, not that they care. It's because Gladdy Gold and Associates hasn't had a job in months. Insecurity has infected them. The girls question themselves. Have they lost their touch? Will they ever detect again? They've become job junkies. They need a fix. Soon there will be bloodshed. I have to do something, but what?

Nine a.m. and we're in the pool, all of us doing our daily morning aquatics exercise. I had to talk them into going. They wanted to skip it and just sulk, and feel sorry for themselves. Finally they gave in, unwillingly.

This is one lackluster non-effort workout today. They look messy. The girls haven't bothered to comb their hair. They're wearing old, stretched-out bathing suits. Ida has on an unattractive torn bathing cap. They don't care how they look anymore. They moan and groan as they walk, back and forth, from one shallow side of the pool to the other, their usual morning pool exercise. Dreariness has set further in.

And there he is. Standing at the side of the pool, leering down at us. We are trapped at last. There's no getting away from Hy this time. Is he going to jump in the pool with us? No. He isn't in a bathing suit. Thank goodness.

'Hey girls, lookie here,' he chirps, smiling phony grins. We all turn to see what he wants.

With that, he whips out a camera from behind his back. The girls make stupid faces, shake their fists, and yell at him to back off. Anything to annoy him.

'Say lox and cream cheese,' he snickers. Hy is undaunted. And in a moment's flash, he's snapped our photo. Once accomplished, he skips merrily away.

I can see super-spy Lola, hiding in the bushes, giggling.

What was that all about?

THREE

Hy's Evil Revenge. We are Saved

It's driving us crazy. What was Hy up to? What was the point of that weird, quick snap of our photo? By the end of the week, Evvie and I suspect something is awry. Neighbors stare at us. Some of them point. A few snicker. Others giggle. But they don't want to tell us why. I have a strong hunch it has to do with Hy. What else could it be? In the black moods my girls are in, the three of them don't seem to care. He's staying away from us, is all that matters.

We happen upon Big Tessie the next morning. We find her at her open mailbox, looking perturbed. She swirls her hand around the obviously empty mailbox, searching for something that isn't in there. All she's getting is dusty hands.

She tosses out at this little tidbit to us, 'Boy, do I have something naughty about you.'

'Oh,' I say carefully, 'that's interesting.' Tessie always needs to be handled properly. It always comes with a price.

That comment seems to pull my girls out of their stupor.

First we need to listen to Tessie gush about how much she misses her Sol. And questions, she has so many questions. 'Why haven't we heard from the guys yet?' Without taking a breath, 'Does he have malaria yet? How can he be eating healthy on a safari? Do they know this is a man who lives for French fries soaked in ketchup? Where will he find ketchup in the wild? They're probably making him eat African food, whatever that is. I saw pictures, in the *National Geographic*. I sometimes look through them at the library.'

What a character. The guys are only gone a short time. And she expects letters?

Ida is already tapping her feet. Ms Impatience. 'So what do you know, that we don't know?'

Big mistake Ida; that is not the way to get to Tessie. I motion her to back off. She does it reluctantly.

Tessie is still on her riff. 'The magazines had pictures of what African natives eat – roasted ants and fried grasshoppers. Can you believe! I kept reading it, even though it was making me sick to my stomach to imagine.'

This brings her to the next tirade on her husband and the food chain. Shuddering, 'Maybe, by now, a lion has eaten my Solly? I'm having nightmares from not knowing.' She says all this while squeezing out a tear or two. She doesn't wait for any comments.

She blurts on, manufacturing a few more tears. 'I hear nothin'', not a phone call. Not even a text. Not a letter.'

Bella is impressed. 'You know how to text?'

'Of course not,' she says with pride. 'Do I look like the type who would own one of those hinky phones or a computer? I'm low tech. And proud of it. I'm no nerd.'

I try to calm her. 'I'm positive our men are still uneaten, and are fine, and having a good time.'

Tessie sniffs, 'That's what I'm afraid of.'

Ida has had enough of her whining. She demands answers. 'What's going on? Why is everyone looking at us funny?'

'Of course I know.' She stops short, suddenly busy giving her empty mailbox another swipe.

Bella says timidly, 'What do you know?'

Tessie huffy, 'Why should I tell you?'

Oh, oh, I predict Ida will soon blow. Not good. Ida, with arms folded, legs spread apart, in get-mad stance, attacks. 'And just why won't you share your knowledge with us?'

Tessie copies her body position. 'And what's in it for me?'

It's become necessary to take sides. My girls line up behind Ida. Passing neighbors merge and back Tessie. They have no idea what this is about, but they think they should even up the odds.

Ida mimics Tessie. 'What's in it for *you*? Wadda ya want, a bribe?' She brandishes her fists. 'I'll give you a bribe!'

Cowardly Tessie backs down. A tiny bit. 'It's on the computer.'

Evvie prompts her. 'What's on the computer?'

Tessie giving out information is like pulling teeth out of a raccoon. My group glares at her.

She finally gives up. 'All right. All right! Since I don't own any computer, Lucy, next door to me, let me see it on hers. There were six of us watching. We all had a good time. You're famous. Soon

I'll ask for your autograph or maybe you'll be selling T-shirts with your names on. Make sure to carry extra large for me.' She stops and takes a deep breath.

Uh, oh, I think. This sounds ominous.

Evvie exchanges a worried look with me. She urges Tessie to go on. 'Please tell us what you heard and saw.'

Tessie preens. Being the spreader of gossip is as good as it gets. Furtive, bending down. Whispering. A spy disseminating vital information. 'I haven't a clue what it means but Hy has "uploaded the video to his channel on YouTube".' She stops, taking a breath.

Sophie asks, 'That's it? What's that got to do with Hy? What's a yutube?'

Ida's tone promises pain again. 'Get on with it, already, or else . . .'

The watching crowd backs out of the way. Will there be a fist fight?

Tessie, also distancing herself away from Ida, continues to drag it out; her voice somewhat squeaky this time. 'He took a movie of you in the pool and put it on that YouTube thing.' She stops again.

Ida hisses, twisting her arm. 'Spit the rest out or I'll hurt you.'

I look at my girls. I can hardly recognize them. Threats? Physical pain? Evvie is also dismayed by their attitudes. 'Shhh,' I say to cool down the temperature. 'Let Tessie tell it in her own way.'

Tessie pulls herself away from Ida and plops down on the nearest bench, fanning herself with a tissue. She blabs, 'He put that movie on the computer and under it, it says, "Hy's Harem, Fort Lauderdale, Florida. Elderly broads on a bad hair day, in the pool".'

Ida shrieks, 'We're his harem? That *vonce*! That bedbug!'

Tessie says, 'They say it's gone viral,' not having a clue about what that means.

Bella is confused. 'He says we're sick?'

Nobody bothers to correct Bella. We leave Tessie, and as of one mind, we all race upstairs to my apartment where our business computer lives.

We can hear Tessie calling out to our backs something about our being ungrateful and make sure we tell her as soon as we hear from the husbands.

*   *   *

Out of breath, the girls egg me on to get my computer booted up. Evvie and I manage to figure out how to look for his channel. We find it on 'Hy's Harem'.

He's really on YouTube? Who knew? And there it is. Tessie saw and heard right. That *goniff* has uploaded a video of us in the pool. Looking awful. Old, torn bathing suits. Bed-head hair. He's making fools of us. They're outraged!

My girls are screeching all at once.

Ida, 'I'll kill him. I shoulda never had that stupid bathing cap on.'

Bella, 'We look awful.'

Sophie, 'How dare he?'

Bella, 'My hair is all knots.'

Sophie, 'My bathing suit is torn at my *tuchas*.'

Ida, 'We were waving at him and screaming. We look like lunatics.' To Evvie, 'You had to mention that harem word!'

'What does that mean – a harem? He has sex with us?' This from Bella, our eighty-three-year-old two-year-old, 'Did we do it? Why can't I remember if we did?'

Ida, yet again, 'I'll murder him.'

Sophie adds, 'What a nerve!'

If smoke could come out of their ears, the room would be fogged in by now.

While they are in rage mode, Evvie and I tiptoe into my kitchen. To brew tea. Herb tea, maybe to calm them down. We are just as flummoxed as they are. But I'm not surprised. Hy is not one to take being ignored.

The girls follow us into the kitchen and the room being a tiny space, we are a mob scene. 'Why?' a chorus sobs out, wanting to understand. I wait. When they are finally finished venting, I say, softly, 'Maybe it was because we were not kind to him. Maybe his feelings were hurt. If we had just included him sometime. This is his revenge.'

Ida tries to fold her arms across her chest. Too crowded to manage in my kitchen. 'Revenge. He wanted revenge? We'll show him revenge!'

Bella tries to pat Ida's shoulder. She can't, no room. 'Yeah!' Then, 'How?'

Evvie sighs. 'Maybe an apology would do more good.'

Gloom and doom, though Bella does ask if I have brownies to go with the tea.

The kitchen phone rings. I answer. My girls hear.

'Yes, this is Gladdy Gold of Gladdy Gold and Associates. Yes, we are available. You have a problem? We would be interested in solving your problem if we can. He's dead, and you think it was murder?'

'Murder?' whispers Ida, rubbing her hands together in anticipation.

'You are located in Key West?'

The girls are clapping. And jumping in place. 'A job again. And in famous Key West! Hooray.' Their depression is over.

'Let me check my calendar.' I wait quietly for a moment, letting the person on the other line think I'm consulting my date book.

The girls are practically jumping on me to say yes, already. A pause, then, 'The dates will work. When would you like us to get there? As soon as possible? In a few days all right?'

Evvie and I stare at one another as I take notes. 'Looking forward to meeting you, Mrs Wassinger.' I hang up. Grins all around.

From Evvie, 'Key West? Where our invisible letters came from? A coincidence? Remember, we don't believe in coincidences.'

They had us at 'murder'. Hy is forgotten.

FOUR

Getting Ready. Back to the Mall

Nothing like the smell of success. It changes everything. We have no idea how long we'll be away, so the girls insist we can use some extra outfits. I can't talk them out of it. Back to shopping at a mall. I take them to another mini-mall.

So we go to Phoebe's Fine Fashions.

Sophie, glowing, 'So much to choose from. I wanna buy out the whole store.'

Ida, smiling, 'How nice the salesgirls are.' Ida smiling? Complimenting someone? Unheard of!

Bella, cheerily, 'I want all these things.'

Ida, 'Lots better than Sawgrass.'

I groan.

Evvie, 'It's two hours already. My feet are killing me. Pick, pay and let's go.'

Sophie and Bella have chosen a half-dozen twin color-coordinated outfits. Of course with matching sun hats and sandals. Lavender and peach are faves. Ida has selected one gray pantsuit which looks like every other gray pantsuit in her closet.

Evvie and I will stick to our already owned clothes.

We follow the happy trio as they stomp into the nearest eatery. They are beyond excited. Evvie and I are numb with exhaustion. This time the girls' cheeseburger is so yummy. The dessert is delicious. Life is good. Suddenly everything is coming up 'rosy'. Sophie is singing and mangling the *Gypsy* lyrics. She keeps saying, over and over, 'A road trip. I always wanna go on road trips.'

Needless to say they pack too much. Also needless to say, they are in and out of each others' apartments re-trying on outfits and sharing visions of a wonderful time ahead. 'Key West, that's like going on a vacation.' Never mind the thousands who come to Fort Lauderdale for all the same things that we have. 'Wonderful beaches.' When have the girls ever gone to our beaches? And drag home sand? Never. 'Beautiful ocean views.' Seen one, seen them all. 'High-rise hotels.' Why would we ever go there for that?

I visit Sophie one morning, intending to talk her into removing items from her overwhelmed suitcase. Bella is already there. The girls are excited. Bella and Sophie are dressed in their twin bunny pajamas and look adorable. Already they babble about their upcoming vacation. Such sophisticates. 'My dear, we simply adore *The Keys*.' La de dah. As if they've ever been. Sophie justifies it with: 'Well, we did see *Key Largo*, and wasn't Bogart divine?'

Since they are floating on cloud nine, I don't bother to remind them that we're going there to work. Someone has been murdered. We're not going there for fun.

I feel remiss that I didn't ask the caller enough questions. We have a list I refer to before signing on a client. Important items that help us decide whether or not to take a case. Sometimes there are pitfalls that should be avoided. But the girls didn't care for any other details. It was a job and in a place they've never been.

I leave them, forgetting to beg them to unpack unnecessary items, but they wouldn't have listened anyway. Phone calls galore. Three different girls calling each other four times a day. Do the math. Evvie and I get more calls because they have dozens of questions for us, all of them already answered. I tell them, we should leave by Wednesday. I tell them this again and again on Sunday and Monday. They are in a panic, not ready yet. However, to my amazement, Tuesday night, they are packed and raring to go. I won't bother to report on how many times they phoned on Tuesday.

Sometimes I feel like the parent of three rambunctious children, who happen to be in their second childhood. Loveable, but draining.

FIVE

Wednesday We Exit. Now Minus One?

Finally, Wednesday arrives. Early morning sneak-out, so Hy won't catch us leaving and create a fuss. The plan is to meet at my car by seven a.m., not a minute later. Evvie, naturally, is first to arrive. She and I place our few backpacks in the rear.

Like the Bobbsey twin-some they are, Sophie and Bella, as if they arranged it ahead of time (as was usual), exit each of their apartments, and arrive at my car at almost the same second. Each is *shlepping* two enormous, seemingly overwrought suitcases. They lumber forth weighed down by their belongings. No use saying anything. We'd only get, the usual 'but we might need all these things'.

Evvie says, glaring at the travel suitcases, 'This is ridiculous. We might be there for only a few days. At the most, probably a week.'

Sophie jumps in. 'But what if it's a month?'

Bella joins the duet. 'Or maybe two months? We might need all these things. I couldn't leave my hot pink taffeta Empire gown with tiara and matching shoes and purse. What if we needed to dress up?'

Evvie sighs, a sigh based on much aggravating experience with the two of them. 'We're leaving to solve a murder. I don't foresee tea dancing in the near future.'

I add, tamping down the sarcasm, 'But, should a cotillion be in the offering, I hear that they do have stores in Key West.'

Evvie helps me shovel their four cases in the trunk, grunting at the weight. But wait! That's not all. The two of them have prepared the extras the way we've done it on stakeouts. Adding in the back seat, snacks. Drinks. The makings of three meals. Pillows. Blankies. Flashlights. Decks of cards. Knitting. Books on tape. Oy!

I study my watch. But where is Ida?

Suddenly, Sophie pokes me and points. Not wanting to speak and possibly wake up the sleeping non-giant, short, spiky Hy.

We all stare up at the landing in front of Ida's apartment. Our fifth member is standing there waving frantically at us. In pajamas. In pajamas! Not dressed and ready? That bodes problems. Practically flopping over the railing, indicating that we should come upstairs, Ida continues to wave at us.

What the heck? I start for her elevator. Of course, my gang of two plus Evvie follow.

We reach Ida, who is looking strangely pale. With finger on lips to remind us not to speak, we pile into Ida's apartment.

Confused. At the door is her packed suitcase and handbag, ready to go.

The parade continues as Ida leads us into her bedroom where she climbs back into bed and pulls her covers up to her neck.

'I'm sick,' she announces, at the same time emitting a hacking cough and humongous sneeze. As testimony, she is surrounded by crumpled tissues, various medicine-like bottles, teabags leaning out of used teacups and empty water bottles. 'I think it's the flu!'

'Oh, no,' we chorus in alarm.

Bella and Sophie immediately pull away from the bed in dismay, eyes wide with fear, as if she's said she'd come down with black plague.

'What? When?' I ask. She does look pasty and exhausted.

Through a throat filled with phlegm, she cries out, 'I was up all night. I didn't sleep a wink. I'm a mess!'

A few moments pass as we take it all in.

Evvie comments, 'Well, I guess we'll have to put the trip off for a while.'

Another kind of chorus – a whimper from the twin-set. 'And unpack again?' *kvetches* Bella.

Ida makes a pathetic crawl up her sheet and pillow to half-sit up; a dramatic performance rivaling the famous old-timer Sarah Bernhardt. 'You mustn't cancel. They're expecting you. We need this job.' Another huge sneeze into what must be the fiftieth tissue of the night.

'Have you a fever?' I ask.

'I can only guess,' she says pathetically. 'Can't find my thermometer, but it feels like 102.'

What to do? This is something unexpected. Ida is an important part of our group.

Ida insists, 'Don't be silly. Go on without me. You have to.'

'But we're a team,' Bella says unhappily. Sophie nods with her.

All look to me, their leader. 'I don't think we have a choice. We promised we'd be there today and our new clients sound anxious.'

Ida manages a pitiable smile. 'Don't worry about me. I'll be all right.'

With last calls of advice on how to medicate, we leave Ida to her sickbed.

Positive that Hy and Lola's window shades are still closed, we leave for our road trip. We're lucky, Hy is probably still asleep, and so we steal out successfully. The last thing I see is Ida sneezing and waving from her bedroom window.

We exit, minus one.

We have no time for Hy at this time. Revenge will have to wait.

SIX

The Road Trip. Agony and Ecstasy

Day One

At first all is jolly. The girls are revved up for a wonderful time. However, my Chevy wagon is packed to the gills. Sophie and Bella are seated in the back seat with all the extra things they brought along surrounding them; behind them, under their feet, on their laps. Even without Ida, they barely have room to breathe.

'Okay back there?' I ask.

'Peachy-keen with me,' says Sophie.

From Bella, 'Happy. Happy.' I can see her through my rear-view mirror, waving a lollipop. Though I sense Bella is relieved that Ida isn't with them. She is usually stuck in the middle between Ida and Sophie. Certain she has wiggle room, and smiles a lot.

Sister Evvie always gets to sit comfortably next to me in the front. To say we are totally cramped is an understatement. And whose fault is it? Did they need those four full huge suitcases? Their answer was a resounding . . . yes!

Are they comfortable? They are all smiles, despite the lack of room. We are traveling 110 miles and will be crossing forty-three bridges. I don't look forward to when eagerness fades and the misery sets in.

The twosome can't agree on what CDs to listen to as we ride along. Bella's choice is 'Oh, My Papa' and other Eddie Fisher favorites (groan). Sophie wants 'Great Songs' by Liberace. At his piano. With candelabra. (Other groans.) No agreement reached, so it is decided (by me) that Evvie will read from a travel handbook she brought along, describing places and facts about our destination.

'Don't you want information about what we can look forward to doing?' I ask.

There are mumbles, I think in agreement. But maybe not. For Sophie and Bella, travel is all about what restaurants we'll be eating in. Travel is also about getting out of the same rut day after day back home. So travel is about just doing something different. With a bit of fear of the unfamiliar thrown in for good measure. But first there's lots of tourist-like gazing out the windows as I drive US 1, the Dixie Highway. Also called the Overseas Highway, as Evvie informs us.

Happy. Happy. Until the beginnings of paranoia. The two-way highway is quite narrow, with the whole Atlantic Ocean to the left of us and of the Gulf of Mexico on the right. The girls look timorously from side to side. Water, water everywhere. Bella wants to know if sharks can jump. Like from out of the ocean and into a car. 'No,' I swear. 'Sharks are not for leaping onto shore.'

As soon as one car passes us too closely, hearing the whirring noise modern cars give off to warn drivers of that very danger, the real fright begins. This time from Sophie. 'Can a car bump us hard enough to shove us into the ocean or the Gulf?'

Again, 'Not likely.'

However, when a car does pass, the back-seaters shut their eyes, and cling to one another, in anticipation of disaster.

'Gladdy, close your eyes!' Bella cries out to me when one car swerves way too close, promising near collision. Her eyes are glued shut.

'If I do, you'll be sorry. After all, I *am* the one driving.'

'I forgot.'

A while later a speedboat passes by on the Gulf side; fast and furious, splashing us in its wake. The girls shriek. There is much hugging of each other once more, and gripping their worn-out blankies. Second childhood, remember?

Other paranoid comments:

'This is a weird road. It's awfully narrow.' From Sophie.

'Yes, it is,' I say.

'Why didn't they make it wider?' From Bella.

'Maybe too expensive.' From Evvie.

'It goes on for a very long time.' Sophie whines.

Evvie states, 'Well, we have all these keys to pass. Plus all the islands off the side of the keys. This is the only way to get to them.'

Mumble. Mumble. They are comforting one another.

Oh, oh, now what?

Sophie asks Bella, 'Did you ever get around to making out your will?'

Bella answers, voice full of doubt. 'I don't remember. Didn't you go with me, when you went to the lawyer?'

It's Sophie turn to be unsure. 'I don't remember either. It was years ago. We were much younger.'

Bella giggles. 'Much younger. I think we were seventy-five.'

Evvie can't take any more. 'You. Will. Not. Die, on this road!'

She whispers to me. 'I wish we could pull over so I can kill them.'

Sophie growls. 'I heard that!'

It is *I* who now has a mantra. *We should have gone by plane. We should have gone by plane. We should have . . .* Like an unwelcome tune, it ricochets off my mind.

I suggest they keep their eyes closed and try to relax while Evvie reads to us about our destination. Anything to keep them quiet.

Evvie starts her travel book lecture. 'There are seventeen hundred islands that make up the keys. Most can only be reached by boat. There are about thirty-seven keys. They are separated into three branches. The Upper Keys, closest to Miami, include Plantation Key, Islamorada Key, Marathon Key, Key Largo . . .'

Sophie, mildly interested asks, 'Why are they called keys?'

Bella giggles, ''Cause somebody got locked out.'

Evvie ignores her, reads: 'Two explanations here. The Spanish called them *cayos,* meaning very small islands. *Isla* for regular-sized islands. Ponce de Leon, when he landed, called them *Cayos de los Martires*, which meant tiny island of martyrs . . .'

A muffled voice, Bella interrupts, asks if we can stop at Key Largo. 'Could I meet Humphrey Bogart? Maybe he still lives there. He was so good in that movie.'

Evvie says impatiently, annoyed at being interrupted, 'No way, Bogart is dead!'

Bella is shocked. 'Oh, how terrible.'

Evvie says, 'It was a long time ago.'

I add, 'But no stopping yet, we need to go further.'

Bella says, 'Okay.'

That didn't last for long. With each sign telling us we're passing or about to pass a new key, the girls in the back seat would start *kvetching*, 'Let's stop at this key. We don't want to miss that key.' Key after key after key. So we did stop, if this counts. In and out for minutes at a time, snapping photos, just to be able to say we've been there.

Will we ever forget Islamorada Key where we just *had* to take the trolley tour with its twenty-nine points of interest?

There we are standing in a long line, only to find out when we finally get to the front, that these rides must be booked way ahead of time. The trolleys are used for large groups of people only. Usually for an event, like a birthday party or a wedding. And are plenty expensive. So much for trolley rides.

And let's not forget the key we left within three minutes of arriving; Just about to head for their main street, when the insects that are call no-seeum attacked. Evvie identifies them as biting midges as we race back into the car, scratching, slapping and moaning, waving our arms to shove away the horde.

Gasping, when finally safely back in our seats. A close call. Don't want to remember what key that was. Brrrr.

And Bella pining for stopping at Pine Key, where we just had to visit the white-tailed deer refuge. I need to inform her that we do not have time to search for them. It was suggested at the information desk that we should plan for at least two or three hours to go exploring in the fourteen square miles of paths. What few deer we saw as we headed back to the car disappointed Bella that Bambi wasn't among them.

And let's not overlook the many restaurants we dropped in at considering the huge number of snacks they brought along. And just plain climbing, needing to stretch those weak muscles.

'What about bathroom breaks?' asks Sophie.

'We will have them,' I promise.

'And lunch?' From Bella, ignoring the fact of all the food they're carrying.

'We've already eaten, visited a key or two, or three and already took time to stretch and find bathrooms,' I assure them. Do they hear the weariness in my voice?

Only ninety-eight miles more to go. Only! I think wishfully that we had what taxis have. A drop-down window that closes off the back of the car from the front. A window that can stay shut.

Twenty minutes later, a little voice peeps up. 'I'm ready for another bathroom break.'

Evvie turns to face Bella, who's looking winsome, like some adorable mewling little kitten. 'I really mean it.'

Evvie knows better. So do I. Evvie asks with a tad of cynicism, 'It doesn't have anything to do with the sign coming up saying next stop, Key Largo?'

Sophie, caring that Bella has been caught out, tries to help her. 'I wouldn't mind a bathroom break, too.'

Evvie shrugs. I give up. The twosome win again. I drive into the town of Key Largo. 'All right I say, here we are.' I park the car in front of the nearest hotel.

Bella and Sophie quickly leap out of the car, immediately go into dramatic stretching movements to doubly justify the stop at this key.

Evvie and I get out. Might as well walk around a bit as well.

'Bathrooms straight ahead,' I indicate to the twosome.

The girls scamper inside the hotel.

Evvie grins. 'Money bet, she'll want to find Bogart while we're here. Even though he's dead and not buried here. She'll want to go where they shot the movie.'

'No bet,' I say.

Sure enough. The girls come out, looking ever-so-guilty. They had a discussion inside and here comes their plan. 'Well,' says Bella, 'as long as we're here . . . might as well see where Bogie starred in the movie.'

With teeth gritted, I walk them back to the doorway of the hotel where a bellboy stands on duty. 'Ask him,' I suggest, convinced they won't believe me if I tell them. 'He lives here. He'll have information all about it.'

Evvie and I stand next to the bellboy, arms folded, smirking. Getting ready for what is to come.

Timidly, Bella approaches and asks her question, sounding oh so sweet and needy. 'Where might the place be where they made the movie Key Largo?' Spoken like the true movie buff she isn't. She is all saccharine grins waiting for the answer.

The bellboy is polite. 'Sorry, Mrs,' he answers. 'The movie was probably shot in Hollywood, or somewhere else. Not here.'

Bella and Sophie suffer mightily.

The bellboy tries to be helpful. 'You could tour *The African Queen* boat. Bogie and Bacall. Been here since 1951.'

The girls look dolefully at him. Bella shrugs. 'Not the same thing.'

They look so dejected; bellboy offers another choice. 'You could swim with the dolphins . . . it's a big thing to do here.'

'No thanks.' Bella is looking as if that same kitten just got clobbered. She heads back to the car with Sophie following, head bowed to show her unity.

Evvie continues her lecture where she left off. 'The Middle Keys have Big Pine Key, Conch Key, Sunshine Key, Scout Key, to name just a few, The Lower Key is where Key West is; our destination. It's the south-west tip of the United States, only ninety miles away from Cuba . . .'

'Maybe we can take a side trip to Cuba,' Sophie suggests eagerly, trying to undo the damage of Key Largo.

Evvie says, 'I doubt it. We'd need a boat. And probably a passport and visa . . . and whatever else.'

She continues her travelogue, 'Come to the sunset celebrations moonlit nights at Mallory Square. Dancing, dining, everyone comes to watch the spectacular sunsets.'

I nudge Evvie and whisper, 'They're almost asleep, don't stop.'

Evvie gets it. Her voice dials down to monotone. 'The keys are famous for their festivals. The Seafood Festival, grilled lobster and stone crab claws are some of the delicacies . . .'

I nod to Evvie to keep up the good work.

'The food and wine festival cranks it up with exotic gourmet meals, with quality wines and other beverages. Including seminars on wines. Then we have the T-shirt & Shorts fair, with music and art. And an always favorite – the Key Lime Festival with rewards for the best baked pie. And Margaritaville . . .'

'Time to stop: your monologue put them both to sleep. You're better than Tylenol PM.'

Evvie sighs in relief. 'Thanks. Quiet at last.'

For the next half hour or so, she and I go through our plans for when we arrive. I say, 'We first stop at the Brown Pelican Inn, a charming Victorian B&B and check in.'

Evvie says, 'Hmm, that sounds familiar.'

I smile. 'Yes, that's where Jack and I, early in our relationship, once went to be alone. And had to leave as soon as we arrived. We needed to race home with a hurricane breathing down our necks.' I sigh. 'We never got to see anything. We missed everything Key West had to offer. Not a chance to spend any romantic time with Jack. Oh, well, it might have been wonderful.'

'The good news is that Jack is your husband.'

'Amen to that.' I continue with our schedule. 'After we get checked in, then we head for the Wassinger house and meet Sadie and Louie, our clients, and hope to hear about their mystery death case.'

'And maybe unravel our own little mystery – the blank page letters you've been receiving in your mailbox for weeks.'

'Amen, again.' I send out a silent prayer – let the girls sleep a little longer.

A few miles later, I ask Evvie, 'A penny for your thoughts.'

'I was just thinking of Ida. She was really looking forward to this trip. She must be feeling sad and so lonely. Poor Ida.'

SEVEN
In Ida's Bedroom. The Same Time

Ida cautiously climbs out of bed, heading slowly for the bathroom; concerned about possible dizziness. She stops suddenly, surprised. She doesn't have to creep along; she's able to move at a better pace. She suddenly realizes that she feels okay. Touching her forehead, she smiles; she no longer feels feverish. The walk becomes a hop and a skip. And then a small run. She feels just fine.

She thinks, I'm not sick anymore. I could have gone on the trip with the gang.

Romantic Key West and a brand-new case. A place I always wanted to visit. Darn it. Darn it. Darn it. I'm missing all the fun!

In the bathroom, she finds her thermometer and checks her temperature. Sure enough, she is normal. What the heck? She was sick and now she's fine.

She walks easily back to her bed, with a stop first to peer out the window. And guess who is standing outside, all by his little self. No one else is up and about yet. And guess who he's searching for? Why Gladdy and her girls, of course. To torment all of us, Because of that video? To see us quiver and shake at his revenge for leaving him out.

Hy stares at the vacancy in Gladdy's usual parking space. Then turns, puzzled. Where can Gladdy be, he must be wondering. Where would they go this early in the morning?

Tee hee. Too late, Hy, baby.

The chickens have flown the coop.

EIGHT

Arrive Key West. Astonishing Adventure Begins

The trip is over; enthusiasm is returning, even though we're exhausted and sweaty from the long hours. Clothes are wrinkled and smelly. Food crumbs on the back floor of my badly-treated car will crunch when Bella and Sophie climb out.

At last we've arrived at the one and only key we were supposed to land on, this, the last and southernmost of the keys, our destination. The sun has dipped down into farewell. It's the evening's turn to shine. We drive slowly, because the streets are filled with people. We gaze, with much oohing and ahhing, at one colorful lit-up mansion after another. One busy street after another. We cross Duval Street, the most famous of them all. Mobbed; so many people outside, strolling and eating in outdoor cafes. The wondrous smells of brand-new foods to taste. Music coming from bars, restaurants, homes, as well as on street corners. Folks, wearing bright-colored outfits with multiple strands of plastic beads, dancing merrily weaving in and out of slow-driving cars. Some are drunk; many are just happy. A few drivers wanting to move faster, are annoyed, honking their horns. They're ignored.

We're barely moving. An older man knocks at the window of our nearly stopped car indicating that he would like one of us to come on out and dance with him. Evvie is tempted, the girls in the back cling to each other in terror of this man in his strange costume of a red devil. The red devil pulls open Evvie's door and, surprised, he pulls her out. She shrugs and goes along with it.

Bella and Sophie nervously watch Evvie join him in a long line of dancers, with arms around the person in front, doing the Conga.

I turn off the motor and climb out of the car and reach the moving line. I tug at my dancing, foot-kicking sister, who is having a good time. I say, 'Hi, Ev, just need to remind you that we are long overdue to the inn and then to meet the Wassingers.'

Evvie drops out of the line, saying goodbye to the dancing devil, 'No, sorry. Gotta go.' He shrugs and continues on, his feet still prancing to the music.

Laughing, we both return to my car, now holding up traffic. I join in once again in the slow progress.

We can sense the natives and tourists alike are motivated by simple pleasures and an entertaining lifestyle. Key West looks like an exciting place. And we are no longer tired; we are getting energized.

Sophie asks, exhilarated, yet a worry-wart to her very heart and soul, 'Did we bring the right clothes?'

'Not to worry,' I calm her sarcastically. 'Look at all those stores, one after another. Worst case scenario, we can always go shopping.'

Evvie groans. 'Not again. I am not going into another clothing store. Not a single one.'

Bella cries out, delighted, 'Look at all those palm trees.'

Killjoy me reminds her, 'We have hundreds of palm trees where we live.'

Bella, shot down, says, 'Well, these look different.'

Sophie, ever her back-up, puts in, 'Well, they might be a different brand of palm.'

Evvie and I ignore them, as they eagerly call out the names of various boutique shops. Places they simply must enter while we're here.

Following our clients' directions, as well as my memory from my previous trip, I find the Brown Pelican Inn, our destination. One of many stately Victorians on a palm-lined street. The street lamps' lights glow gently.

The inn is a subtle, pale yellow building, nothing brown about it. It is lit up and beautiful. And welcoming.

Evvie, still in travel maven mode, comments, 'This is a copy of an early English Victorian mansion. Sometimes referred to as gingerbread.'

'And just as charming inside,' I add.

We enter the inn, leaving our luggage in the car.

Inside, the girls are suitably impressed with the beige wicker furniture with charming navy blue pillows, slatted window treatments, ceiling fans blowing gentle wafts of air, colorful rag rugs and charming knick-knacks on the shelves, mostly with ocean themes.

I check in with the pretty, forty-ish owner, Teresa LeYung. I still recall the petite lady, with straight long, dark hair, and slim body. She was wearing an Asian long, thin satin dress when I was there last time. Today she wears a pale blue business suit.

She also remembers me. 'You were here when our last hurricane hit. Two years ago. Your romantic trip was cut very short as we all ran for our lives.'

Ruefully, I agree. 'That was me, Ms LeYung.'

'Well, not to worry. The weather is perfect this time. And please call me Teresa. We're pretty casual around here.'

I notice a young man lugging in those heavy suitcases that belong to the girls. Like Teresa, he is of Asian descent.

Teresa calls out to him. 'Jin, say hello to Miss . . .' She hesitates.

I inform her, showing my ring, 'Now Mrs Jack Langford. Call me Gladdy, please.'

'Congratulations,' she says warmly, meaning it. 'Jin, this is Mrs Langford; Gladdy, meet my nephew, Jin.'

Jin looks in his twenties. Tall, thin, almost pretty. Black crew-cut hair, tight jeans. Tight red and white striped shirt. And are those ballet slippers?

I introduce Evvie, Sophie and Bella and explain that Ida Franz, one of our group, is not coming. She strikes Ida's name from the registration book.

Teresa informs me, 'Jin helps out at the inn when he's not at the theatre.'

Her nephew smiles. It's an appealing smile. He is sincerely friendly. He addresses us. 'I'm an actor. Also a singer. A so-so dancer. Playing in a musical, in a theater down the street. If you like plays, you might want to take in our show.'

Sophie is eager. 'We adore musicals. What's it called?'

'*La Cage aux Folles.*'

She looks confused. 'That sounds French. Is it in English?'

Jin and his aunt exchange amused looks. 'Definitely in English. It has been translated from a French farce.'

Evvie and I pick up on their meaning. We've heard of the show. We might have to do some explaining to the girls.

Evvie says to Jin, 'I'm certain we would enjoy it.'

I add, 'But first we are here on serious business.'

Teresa reacts. 'Of course. The Wassingers made your reservations under their name. You're to be their guests.' She and Jin are worried. Why?

My antenna immediately goes up. Something amiss? 'You are familiar with the Wassingers?'

Teresa nods. 'Of course. You've heard what they say about small towns. Everybody knows everyone.'

Jin adds, grinning, 'And knows just about everybody's business.'

Teresa looks justifiably sad. 'You're here because of Robert Strand's death. Terribly unexpected news. Such a well-liked, nice man. Dying on his fishing boat like that, in such a bizarre, tragic accident.'

Sophie is surprised and blurts, 'But we were told he was murdered!'

Jin blurts as well, 'That's what the Wassingers think. No one else does.'

Teresa and Jin are suddenly rigid. We sense that Jin shouldn't have said that. By our startled looks, it's obvious we weren't told anything like this by the Wassingers.

'I thought you were related by family or friends,' Teresa says quietly, 'here for the funeral.'

I shake my head, no, with a chorus of group head-shaking to agree. 'We have no family connections in Key West. We never knew Mr Strand.'

'Then why are you here?' Teresa asks.

I'm suddenly aware of how little knowledge I have about this case I signed on for so quickly. Why didn't I find out more before I grabbed it so fast? Where was our due diligence? Just because the girls were bored I acted too quickly.

The Wassingers said 'murder' and we hear 'bizarre accident'. What's going on? I have a feeling Teresa might be able to give us information we don't have.

I say, 'We were hired by the Wassingers to investigate Robert Strand's death. We're private eyes.'

Teresa is incredulous. 'Hired? Oh, no. Not again. They didn't? Those poor misguided people.' Then, more confused, 'You? Private eyes? Really?' She stares at us, unbelievably, as if to question how all these elderly women could possibly be here to investigate a crime.

Evvie adds, 'Our company name is Gladdy Gold and Associates.'

I ask carefully, 'Are you saying that only the Wassingers think Mr Strand was murdered?'

She answers me just as cautiously. 'Robert Strand had no enemies. None that anyone heard of. A good man, beloved by all who knew him. He went fishing one day. Alone. He went fishing often and was quite good at it. What happened was freakish. He had a huge marlin on his line and he was gored by that huge fish as he tried to pull it in.'

Evvie is startled. 'A fish killed him?'

Teresa sighs. 'The truth is, there is positive proof of this. Even though they never found his boat. The whole city is positive this is the case.'

I insist, 'But the Wassingers were so sure . . .'

I'm just about to ask her for more information, when I'm stopped by Teresa. With a quick look at the iPhone in her hand, she changes the subject, maybe pretending there is a text message; something of importance. And as for her demeanor, she's business-like now. 'Jin, get the rest of the luggage from the car.'

She turns to me and hands me two sets of room keys. 'My nephew will show you to your rooms. I must go to my office.'

With that she hurries from the lobby and disappears down a hall.

Uh, oh, what have we gotten ourselves into? Here's a different kind of mystery.

'Follow me,' says Jin too quietly, not looking at any of us. 'After you unpack, I'll give you directions to the Wassingers.' He, too, is suddenly all business.

I have a feeling his aunt will be giving him a lecture while we are unpacking about keeping one's mouth closed.

Evie and I share a room. We quickly get settled unpacking the one backpack each that we brought. The other two girls are down the hall. I imagine they'll be up half the night unpacking all their unnecessary clothes and chatter-boxing about the events of the day.

I hardly notice how stunning our room is in its pale peach and beige décor. Soft beige walls. With Laura Ashley peach curtains with white lace trim and peach duvet covers on our twin beds. The smell of lavender on the down pillows is subtle.

I remember for a moment the room Jack and I shared that tumultuous night we were here as the hurricane hit. Our room had a king-sized bed and faced Mallory Square where so many people came to watch the sunset.

What I see out this window is the street, but I can hear from that other side of the building the air horns of cruise ships coming and going.

My mind replays what I heard from Teresa, and there is something she is not saying.

'What's going on here?' I say to Evvie. 'The Wassingers never mentioned anything about an accident. And the fact of all those disagreeing with them; I wish we'd been advised of this.'

Evvie nods. 'No kidding.'

'Did you hear Teresa say the Wassingers were misguided? She also said, "not again". What did she mean by that?'

Evvie shakes her head. 'I'm positive we'll find out more once we meet them.'

We're ready to go back downstairs. She adds, 'Teresa didn't think much of the fact that we were professionals.'

'I guess not. But don't forget, she's under seventy-five and according to our motto, we don't trust *their* opinions.'

Evvie grins. 'I wonder which surprised her the most: that we were women investigators, or that we were old? Or that we are not here for a funeral.'

I nod. 'Probably a little of each.'

I call the Wassingers to make sure they still want to see us today, or would they prefer tomorrow, since the day is almost gone. I am hoping we'd get a chance to rest, but, no, come right away was Mrs Wassinger's answer. We have an appointment and she gives us the simple directions to their home.

When we go downstairs, Teresa has not come back to the lobby. Jin is there, waiting for us.

He greets us, but he is clearly uncomfortable. He stiffly hands us a few brochures; his voice is a monotone. 'If you like key lime pie, this is where it was invented, and there's a building in town with a plaque to prove it. Parasailing? No, I guess not.'

Yes, Aunt Teresa did have that chat with her nephew. He's nervous with us.

'I do recommend the Shipwreck Museum and Harry Truman's winter home and of course, the mansion. You won't want to miss . . .' He stops himself, choking on his words. His face turns red, because once again he's about to reveal something else he shouldn't; but what?

Jin quickly opens the front door and urges us out. 'You don't want to be late.'

Before the door is completely shut, I hear Teresa's voice. 'Have they gone yet?'

She is hiding from us? What is going on? What don't they want us to know? Are we going to be sorry we took this trip?

Evvie and I are aware of Teresa and Jin's tension; Sophie and Bella are oblivious. My sister and I are puzzled. What next?

Ready or not, we're off to meet the Wassingers. Whatever they throw at us, we'll be able to manage.

Or will we?

NINE

Ida's Apartment – About the Same Time

Ida has not dressed today at all; she is still moving around barefoot in her living room. A radio is playing loud, intense hip-hop music and Ida, who has discovered she isn't ill at all, is celebrating by dancing up a storm. And remembering the way things were when she first came to Lanai Gardens sixteen years ago.

Ida was a loner. She had decided to stay that way when she moved in. She came loaded down with a mysterious, despondent past and if she'd had her way, she'd have curled up and lived closed-up and alone. Away from all feelings. Feelings and memories that made her cry.

But the survivor in her knew that isolation was bad for her. She had to pull out of her depression with her own mantra, 'Get over it, get over it.' The real Ida wanted to live her life and forget a past that she couldn't fix.

And so, years ago, she befriended her neighbor, Sophie, who introduced her to Bella and then to Gladdy and Evvie, and she knew her decision had been right. She'd found good friends. And finally, a feeling of having a home. And then a bonus; a happy and useful senior life once they became investigators. She had become the new and improved Ida Franz.

And a quick unwanted thought about not being in Key West tonight ran through her mind. No sense crying over spilt milk.

She looks at the time, clicks off the radio and turns on the TV to her favorite night-time soap opera. Her chicken is roasting in the oven, her veggies are waiting to be steamed; she's not hungry yet. So she plops down on her couch, ready to enjoy her program, *Lust Among Lovers*. She's addicted to this corny soap, and she doesn't care that others think it's silly. She's hooked.

In a few moments, the phone rings. She debates whether to interrupt her happy viewing and decides to let it ring. If it's important, whoever it is will leave a message.

And someone is leaving a message, one that surprises her. She listens to the near-hysterical Lola Binder practically screeching. What on earth can Hy's wife want with her?

She hears: 'Ida! Are you there? I've left six messages already on Gladdy's phone! She's not answering. Doesn't she ever pick up the phone anymore? What if she got important calls? I need to talk to her. It could be a matter of life or death . . .'

With that, Ida lowers the sound and with one eye still on the television, picks up the phone and interrupts Lola's hysterical chatter. 'Lola, yes, I'm here. You can't reach Gladdy 'cause she's out of town. Can I help you?'

'No, I need Gladdy. I have a serious problem for her to solve for me.'

'I'd be glad to be of service . . .'

'When will she be back?'

'I really have no idea.'

Lola is still fairly shouting. 'Where is the Gladdy of Gladdy Gold and her Associates? What kind of business does she run to not be here when she's wanted? I need Gladdy, not you! Find her and have her call me right away! You know my number!' With that she hangs up.

Ida mutters something obscene under her breath. What the hell can Hy's wife want that's so important? She raises the TV sound, drops back down onto her couch, looks at her clock. Her chicken needs ten minutes more. She goes back to enjoying her program. When her favorite male star, Kit Kittredge, comes on screen toying yet again with his long-suffering girlfriend's desires, Ida gives him badly needed advice, 'Kiss her already, dummy.'

TEN

Meet Clients. What is Happening Here?

Accepted to our map, and directions, we are traveling only three blocks from our B&B. We could have walked. Our plan is to meet and greet the Wassingers, then go out to dinner. We've never stopped eating in the car on the way up, and had lunch in one of the keys, so how can they still be hungry? But they can't wait to go to Margaritaville – whatever that is – and try some Caribbean seafood. And maybe sample the key lime pie. That's what they are eagerly looking forward to tonight. But for me, it's been a long, exhausting day and all I want is a hot bath and early bed.

According to Evvie's travel guide, 'We are just around the corner from a famous tourist location. 900 Whitehead Street was the home of Ern—' Before she can finish her sentence, we've arrived at our destination.

After the well-kept B&B where we are staying, and the many gorgeous mansions we've passed, this building is a disappointment. It's a shabby structure covered with gray clapboard, in desperate need of paint. Three storeys above there's a widow's walk on the roof. Evvie points it out and informs the girls that fishermen's wives used to stand on their high balcony, waiting for their husbands' ships to come home. Many husbands never returned, never to see their families again. Many tearful women learned that they had become widows from on that high floor.

The girls aren't paying too much attention to the history lesson, more interested in wondering about this house we're standing in front of.

Bella comments, 'It needs a lot of work.'

Sophie adds, 'It looks real old. And falling apart.'

The bell doesn't seem to work, so I knock. Then I knock again. After what seems like a long time, the door opens and an elderly couple stands there to greet us.

Obviously the Wassingers.

Bella whispers, 'So are the owners. Very old. And falling apart.'

Evvie pokes her. 'You should talk, *alta cocker*. You're almost as old as they are.'

He says, 'Welcome. Come in. She is Sadie.' A quivery voice.

She says, 'Come in. Welcome. He is Louie.' An equally weak voice.

We follow our clients inside. I introduce the girls.

They repeat our names twice. 'Gladdy. Evvie. Bella. Sophie. Gladdy. Evvie. Bella. Sophie.' Their way of remembering names. Good luck with that.

The Wassingers move at a snail's pace. We slow down to keep up to them. Aware of my girls' fears and foibles, I can read their minds as we walk through the dark hallway with dim lightbulbs hardly doing the job. A sharp contrast to the brightness of our B&B. Bella is already looking at the ceilings, expecting spiders and their webs and getting ready to faint.

Even Evvie is responding, unlike her, but somehow needing to touch tabletops and moldings for dust, her sleeve and fingers getting dirtier by the minute.

Sophie is sniffing – here she goes with her favorite aversion; the house smells of cats. She is allergic to cats. She's never been in a house where there's been a cat, so she's never tested that theory, but she's convinced she's afflicted. She can't help herself; she is sure the cat odor is causing her to sneeze. Finally, unable to resist, she addresses the backs of our hosts and whispers timorously, 'Do you have a cat?'

Sadie and Louie turn, smile sweetly at one another. Sadie says, 'We did a while ago. Snow White, number Seven. She was such a dear; she loved to sit on my head . . .'

Louie finishes it. '. . . and she was a great mouser. We miss her.'

They continue at their pathetic slow rate. Sophie is still sniffing unhappily. Evvie's sleeve and fingers are still dusting.

Bella continues to peek up, then down, with a new worry. No cat? Then there must be mice under foot. She tiptoes her way through the darkness.

I need to describe our clients. Both are tiny people, seemingly shriveled, with long, narrow faces, bodies pitifully thin. They are probably in their nineties. They wear gray, the same color as their outdoor house paint and the same shade as their hair. He is in a drab gray shirt and loose gray pants, no socks and house slippers, she in a gray loose-fitting, longish tent-like dress with heavy gray socks and also house slippers. Both use canes. They seem ancient.

I hope the girls are counting their blessings, since our ages are getting closer. We are all still able to get around; these folks seem shaky and feeble. Nearly helpless.

Sophie turns to me whispering, concerned at the shabbiness surrounding them. 'Can they even pay?'

I touch my finger to my lips, shushing her.

The Wassingers lead us into their kitchen for, as they call it, high tea. I haven't seen an old, avocado-colored fridge and stove like that since maybe the 1970s. The whole room looks like a painting out of a long ago *Saturday Evening Post* cover. I imagine the rest of the house is similarly furnished.

'Please sit down.' Louie points lovingly to his wife. 'Sadie will pour.'

'Please sit down,' she says, equally lovingly. She goes to the stove, where a kettle is turned up on high, steam hissing, almost clouding up to the ceiling.

I go through the routine of introducing our group, once again, our names already forgotten. 'Gladdie. Evvie. Bella. Sophie.'

With much nodding, they indicate that this time they'll remember. They won't. We all, but Sadie, take a seat; albeit on an aged, wooden, ladder-back, rickety chair. The room smells of mold and dust.

Sadie is advancing toward us from the stove holding the boiling hot kettle to pour water into teacups. We watch, with tremulous apprehension. Her hands tremble; we expect disaster any moment. She is close to scalding her hands. But somehow the cups are filled safely. We busy ourselves, being good guests, with the milk, sugar and dunking our tea bags, as Sadie calls them (they look used!) and drinking . . . boiling hot but utterly weak tea.

We all look about for maybe scones with clotted cream. Or jelly. Not a muffin, not a cookie. Nothing. This is high tea?

To make conversation, since my girls are silently trying to hide their disappointment, I ask the Wassingers how they found out about us.

Louie says, 'We read your ad . . .'

Sadie says, '. . . In the newspaper. We cheered at your . . .'

Louie says, 'Slogan.'

They both giggle. Sadie sips her tea, purses her lips and recites, 'Never trust anybody . . .'

Louie pinches Sadie's cheek in glee. 'Under . . .'

'Seventy-five.' Sadie pokes him on his shoulder and finishes the slogan. Both are pleased with their recitation.

We sit there, waiting for them to comment on the case. I have to keep from yawning. It's been a long day of driving, and the heat in the room is making me sleepy. Evvie is busy looking around this ancient room. Sophie and Bella keep lifting their feet up, worried about what germs might be on the floor.

Louie takes charge. He pounds his fist weakly on the scarred and wobbly wooden table. 'Let the meeting come to order. First, we formally welcome our guests.'

Sadie. 'You are so welcome in our humble home.'

'Thank you,' we respond.

'It was good of you to come,' says Sadie.

I say, 'We are pleased to be of service. Shall we discuss the case?'

Sadie pushes at Louie. 'Tell them it's not true.'

'I know dear, it's not.'

'About Robert, did you know Robert?' Sadie asks us.

'Mr Robert Strand?' I ask.

Evvie answers her, surprised, 'No, because we don't live here.'

That was a mistake. They want us to take a left turn in the conversation to discuss yet another topic. 'Where do you dear ladies live?' asks Louie.

Surely they remember that they contacted us where we live? I try to keep it short to get this slow-moving show on the road. This very long day is getting longer. 'We live in Fort Lauderdale.'

Sadie shows surprise, 'All of you?'

'Yes, all of us.'

Louie jumps in. 'Is that anywhere near Orlando? We once had a friend who lived in Orlando.'

Sadie adds, 'We always intended to visit. But we never got there. We traveled to Rome and Paris and London,' she giggles, 'but never made it to Orlando.'

Louie sighs. 'Poor Oliver. He died too young. He left a large family and many debts.'

Sadie musing along on her own pathway, 'I think Venice was my favorite city. Traveling on the water in gondolas.' She hums a bit of *O Solo Mio*.

I assume he's still mentioning the friend in Orlando, Florida. And she's going to take us through her full travel itinerary. I think it's time to get them back on track or we'll be here all night. 'Tell us what facts you have about Robert Strand.'

Sadie rotates her head, back and forth. Quivery, like her hands. 'He was our only hope.'

Louie adds, equally frail. 'They'll take it away, that's what they'll do.'

Evvie asks. 'Who wants to take it? Who wants to take what?'

Sadie looks at her, eyes tearing. 'Why, our house. That's why they killed him.'

Louie shows anger by squinting. 'What they did was to make the police believe we've lost our marbles. Robert's lawyer partners will put us away in some nut house. Sell our home out from under us. That's their plan. And what will happen to Papa?' He pounds pathetically on the table again.

Papa? These two people in their nineties can't have an older parent. A brother? Some relative? A leftover somebody from Orlando?

Sadie has absented herself. She's wandered down memory lane

in a world far, far away. In another galaxy? 'Do you have any idea how many hurricanes Gray Lady has been through?'

Sophie asks, 'Gray Lady?'

Louie, 'That's the name of our house.'

Sadie comments, 'Almost got us in '51 when Easy hit.'

Louie disagrees. 'Worse in '66 when Inez really packed a wallop.'

Sadie, 'Betsy in '65 was worse than Inez. You know that.'

Sophie whispers. 'They're talking about hurricanes. Why are they talking about hurricanes?'

We've lost them to ancient history. The girls are looking to each other, puzzled.

Louie, 'Floyd in '57 beat Betsy.'

It's turned into an argument, with heated, though still shaky, voices.

Sadie, 'Donna in '60!' With trembling lips as well.

They are working themselves into a tizzy. Bella and Sophie are totally confused.

I knock gently on the table to bring them back to the real world. Now the table has its own quake as well. I hope it won't collapse.

'Louie, Sadie, we're here, how can we help you?'

They pull themselves back to the present time, looking around as if to remind themselves of where they are.

'Sorry,' Sadie says.

'Sorry,' Louie says.

Evvie comments, 'We were recently given to believe Robert's death was an accident.'

Louie, upset, tries to get up, totters, changes his mind and drops back down. 'Robert, he was the good guy, not like the others. He protected us. They won't.'

'And we know that for sure it was not an accident,' Sadie says, firmly.

Evvie pipes up, 'How could you know that?'

Louie again. 'We just do.'

The Wassingers grin at that.

'Why are you so firm it was murder?' I repeat. We need to get them on point again, before they go off on another useless tangent.

Louie says, grandiose, 'Because we . . .'

And sure enough, Sadie takes her turn, '. . . have a witness!'

Louie next, '. . . who saw it all,'

And Sadie completes it. '. . . Papa saw Robert being murdered.'

Evvie asks, 'Did he go to the police and report it?'

Sadie, uncomfortable. 'Of course, not.' They both snicker.

Evvie asks, 'Why not?'

I ask, 'Where is your witness? We ought to talk to him.'

Sadie, 'Louie, I'm right and you are wrong, sweetheart. Donna nearly finished us. Shattered all the windows, made us run for our lives, poor Snow White, number three, was terrified. Or was she number four . . .?'

Louie, 'It was Snow White number six, and wrong, it was Floyd!'

Sadie, 'Not Floyd, Donna!'

Louie is at fever pitch, 'Hurricane Andrew in 1992 was the most destructive hurricane we ever suffered through! It was twenty-five years later that Irma made the list for worst! So, there!'

Sadie, sweetly, 'Yes, dear.'

Uh oh, lost them to hurricaneville again.

I get up. The girls quickly do the same, pushing away from their unsteady chairs.

'It's getting late and I'm sure we need to have dinner. Perhaps we can come back in the morning?'

The Wassingers rise and look perplexed. They head, house slippers skimming the floor, inch by inch, again for the front door as we follow.

Much shaking of hands. Louie says, 'Yes. Tomorrow. For breakfast, coffee. Sadie prepares a lovely coffee.'

Like the high tea?

Once outside, we group in front of my car for a few minutes, and just stand there. Numb. Sophie is making a big deal out of breathing cat-less fresh air. Bella has stopped looking upward in the sky for cobwebs.

Evvie brushes her dusty clothes, and says, 'What was that all about?'

I haven't a clue.

ELEVEN
Ida on the Phone Late Night

'Hi. Gladdy, is this a good time to call?' Ida is seated at her kitchen table, in between balancing the phone and munching on her late dinner of roast chicken, veggies, French fries and a Coke. She figures ten p.m. isn't too late to call.

'Hi, Ida. Perfect timing. We just had our first meeting with the Wassingers. In fact, we're all sitting in my car right outside their home, trying to figure out what just went down. It was quite an extraordinary experience.'

'Tell me. Tell me.'

'Let me put us on the speakerphone so we can all hear. The girls are leaning in, and don't want to miss a thing.'

Ida smiles at the chorus of the girls saying hello. She calls hello back to them.

Sophie jumps in. 'You wouldn't believe our clients. Two itsy-bitsy people, who are very, very old.'

Ida sips at her Coke, laughing, 'Older than we are?'

Bella, 'Lots older. Lots and lots. They're very, very old. Not like us. We're good old.'

Sophie, 'They're so funny. They finish each other's sentences.'

Gladdy adds, 'And it's difficult keeping them on track.'

Evvie, 'You should have heard them talking about all the hurricanes they went through. They were so funny; they forgot we were even there.'

Sophie, 'They're very secretive.'

Bella, 'I'd call them weird.'

Ida, still eating her dinner, sucks away the bone marrow on the chicken bones. 'That is amusing. But what about the case?'

Gladdy answers that one. 'There seems to be a difference of opinion; it comes down to the Wassingers being the only people in Key West who think Mr Strand was murdered. Everyone else insists it was an accident. I wish we had known that before we left. We should have asked for more information.'

Ida is tackling her French fries. 'Sounds like you've got your work cut out for you. At first it sounded open and shut.'

Gladdy says, 'True.' She pauses. 'But most important, how are you feeling?'

Ida is finishing the last of her French fries, and she wipes her greasy fingers with a napkin. 'That's why I called. I have two things to discuss with you.'

Sophie sings out into the phone. 'I thought it was just because you missed us.'

Ida starts on her strawberries and whipped cream dessert. 'That, too. But first, big surprise. I don't have the flu. I must have had some odd bug, because, it's gone. Totally. I'm one hundred percent back to normal. I feel healthy and happy.'

Bella, 'That's nice. 'Cause, when we saw you, you looked like you were dying.'

Sophie interrupts, 'That's good news. Then come and join us.'

Bella, 'Yeah, jump on a plane; you'll be here in minutes. Well, maybe an hour.'

Sophie, 'We'll be so glad to see you. You'll get a kick out of the Wassingers. They're a hoot.'

Ida wipes up the rest of the strawberries with one finger. 'Girls, you don't remember. I hate to fly. I never fly. I only did it once and it scared the heck out of me. I would shoot myself in the foot before I get on an airplane again.'

Bella apologizing, 'We forgot. I got another idea. Rent a car and drive down all by yourself and join us.'

Sophie, 'Great idea. Too bad you won't have us for company.'

Ida examines the dish, but it's empty. 'No. No. No way. I gave up my license years ago. That's when I also sold my car. Remember? And besides, I would never drive such a distance alone. So forget about it. I'm stuck here.'

Bella and Sophie together, 'We forgot.'

Evvie, 'Sorry about that. You'll just have to get updates from us. We'll keep you posted. But, what was the second thing?'

Leaning her phone on her shoulder near her ear, Ida picks up her dirty dishes and heads for the sink. 'Gladdy, you're getting a lot of calls from Lola on the business phone.'

That's a surprise to her. 'Lola Binder? Whatever for?'

Bella giggles, 'Maybe she heard we're mad at Hy and she wants to save his silly butt.'

Sophie joins in the giggling, pretending shock. 'Bella, don't talk dirty, it's not nice.'

Ida is disappointed, nothing more to eat. 'No, she sounds worried. She says things like it's a matter of life or death.'

Gladdy says, 'Really? What's wrong? Did she give you any details about what the trouble was?'

'That's just it. She refuses to tell me anything. She has a problem she wants only you to solve. She's so mad because she can't talk to you directly. It's gotta be about Hy, 'cause he wasn't there in the apartment. I told her you were out of town. But she was adamant. She only wants you.'

'Well, that's silly. You call her back and tell her that while I'm away, you are in charge of our business. Or she can go elsewhere. Be strong. Be tough.'

Ida pretending meek, 'Yes, ma'am.' Ida thinks about this.

Gladdy says, 'Well, that's settled . . .'

Evvie says, 'The Wassingers are keeping something from us.'

Ida laughs. 'I'm positive you'll figure it all out without me.'

Bella, 'Say goodbye. We're tired and hungry.'

Ida, 'I heard that. So, goodbye.'

The phone call is over. Ida puts the dishes in the sink to soak and addresses her mirrored reflection on her glass-windowed stove. 'Be strong. Be tough. Strong. Tough.'

She whirls around. 'I can be that.'

TWELVE

Clarity. Jasmine Tea. And Real Facts

We didn't get around to Margaritaville or any typical Key West restaurants tonight. We weren't going to watch the sunset with a hundred or more people at Mallory Square. Too late. We hop into the nearest all-night coffee shop and order hamburgers and sodas. I order a small salad. I can't believe they were still hungry after all that food today.

Gladdy Gold and Associates are flummoxed and exhausted from keeping up with the Wassinger rigmarole. The subject of the Wassingers is like an itch we keep on scratching. In between chewing, we can't stop our curiosity.

We had asked questions that got us no answers.

'Was there really a cat inside?' Sophie asks, while eating her burger, medium rare.

'Did anyone see any spiders?' Bella asked worriedly over her burger, also medium rare. Naturally, she orders what Sophie chooses.

'What was that comment about lawyers?' Evvie asks while having her burger, well done.

More and more things to ponder while I'm just picking at my salad. What really was the worst hurricane? Did we care? Where does their papa live? And what has he got to do with this crime. Is it even a crime? Who was the witness to a crime that may or may not have taken place?

My own question to myself: why are we here? Really? This is giving me a headache.

Evvie reminds me, 'We never had a chance to ask about the mystery letters in your mailbox.'

We need to talk to someone who makes sense. Someone who can answer these puzzling questions. I drive us back to our Brown Pelican Inn and hope Teresa, our manager, is still awake.

We arrive back at the inn. Lights are dimmed. All residents are either night owls and out on the town or sound asleep. The lobby is quiet. Too late to find Teresa. I'm disappointed.

Suddenly, surprisingly, Teresa appears. She's glad we came back and looked for her. In fact, she tells us, she was waiting for us. She apologizes for her strange behavior earlier. She invites us for tea before bedtime, and feels she needs to explain.

This time we are served jasmine tea in the lobby, enjoying a much-improved tea served with lemon cookies.

When do my girls stop eating? I speculate.

'You really are private eyes?' Teresa asks, looking us up and down more closely. She doesn't say it but I guess she is wondering how this is possible.

'Yes, we are. And have been for three whole years,' Evvie chimes in.

Sophie preens. 'With a perfect score of closed cases.'

Bella nods, twin-like. 'Perfect. No case too big, no case too small. We win 'em all.'

Evvie explains briefly. 'We deal with seniors' problems and being seniors ourselves, we understand. It works.'

Teresa is pleased. 'Well, good for you. And lucky for all the seniors you've helped. However, I feel I should say a few words up front. You are nice women, and forgive me for being presumptuous by poking into your business, but I believe you've made this trip needlessly.'

The girls stare at her in distress. Not I, because that's what I've been thinking to myself. Unusual for them, they stay quiet and don't interrupt.

Teresa passes us the plate of cookies. Only Sophie and Bella take more. Sophie reminds me of that little joke about when you're on vacation the calories don't count.

Teresa leans forward in her chair. 'Let me start from the beginning and perhaps you'll understand. I'm well aware of how worried my friends, Louie and Sadie, are. And rightly so.'

Evvie asks, 'You know them well?'

Teresa nods. 'Of course I do. For years. They originally were the Wassinger Worldwide Travel Agency. They helped tourists plan trips for those who visit the keys and foreign travel as well. It was a highly successful business. Then they retired at age sixty-five.

'For many years after that, they traveled a great deal themselves to enjoy the trips they had suggested for others. But, as Louie would say, and has said many times, they've lived too long.

'After they decided that, because of their age, they didn't feel capable of travel anymore, they returned home for good. They'd planned ahead with a good retirement plan. They were happy to spend what they described as their last good years in their precious house. She gardened. He belonged to the Historic Society, which helped restore and protect famous homes that had become national treasures.'

'But?' Evvie commented, 'There's a "but".'

Teresa pours us more tea. '*But*, once they hit their eighties, they eventually ran out of the pension money. They couldn't keep the house up. They watched its slow demise in despair. A roof that leaked. Floors that needed repair. Painting required inside as well as out. They couldn't pay for any of it. They eked out money from the equity on their mortgage and that's what they're living on.

'They're in their nineties and nearly senile and I worry about them. They aren't afraid of dying, but they are afraid for their house. They don't want to sell it and go into a retirement home. They don't want it sold, even after they are gone.'

I think that's odd. Wouldn't the house be inherited by someone?

Evvie jumps ahead of me. 'That's where this Robert Strand came in?'

'Yes, as a partner in the law firm, Strand, Smythe and Love, Robert was getting close to his retirement. He stayed on to keep the Wassingers as his only clients. He promised them he'd get their house listed with the Historic Society and it would be preserved.'

I finally ask the question. 'They have no heirs?'

'Robert Strand was to inherit.'

I wonder about their papa, but I don't want to break Teresa's train of thought.

'Now Robert Strand is gone,' Evvie says, refusing a third cup of tea. She raises her hand, as if in school. 'I think I see where this is going.'

Teresa nods, answering her unasked thought. 'It will then be passed down to the other lawyers, who they fear will immediately turn it over to realtors. The house will be sold to people who probably will tear it down. There is a real estate company that is already sniffing around.' She wrings her hands, distraught. 'Long ago, I advised the Wassingers to leave it directly to the Historic Society, but they felt more secure knowing Robert would handle it.

'And right now, they seem too paralyzed to do anything. They are mourning Robert.'

I ask Teresa, 'What do you think happened to Robert?'

She waits for a moment, as if in battle with herself. Finally, sadly, she shakes her head. 'It's as I said before, it was a freak accident.'

Sophie finally needs to talk and makes an assumption. 'Is that why the Wassingers need to think Robert was murdered?'

I'm stunned. 'Surely they don't think someone killed him because of the house?'

Teresa nods, again. 'They do believe precisely that. They're adamant and won't let go of it. That's why they called you.'

A few minutes of silence as we digest this.

'But they're the only ones who think he was murdered,' Teresa continues. 'The police are absolutely convinced it was an accident.'

'The coroner?' I ask.

'An accident,' Teresa answers.

Sophie is up next. 'Robert's law offices?'

'An accident. The law firm assured the Wassingers that they would take good care of their house for them. The Wassingers don't trust them.'

The time is now. I can't put it off any longer. 'I have a funny question to ask. If they don't have any heirs, or relatives, and they're obviously not interested in getting whatever money they'd get for the house sale; then what about this papa, who says he is a witness, and why hasn't he stepped forward?'

Teresa suddenly stiffens and stares, like the proverbial deer in the headlights. Then she stretches and yawns. 'Bedtime. I think I've bored you enough.' She gets up. 'Sleep well.' And she walks quickly away. Leaving all the tea things.

We stay silent for a moment, then Evvie smirks. 'What a phony yawn.'

'Obviously that question shut her down,' I say. 'But why?'

Evvie, 'I guess their witness can't go to the police. Or won't. But why?'

I say, astounded, 'And Teresa has the answer but refuses to tell us.'

There's much to discuss about what we've just been told, but all agree; they are exhausted and just want to sleep. It can wait until tomorrow. Obviously, the cookies can't; Sophie and Bella grab what's left of them.

Though, for a while, we can hear Sophie and Bella down the hall probably chatting about this odd day. Or maybe discussing all the food they ate. Or maybe chewing on the rest of the cookies, followed by Tums.

I wonder what tomorrow will bring.

Evvie is thoroughly exhausted and asleep within minutes.

I toss about, puzzles in my head that won't leave me alone. Who is their papa?

THIRTEEN

The Raincoat Man and his Episodes

Ida rushes through washing the dinner dishes, scrubbing the pots, tossing the leftovers in the trash, cleaning off the dining room table. All the while her plans spin wildly about in her head. Always the perfectionist, she is surprised at herself for doing a slap-dash job with clean-up. Methodical, she calls herself. It's her middle name. But she is so focused on what lies ahead, she gives her perfectionist self permission to wait until the morning to finish up the job according to her purist obsessive nature.

She dashes from the kitchen into her bedroom; an excited woman with a mission.

Mumbling, 'Be strong. Be tough. You're in charge. Yeah, mama!'

She pulls open her closet door with vigor. A closet that is never visited by anyone else. It's not the hung clothes that matter; she'd wear the same gray pantsuit daily and not care. It's the inside back of the door.

A full-sized poster, badly aged, with colors dulled, has hung there since the day she moved into Lanai Gardens around sixteen years ago.

Her secret fetish. A life-sized photo of her hero, TV star Peter Falk as his most famous character, Lieutenant Columbo, wearing his famous wrinkled raincoat over some kind of light-colored suit and white shirt and tie. She'd seen just about every episode in the ten seasons the show was on the air. She throws his faded image a kiss, then digs into the rear bottom of her closet, and pulls out a ragged cardboard box, one she hasn't thought about nor opened in years.

She addresses the poster. 'I knew we'd be together again, Peter, darling.' With that she digs in the box and drags out a beige-ish, or maybe it's a green-ish, lump of an outfit; the long shabby famous raincoat she bought at a fans' auction. They told her that it was the original worn by Falk on the show. They also gave her a receipt with its *provenance* – the proof of its integrity. She paid plenty. It was worth it. A treasure to Ida.

She puts the wrinkled garment on over her pajamas. She's delighted that she hasn't bothered getting dressed since the girls left. What freedom! To do what she wants when she wants to. She admits to herself that always hanging around with the girls has hampered the inner Ida. It was always a group decision about everything. When and where to eat. What movie to see. When to swim at the pool. When to go shopping. To the food market. To the bank. To the dentist. Even doctors' appointments were made as group trips. Where was her individuality? Stifled, that's where.

Now, she can enter her long-lost fantasy land.

In front of the mirror on the outside of the door, she pretends to light a make-believe cigar and then pivots her body about into a casual, relaxed position. Her voice changes to what she thinks is a great imitation of her hero.

'Don't think you're gonna get away with it, Faye Dunaway. I'm on to you.' Then, holding onto the doorknob, as if she's leaving but has abruptly changed her mind, she quotes, and acts out, the lines Peter Falk made famous – his parting shot in many a final scene. 'Just one more thing before I go.' Columbo is onto Faye. The jig is up. That she and her evil partner, Claudia Christian, are the murderers of their two-timing boyfriend. Colombo has figured it out and he can prove it. Yes!

She goes to the phone.

Time to take on Mrs Hy Binder. Mealy-mouth Lola. Ida doesn't care if she wakes her up. She will make an appointment with her for the first thing in the morning. Ida will decide on the time, at her own convenience. And Ida will be tough. She's in charge and power is what she craves. First step on doing it her way.

She dials the Binder number. She doesn't bother glancing at her clock. She doesn't care how late it is.

Ida has a complete list of residents in a bound three-holed paper book they printed years back. She's kept it up to date. Lots of additions when newcomers moved in. Pages of cross-outs of people who've left to go to other cities, or to other states. Those who return to their original towns. To choose, welcome or not, to live with the grown children. And those who made the final journey to either heaven or . . . down below. Ida has notations at each name, keeping track of all of them. A perfectionist in action.

She waits as the Binder number keeps ringing. She giggles. Bet I wake her up. Keep it tough; let her find out who the boss is.

Instantly, Ida hears the gushing, sleep-deprived voice of Lola, who cries out. 'Hy, honey-bun is that you?'

Oops. Bad idea. Take a different tack. Kindly. Understanding. Sound sorry. Like Columbo would do it. 'I hope I didn't wake you. It's only me, Lola, dear. You've been on my mind, so I thought I'd call . . .'

Lola interrupts. 'You know something! What do you know? Tell me!'

Simpering now. 'I only called to make an appointment with you for the morning. As you can tell, I'm already on the job.'

Lola is sobbing. 'Thank you. Thank you. Come any time after eight. I'll be up. Thank you so much for caring.'

She looks at the clock. Three a.m. So much for being tough.

Slowly Ida removes her Columbo coat. She throws it on the floor next to her bed. She's positive Peter Falk would do the same.

FOURTEEN

Ida on the Job. Lola Defensive

Day Two

Eight a.m. Dressed for 'the kill.' First, one last scan in her bedroom mirror door. She puts on her Columbo coat and with it, Columbo's self-assured but seemingly clueless attitude. Peter Falk whispers in her ear. *Let them think you're a simpleton. They always fall for it.*

Ida is let into the Binder apartment. Located across the way from where she lives. The minute the door opens, she's met with,

'Why are you wearing a raincoat when it isn't raining; it's ninety degrees out there?' Lola snarls with biting sarcasm.

Nice beginning, Ida thinks. She's only been there once and that was enough. *Chochkies* throughout the apartment. Every shelf has 'treasures'. Lola's salt and pepper shakers collection, for example. Not just one set, but she's got salt and pepper sets of every size, shape, color, and country of origin . . . blah blah blah. None worth over ten cents in a garage sale (from where she probably grabbed them).

That would be nauseating enough, but there's also the keys collected from each cheap motel she ever slogged into. Then the cream pitcher assortment. And baby dolls with moveable eyes . . . And the smell of potpourri, which chokes the air. How does Hy stand living here? How does he live with that whiny *meeskait*? Ugly, ugly, ugly. Ida stifles an inner giggle. But then again, who'd want to live with Hy? Neither of them movie star quality.

She buries the thought that she is being unkind. Never mind, let's get down to business so she can get the hell out of there. She can't stand Lola and Lola hates her just as much. So they're even. She wishes Gladdy were the one dealing with this mushy stuff. Lola is a powder puff; Ida holds on to her pretend simple self. She hates it; that's not who she is. But she's stuck right now.

They face one another like medieval gladiators. Can there be any two more unlike women on this hemisphere? Lola's wearing a frilly girly-girly sunshine yellow bathrobe. Her stance: hands on hips, queen of her garage sale domain. Ida, as her own hero, down and dirty, pretending sweetness, always sure, always right. Her Columbo.

Ida, still oozing strength coming from her closet session with Columbo gear, jumps in with a tough mindset, 'Never mind about me, dearie, let's hear from you. Spill it. What's a matter of life or death?'

'I specifically asked for Gladdy. That's who I asked for. That's who I want!'

'Well, you can't have her. Gladdy specifically told me to tell you she's on a business trip and not available and I am the PI holding down the fort. Take me or leave me.' Ida has mixed feelings. She'd be glad not to deal with Lola. But then, she loses her chance to shine.

She can imagine Lola's battle within herself. She would be glad to dump Ida, but it seems like she has a problem that is stronger than her loathing.

Lola can hardly get her words out. 'Hy's disappeared! My husband is gone and I'm terrified something horrible has happened to him!'

Lola races out of the room, leaving Ida looking after her. Amazed.

What the hell?

Lola doesn't come back. Should she go look for her? Hold her hand and make her feel better? Nah, let her cry it out. She'll wait for a better time.

Columbo tries for a dramatic exit. She swirls her coat around her . . . and, oh, oh, she's just knocked down a pair of kitty-cat salt and pepper shakers.

'Oopsy,' says Ida. 'I'm outa here'.

FIFTEEN

Another Trip to the Gray Lady

It was a wonderful breakfast of delicious blueberry muffins and excellent coffee at our B&B. What was not surprising about the breakfast was there was no sign of Teresa. It was obvious she was still avoiding us after last night.

Jin is behind the front desk. Polite as he is, he still has not looked at us.

Well, maybe today will give us some enlightenment, before we decide to stay or go home. There will be things to discuss after this meeting.

Here we are, returning to this odd, gray mansion with its odd, gray couple, and right away we are offered coffee. Sadie gaily waves a jar of 'instant' at us. Coffee will be as awful as was the tea. Shuddering, we politely inform our clients we already had breakfast, thanks anyway.

Louie and Sadie face us in the hallway, bright-eyed and eager. They are dressed in exactly the same clothes as they wore when we met yesterday. Or does their closet only hold similar outfits?

To avoid any more side discussions of hurricanes, being businesslike, I get right to the point. 'Shall we visit your papa? Is he aware we are coming?'

They are startled. I sense they intend to waffle some more. Like they did yesterday. Why?

After many shared looks between them with silent whisperings, they have made their decision and beckon us toward that barely lit, gloomy staircase.

Sadie proves me right. 'I have some special antiques you might like to see first.' They are still stalling.

Louie chimes in, of course. 'Vintage china. Ancient brass candleholders. Patchwork quilts?'

Evvie stops that tactic. 'Maybe, later.'

Sophie and Bella are back to their search for spiders and cat smells. I ignore them.

The couple exchange more nervous looks, then shrug as they give up on the delays. They lead the way. The stairway has steep steps. Is it possible their papa lives in this house – up there?

Sadie chuckles. 'Three flights.'

Louie chuckles, too. Suddenly he's the comedian. 'Quite a hike. Hope you wore your climbing shoes.'

Again, they *schlepp* slowly, as if each step were a mile. I'm amazed that they can do this at all. Step one. Push forward with cane. Hang onto banister. Step two, climb another step. Push with cane, etc.

The girls look pained. They find the staircase difficult. At home, we live in easy access, easy steps, and we always take the elevator, anyway.

I hear Sophie puffing and mumbling behind me, in a monotone. 'I'm getting older by the second. I'll be a hundred by the time we get up there.'

'Yeah, me, too,' Bella chimes in.

Evvie. 'Shhh, keep going.'

Louie calls out to the girls lagging behind him, 'I need to inform you; there are strict rules. Papa is quite moody. We must be wary. And very respectful.'

Sadie. 'After all, he is quite famous.'

Louie. 'Speak only when spoken to.'

Sadie. 'He has earned the right to have a big ego.'

By the second flight, the girls are panting hard, and clutching the banisters, positive they will topple if they let go.

The Wassingers are still moving steadily at their snail pace.

At the third flight landing, we stop, gasping for air. At last we're finally at the top.

Sadie says sweetly, 'We're not there yet. Papa enjoys sitting on his favorite chair in the sunshine.'

Louie. 'So up we go. To the roof top, part of which is a widow's walk.'

With dismay we manage to clamber up behind them once again, in a corner of the landing, climbing now on an old creaky wrought iron circular staircase.

Sadie calls behind to Louie. 'Did you remember your homework?'

Louie chuckles, 'I *dassent* forget.'

What are they talking about? Homework?

Finally we are on the roof. The large roof's floor is covered by what looks like a huge oriental rug. A small portion off to one edge was probably used as a widow's walk. We look around. There's an area of about six feet by six feet approximately which is surrounded by a white picket fence. We see a beautiful white wicker chair, with colorful pillows. Next to the chair, a small, round, white, metal and glass table. A frosted goblet on it that looks like a chilled southern rum drink with ice cubes and floating limes. Next to the drink, an empty wooden box labeled in Spanish, which I discern says 'Cigars from Cuba'. *What? Did I just imagine the drink levitated for a moment!*

No one is seated in the chair. We search for their papa. I look around. No one is on the roof but us.

Has he stood us up?

What's this? Louie and Sadie stand in front of the enclosed fenced area and stare at the wicker chair. Louie bows. 'Good morning, sir. I hope your daiquiri is to your liking.' They listen.

Sadie bows. 'Thank you, sir.' She points. 'That's them. The ones we hired.'

The girls and I are stumped. What is going on? The Wassingers are speaking to the empty air. The girls look to me, their uneasy leader, so I plunge in.

'Where is your papa?' I ask. 'I thought we had an appointment.'

The Wassingers are doing what might be called bowing and scraping. An early expression of respect by obsequiously, and with great deference, bending as to a musical conductor or royalty. *What the heck?*

I try again. 'May I ask what you are doing?'

Sadie says, bursting with pride, 'Why, we're conversing with our house guest, Ernest Hemingway, the world-famous writer. Known to all as "Papa".'

Louie jumps in quickly, 'And brave soldier, explorer and boxer; so many things he is famous for. That's his nickname.'

Sadie giggles. 'He just told me for the hundredth time, he hates that nickname.' She waves coyly and prettily. 'Oh, you always say that. You like being called Papa!'

What on earth is going on! I say, very, very carefully and sweetly as if speaking to aliens from a far-off galaxy, 'And how come we can neither see nor hear this famous dead writer-hero?'

By now Sophie and Bella are hugging each other, in fear. Evvie is speechless.

Louie and Sadie smile. In tandem, they explain to the chair, 'Yes, sir, it's our Gladdy Gold and Associates Private Eyes. The ones we phoned in Fort Lauderdale. Yes, we've tried all the locals. These special ladies accepted our invitation and would take the case. We're so lucky. They just arrived.'

I am getting an ominous feeling that we have made a horrible mistake. We've stepped into loony-tune land. Was this what Teresa was trying to warn us about? And was too embarrassed?

The couple, ears pointed forward, listen avidly. They laugh and laugh some more.

Sophie asks, 'What's so funny?'

The Wassingers are uncomfortable; being the voice of the famous dead man doesn't come easy for them. Sadie asks, 'Papa wants to hear how come there are no men in your company.'

I am expected to answer; this is the best I can come up with, 'Just because,' I say, stumbling.

My girls have eyes wide open; they look like they want to flee.

Hold on. No, not all. Bella is motionless, staring at the same point in the air that has the Wassingers in thrall.

Slowly Louie says nervously, 'Papa is famous for quick-making assumptions. He says to tell you he can't believe you are detectives.' Louie gulps. 'He used the word, "pitiful".'

I can tell there is more, coming from Nowhere Ville, but Louie restrains himself, unable to speak. Weird! Are they hallucinating? I wonder about drugs. And how do we get out of here gracefully?

Evvie, ever the realist, is snarky. 'I get it. You're pretending an invisible man is making fun of us. *Really?* Well, such nonsense. Invisible Man from movie-land? I remember the film with Claude Rains. Or are you having a laugh on us? Joke's over.'

Louie and Sadie jump as if they were blown at by one of their famous hurricanes. Louie hisses, 'Shh, Papa is angered by your lack of respect. He is a world-class figure who has written many famous novels and has appeared before kings and queens. He demands you treat him like the royalty he is.'

Evvie says carefully, 'Let me get this straight. Are you trying to say you are talking to a . . . ghost, Ernest Hemingway's ghost and he is answering you?'

Again the couple is startled. And too nervous. This is not going well.

Louie, 'He doesn't like it when he's being talked about when he's right here.'

'Okay, girls. Look at the time,' I say, glancing at my watch. 'We should leave.'

Sophie and Evvie want out of this *mishagosh*. Sophie is racing, so to speak, in her cane-dragging way toward the circular staircase. Evvie is right behind her. I am suddenly rooted to my spot. Wait a minute. What is going on here?

Suddenly Bella chortles.

Sophie stops in her tracks, annoyed, 'What's so funny?'

Bella puts her hand over her mouth to cover her smile. 'He just said a naughty word. I don't want to repeat it.' She waves gaily at the empty chair. 'Hi, there.'

Three mouths open wide. Finally, I manage to find my voice. 'Bella. You can see someone? You hear someone?'

Bella is pleased. She isn't often the center of attention. Perky, happy. 'Of course I can. He's handsome.' She's in stitches as she grins at the chair. 'He just said I'm cute.' She curtsies. 'Why, thank you, sir.'

Is insanity contagious?

I can't believe I'm saying this. 'And what does Mr Hemingway look like?'

Bella, stuttering with delight, 'He's a big guy with a bushy white beard and mustache. He still has all his hair! He's wearing light brown shorts and a jacket . . .'

Sadie interrupts. 'His favorite safari jacket. And straw fedora.'

Louie tells us to pay attention. Just as well, we can't speak, anyway. 'I have to do my recitation now. Whenever I visit Papa, I recite some of his very famous words. It's my homework. This is from *A Farewell to Arms*.' Louie emotes with waving arms and lots of feeling:

'"The world breaks everyone and afterward many are strong at the broken place, but those who that will not break, it kills".'

Louie bows. Sadie claps at his performance.

I think to myself. No wonder I was not a Hemingway fan. I always found his prose choppy. And sometimes just plain bad. What the hell am I doing? A book report? Bella is talking to a ghost and we're behaving as if this is sane! If Ida were here, she'd be choking with laughter.

'Ooh,' Sadie says, wagging a finger at Bella. 'It's for you,' she says indicating the imaginary literary giant.

Bella listens to the air above the wicker chair as we, feeling dim-witted, continue to gape. Her cheeks break out into blushes.

Evvie, unable to stand the ridiculousness of it all, sneers, 'And what did Papa H. just say to adorable you?'

Bella smiles, 'He recited lines to me from the same book.' She tilts her ear, to listen again. And repeats, '"I am not . . . brave anymore, darling . . . I'm all broken. They've broken me".' Bella is touched by his words. She curtsies again.

Evvie whispers to me, 'I'd like to smack her. Damn. I read that book. I think the lines are correct. Boring and banal, but correct.'

I whisper back. 'I read it, too. Remember, you loaned it to me. I also remember those lines. Bella couldn't possibly be making that up.'

Sophie asks me, one step hovering on the spiral staircase, 'What do we do now?'

'I have no idea.'

Evvie can't resist. With a twinkle of her eye, she says, 'Bella, ask your new friend if he sent Gladdy letters back home? In white envelopes?'

Bella turns miffed, 'I don't have to ask him. He's not deaf. He can hear you.'

Evvie grim, 'And what was his answer?' She faces the empty chair. If looks could kill. But then, again, he's already dead.

Bella, reporter *par excellence,* answers, 'Of course he sent it. Louie addressed, stamped and mailed it. Didn't you read it?'

Evvie places her hands on her hips, refusing to face Papa. 'We were supposed to read blank pages?'

Bella listens again, then bows her head. 'He said what kind of detectives are you? You should have been able to figure it out.'

Evvie is annoyed, but can't stop herself. 'And how were we supposed to do that?'

Bella, repeating the master's words, 'Any kindergarten kid knows that you use lemon juice on invisible writing. It was an invitation to come here. Dummies, he calls you.'

Louie and Sadie are glowing. Happy that Papa at least likes one of us.

Louie jumps in. 'Don't you see why he can't be a witness? There are so many unbelievers out there. That's why we hired you. To make the others understand. Papa witnessed the whole thing. He knows what really happened to our poor lawyer friend, Robert. As if a fish could kill!'

Sadie adds, worriedly. 'Papa's been our house guest since 1961. If, after we're gone, they tear down this house, where can he go? He used to live in his own mansion around the corner, but they turned it into a museum . . .'

And of course, Louie finishes her thoughts, '. . . and Papa couldn't stand the crowds, the annoying children or the noise, so he moved in with us.'

Louie stops short. The Wassingers tremble. They are being addressed by their 'house guest'. From their tremors, it must be bad.

Louie recites Papa's final words, embarrassed. 'I cannot abide fools. You silly women weary me. Time for my daquiri and noon nap. *Adios, muchachas.*'

Sadie and Louie shrug. Meeting adjourned.

We start for the staircase. Louie calls out to us. 'Expect a quiz next time.'

I don't bother answering.

SIXTEEN

Aftermath. Still Dazed. Are We Crazy?

We are minutes into my car, windows closed, AC on; right after our meeting with – can I believe I'm even saying this – Ernest Hemingway's ghost.

Bella is cringing in the back seat, all of us staring at her; each with an assortment of expressions of disbelief. Since she is practically in Sophie's lap, her closeness is more intimidating. Secretly, I think she expects her once dear friend to hit her.

Evvie turns so that she can face the two in the back, and says with irony, 'Let the interrogation begin.' Not that our partners would understand that word, but they catch the meaning.

'Well?' says Sophie.

'Well, what?' Bella answers her best friend with terror in her eyes. She squirms, trapped, with nowhere to go.

Evvie. 'So you really chatted with a ghost? You really saw him and heard him?'

Bella, on the defensive, 'You were there. You saw. You heard.'

Evvie again. 'How is that possible? There's no such thing as a ghost. Or zombies or mummies or vampires. Or hungry werewolves!'

Bella, cowers. 'I can't explain it. I just knew.'

Evvie still unbelieving, 'You just knew. Oh, really? I didn't think we lived next door to Baba Vanga.'

Sophie squints, 'Who's Baba Vanga?'

I turn to Evvie at that one. 'Who?'

Evvie answers aggressively, 'A blind Bulgarian mystic. She sort of predicted the end of the world.'

I'm startled. 'Where on earth did you pick that up?'

Evvie is dismayed, 'We read about her in my book club!'

A moment of silence. Lots of glaring going around.

Sophie brings us back to our attack of poor Bella, 'Does their Papa look like a real person?'

Bella, 'I guess, sort of, I'm not sure, like on TV, or a movie when it's a black and white, kind of flat, faded . . .'

Evvie, upbeat for a moment, 'Reminds me of that little kid in the movie. What did he keep saying? "I see dead people".'

Sophie, 'Yeah, we saw that one. Creepy.'

I can't resist, 'And we're supposed to see dead authors.'

Evvie, 'Just one, I hope. What if he has friends?'

Sophie adds, 'Don't go there; we have enough to worry about.' She grimaces. 'That thing, whatever it is, insulted us! What nerve.'

There's a long pause, all of us thinking. It lasts a while as we ponder the preposterous. Finally, I say, 'Bella couldn't have made those lines up. She wouldn't have known those quotes.' I look sharply at our scared partner.

Bella, with arms folded. 'Yeah. That's right. I only read romance novels.' She wiggles as best she can away from Sophie. Who equally wishes she was far away from her.

Evvie. 'This is so nutsy. If we ever told anyone they'd think we were crazy.'

I add, 'Teresa knows. That's why she ended our discussion so abruptly. She didn't want to deal with her friends' eccentricity. But I bet she thinks the Wassingers are senile and imagining that they are living with a famous ghost.'

Bella stiffens, feeling righteous. 'But I didn't imagine him. I swear.'

Evvie sighs. 'There's that. Now what?'

Bella, poignantly, 'We go home?'

Evvie, 'Good idea. And tell everybody we were here on vacation.'

Sophie, 'That would work. But first we need to go to the beach and get a tan.'

I'm feeling dejected. 'Right this minute I wish I was on the safari with the guys. Chasing lions and elephants. It would be more restful.'

Evvie sighs. 'I miss my Joe.'

I join in with her sighs, 'And I definitely do miss my guy.' Another week and he'll be back home. And hopefully, I'll be there to meet the bus.

There is another silence in the car for a few moments. Bella stiffens, waiting for what attack might come next.

Sophie, the lightbulb turning on, 'I wonder, why can't Papa move to another home and save us all this trouble?'

I answer. 'Good question. Why, indeed?'

Bella softly, 'Nobody else would take him?'

'Got that right. He's high maintenance,' Evvie laughs.

Ominous silence.

Bella. 'So what do we do now? I wish Ida was here. She'd know I was telling the truth.'

Sophie smirks. 'Yeah, right. She'd tell us to take you to the nearest booby hatch.'

I say, 'Reason tells us we're in a preposterous situation and we should definitely leave for home, tanned or not.'

Sophie says judiciously, 'Hear, hear. I agree.' She knocks on the back of my seat.

I shake my head. 'Not so fast. We can't ignore the fact that our Bella saw and heard their ghost, outrageous as it seems.'

Bella does her version of, 'Hear, hear, *that's* true.' Banging on Sophie's shoulder.

'So,' I say, at the risk of being considered a madwoman, 'we go back to that nut house one more time, and find out what the ghost, that prime witness, "saw".'

A few moments of absorbing this startling turn of events, Evvie takes on my cause. 'Are we going to let some ghost scare us away?'

'No!' calls out Bella, feeling reprieved.

'What was that about a quiz?' Sophie asks. 'I'm not too good at those.'

Evvie snarls, 'They couldn't get local suckers to deal with a ghost. They had to go as far as Fort Lauderdale.'

Bella, not getting it, grinning, 'And they found us suckers.'

Suddenly we are treating the apparition seriously?

Evvie giggles. 'Besides, I'm curious.'

Dead silence, then, Sophie says happily, 'It's near lunchtime. Let's eat, I'm starved. Soft-shell crab, anyone?'

Bella is so relieved. The grilling is over.

I turn on the ignition.

Food always seems to come first.

SEVENTEEN

Ida and Lola Fight to Finish

Another inquisition. Lola and Ida. Weary. Morning. They've been at it in Lola's apartment, first in the kitchen, then in the living room. Off and on, most of the day with food breaks of course. But that doesn't stop Ida *noshing* as they talk. Ida feels she's at the top of her game, still channeling her hero, Lt Columbo.

'Why won't you call the police?'

'He would kill me if I did that.'

'But if you really think your husband's in danger?'.

Shrill, 'No police. No! That's why *you're* here. Your business is "private" eyes; that means you keep it all confidential!'

'All right, but I need some help and I'm not getting any from you.'

'I told you all I know. I don't know any more.'

'Tell me again,' Ida says, chewing away at her pistachio peanuts snack, enjoying that it bothers Lola. Especially when she spits out the shells.

Reluctantly, 'Sometimes Hy wants to have time out. He needs to be alone.'

'Like Greta Garbo. So where does Greta go when she "vants to be alooone"?'

'How should I know? He takes the car. He goes somewhere. He says nothing. He never stays away at night. He always comes home to me. It's thirty-six hours he's been away!'

'And you let him get away with that? You don't demand that he tell you where he went?' Ida looks down into her empty bowl. 'Peanuts are gone. Anymore hummus?'

Lola is in tears by now. 'You've cleaned out my garlic hummus

and my Greek hummus and even my yellow lentil hummus. I'm
all out of hummuses!'

'Okay, don't get excited. Just asking. I need Hy's cell phone
number.'

'What for? He isn't answering it. It all goes to message.'

'Just give it to me.'

'Okay, don't be such a bitch. Hold your horses.' She jots down
the phone number on a torn-out piece of the daily newspaper and
shoves it at Ida. Ida puts it in her pocket.

Ida makes one last pit stop at the fridge. Opens it and shakes
her head, nothing more of interest. Lola glares at her.

'Where were we? So, this time he didn't come home. Therefore,
going on the assumption that Hy isn't lying in a gutter bleeding
to death, or you'd call the police, I need something to work with.
You give me nothing. Not a single clue.'

Near sobbing, 'What can I say? I'm just a plain, ordinary wife,
a happy wife. I love my husband.'

'Yeah. Yeah. He's Mr Wonderful. That's why you're sitting here,
scared stiff and looking like crap.'

'He's a perfect husband. So, I don't ask questions. I'm a perfect
wife who lets her husband have a little freedom every once in a
while, but I'm worried, he must be in trouble.' Snarky, 'I don't
see *you* with a husband. I can't imagine anyone living with *you*!'

'Hey, lay off of me. You need me, to save your . . . never mind.
You'll thank me after I find your mysteriously missing hubby. But
I need something to work with. Maybe it might be because he's
unhappy in his marriage?'

Self-righteous anger, 'How many times do I have to say it? I'm
a faultless wife. He's a faultless husband. There's nothing wrong
with my marriage! There are no secrets. In fact, just a few days
ago he brought me a beautiful present.' She lifts a doll from the
coffee table in front her.

To Ida it's really ugly, but obviously Lola sees beauty.

Lola holds it up. 'It's an antique Adora doll for my collection.
See how the eyes roll all around? That hair that looks so real,
that's from an angora goat. My darling Hy must have spent a
hundred dollars.'

Ida restrains from giving her opinion of the silly toy. 'Birthday
present? Or anniversary?'

Lola looks puzzled. 'No, just a gift . . . because he cherishes me.' She grins.

Sardonic Ida can't resist, 'Does that often, does he? Plies you with expensive gifts?'

Lola is puzzled. 'No, not really. But isn't it wonderful?'

Ida decides it's time to leave. She's drained the witness, and there's nothing more to squeeze out of her. Nothing more to gain. Nothing more to eat.

She heads for the door. 'So, good afternoon. And if you think of anything useful, call me.'

Lola is begging now, 'Find him, please.'

And in true Columbo style, Ida leans on the door jamb, about to leave and turns and winks at Lola, using the famous line, 'Just one more thing before I go.' She grins, delighting in being malicious. 'How is your sex life?'

Lola throws the empty hummus carton at Ida, who ducks and hurries out.

'Yoo hoo, Ida. Stop.'

She turns around, seeing Big Tessie running toward her, past all the parked cars, arms wind-milling, flabby body parts flying in the breeze, puffing for breath.

'Wait up,' she insists.

'Hi, Tessie. You looking for me?'

'I like to walk when I can't nap and I can't get my regular nap when my darling Sol is away to share it with me, though that's none of your business. Anyway, I've been looking for you.' She pauses. Tessie stares at Ida, taking her in from up to down. 'What are ya wearing a raincoat for? There's no rain here. I don't see no raindrops.'

'Yeah. Yeah. And it's ninety degrees. So what do you want?'

'How do you know I want to talk to you?'

Ida smirks, 'Because I'm a detective. You were waiting for me to come out of Lola's apartment.'

Tessie smirks in return. 'You get any clues from Lola?'

She leers at Tessie, who looks to her like a demented basset hound, drooling spit. 'You know about Hy?'

'Of course I know about Hy.'

Why am I surprised? The *Yenta* Brigade is always on duty. 'So what do you know?'

She does a kind of jig around Ida. 'I know plenty.'

'So, spit it out, already. The day is no longer young and, ditto, neither are you.'

'What's it worth to you?'

'Oy, here we go again; twice in one week. Bribe-arella. You're gonna want me to pay you for information? Fat chance.'

'What I know is that the boss of your group is out of town so you're taking over for Gladdy and this is a new case. And I have vital information.'

'And you are my snitch?'

'Call me anything you want, only don't call me late for meals.' She chuckles at her pathetic joke.

Ida shakes her head. What a dimwit. 'Okay. Payola. One free breakfast at The Original Pancake House. Anytime.'

This gives Ida an idea; she's gonna start keeping a list of expenses, starting with bribery.

'Big deal. No deal.' Tessie is not impressed.

'I take you there for "All The Pancakes You Can Eat" Day.'

Practically salivating, 'You're on.'

I lead my chubby informer away from any possibility of Lola watching us from her living room window. We hide to do our spy thing under a massive palm tree, with our feet enmeshed in fronds.

'I'm all ears, wadda ya know?'

'Sol was at Levy's bar the day before he left on that safari thingy . . .'

'Wait, where's there a Jewish bar?'

'So it was a deli that also served beer.'

'Get it out already. Before it turns into night and I'm on overtime.'

'So, Hy is there with some guys and my Sol, and he gets a ding-a-ling.'

'In a deli?'

'I know what you're thinking. You have a dirty mind. Hy's ding-a-ling is his phone that rings a stupid song when he gets a text message. You figured out what it sings?'

'I've heard it a million times, *King of the Hill*. Move it along.'

'Hy reads his text message. My Sol says he turns red as a ripe tomato, and says he needs to piss, and off he goes, texting like crazy on his phone.'

'Then what happens?'

'How should I know? Sol wasn't in the bathroom with him.'

'I meant when he came out.' Idiot.

'He comes out of the bar, whistling. And orders another beer.'

'Where is the call or text from?' Oy, this is like pulling teeth out of a squirrel.

'He says, Miami. He has a friend who got in touch to say hello. He quickly says it's a guy so Sol knows he's lying. Besides, you don't blush all over when you're talking about a guy. And he's grinning from ear to ear.'

'But he didn't go anywhere after Sol and the guys left on that trip. What's the big deal?'

Tessie is sly, 'However . . . he left, poof, right after your gang took off for Key West. He's gone overnight, and Lola is trying to pretend he's still around.'

'Wow, did Sol say anything else when he was in that bar . . . the deli bar?'

She smiles wickedly. 'My Sol said,' murdering the French, '"*Shersay la female*". That call was from some broad.'

She walks off, head high, 'See ya at the pancake house.'

EIGHTEEN

The Rest of the Day Off

I give Bella and Sophie a choice. Some sightseeing? The beach? Or a movie. Visit any of the places Evvie read about in the travel book? Go wandering on their own? They surprise me and suggest seeing a movie. They probably need something quiet to erase the mind-blowing latest experience with our ghost. Some lightweight movie with no big messages. Ditto, for dinner. No evening exploring, either. An early night in and much-needed sleep.

We split up. They take a cab to a movie theater while I drive over to the nearest library with Evvie, who of course, is at my side. We have a quiz on our minds.

It's been a long time since I studied the Arts in college. And an equally long time since I was a librarian.

Evvie and I are equipped with computers for Google searching. Though I intend to peruse the books on the shelves for a crash course in reminding me of the life and works of the famous, or should I say infamous, novelist-adventurer, Mr Hemingway. Not *my* Papa.

I am still simmering over his demand to test my knowledge of him, instead of giving me the information we need. Crazy, all of this. As if there really is a dead writer, with his spirit still hanging around. With a deadly clue. It's a strange out-of-body experience we are having.

I really do wish Ida was with us. Would she take any of this seriously? Why are *we* taking this seriously? Why aren't we on our way home right this minute?

I'm making a guess as to what will happen at our next meeting. I expect the big, important dead man to do what he's done all his life. To prove himself better, smarter, stronger than anyone else. I have to find the way to defeat him. A mighty task, which calls for a plan. Plan A, and if that fails, a plan B.

So, here we are at the library. Evvie has been given the job of noting oddities about Papa and listing them in her computer. I watch her studying. At various times she giggles, or cries out in disbelief, 'Omigod. He couldn't. He didn't. But he did. All those marriages, divorces, affairs, world travel, wars. Famous friends and famous enemies. Battles, real and imagined. The suicide attempts . . .'

I tell her to keep going. Knowledge is power. But does power work with a ghost?

The astonishing part of all this, is that I am actually expecting a *ghost* to take me on in this quiz thing.

I'll handle what he throws at us. But then he's got to answer my one and only quiz question. What did he witness on Robert Strand's boat? I'll bet he's going to say his spirit hung over the boat and watched a crime being committed? Oh, stop mumbling to yourself.

We spend hours doing research. And yes, indeed, he had an amazing life. Such highs and lows. Tremendously impressive, the number of books and stories and articles he wrote. The awards he received. The bad things; so many illnesses, so accident-prone, his alcoholism that finally destroyed him. It lost him his friends, it took away his ability to write, and eventually he became depressed and paranoid. His bizarre mother. His father who committed suicide; and years later, he killed himself. Wow!

When we decide we'd had enough of our quick re-education course, which by now depresses us, Evvie has only one thing to say. She sums it up. 'Let's get out of here, I need a drink.'

I look up, wondering if he's hovering over us right now. Only Bella would know.

We meet up with Sophie and Bella later, back at the B&B.

Evvie asks, 'So what movie did you see?'

Bella, 'I don't remember the name of it.' Sophie nods in agreement.

I ask, 'What was it about?'

Sophie, 'Vampires. Sucking the blood out of pretty blond actresses' necks.'

Evvie is surprised. 'You both hate violent movies. Especially anything with vampires. Why did you choose that?'

Bella says, 'It was the only one playing.'

Sophie jumps in, 'Not to worry. We closed our eyes in all the bad parts.'

Teresa is still avoiding us.

Tomorrow will be quite a challenge.

NINETEEN

Another Phone Call. Now About Midnight

'**G**laddy. Did I wake you?'

I grope for the phone, eyes still shut. 'Ida, is that you?'

'You were expecting maybe George Clooney? Of course it's me.'

Looking at a clock, whispering so I won't wake Evvie. 'It's midnight.'

'Really? Time does fly when you're making progress.'

'Does that mean you've found Hy?'

'Not yet, but I'm getting closer.'

Yawn, 'Can it wait 'til morning, then report all your news?'

'I suppose, but I feel like I'm excited this minute, and don't want any grass to grow between my toenails. I just have one question.'

More yawns, 'Hurry, my eyelids are drooping; my mind is at zero brainpower.'

Talking quickly, Ida states, 'I found out that Hy has run off to Miami and I think he's with a woman. What should I do?'

'He's with Lola?' Half-asleep, I'm slurring my words.

'No, I was just with Lola, it's definitely another woman.'

I manage to open one eye at this. 'Hy Binder, cheating on Lola? The mind boggles. Not possible.'

'Why not, he's a man, isn't he?'

'Why? Not? Because Hy is a yellow-bellied coward-man. He knows Lola would slash him 'til he bled, if he strayed.'

'Get this, you'll love it. Just before he disappeared, he bought Lola an expensive present. Something he hardly ever did before. What does that tell you?'

'That's sounds like male guilt. Guys give wives expensive gifts when they're hiding something. When they're up to no good.'

Ida agrees. 'That's just what I thought. He's got a girlfriend. And he's run off to be with her. Wow.'

'And that was your one question. Goodnight.'

'No, no, that was just an aside. That doesn't count. My question is, since Miami is large, how do I find him there?'

'mmddkjfvkjfl.'

'What did you say?'

More yawns, 'Sorry. I was falling asleep. Do you have Hy's cell number?'

'Yeah, but he isn't answering.'

'If he's with another woman, he would never answer. Death would be on the other end of the line.'

'Gladdy, I could use your help. What should I do?'

'Easy-peasy. Call Morrie Langford and he'll track him down for you.'

'That's a wonderful idea. I would never have thought about it. Thanks. How about you and the girls? How was your meeting with the mysterious witness? . . . Gladdy?'

No answer. Ida is chagrined. Gladdy is asleep again, snoring. Ida grins and hangs up. 'Easy-peasy.'

TWENTY

The Cop and the Acting Detective

Day Three

Ida is still wearing her Columbo raincoat. She is finally out of the house, wearing one of her usual gray pantsuit outfits under the coat.

By appointment, she's in Morrie Langford's office at the local police station. Morrie offers Ida a cup of coffee. He sits at his desk drinking his.

Ida sips and sighs, happy with the brew and his company. 'This is so nice of you to take time off to see me.' Ida, the grump, knows when to curb her vitriol and play nice. Especially with Gladdy's good-looking cop son-in-law.

'My pleasure. So Gladdy suggested I could help you out. Where is she, by the way?'

'In Key West, on a new case.'

'Lucky them. It's a beautiful place. And they'll see some wonderful sights.'

Ida, not wanting to hear more about what she's missing, gets on with it, 'I know you can help me.'

'About that raincoat . . .'

Ida, chagrined, 'Oh, no, not you, too.' Disappointed, 'Say it! You're gonna tell me it's not raining . . .'

'No, I was just trying to remember who used to wear that kind of coat, it was somebody famous.'

Ida is about to give him the answer, but he holds up his hand to prevent her from spoiling his fun.

'No, let me guess. Wait a minute. It's coming back to me. On the tip of my tongue.' Excited, 'Columbo! The TV detective! Of course! I loved that show.'

Ida is amazed, 'You did? But that show was way before your time. You were a kid when that show was on.'

'I saw every retro re-run. He was the guy! Always looked like an unmade bed, and even though he had a glass eye, he always got his perp.'

Ida is in seventh heaven. She's finally met someone with her good taste.

Morrie walks away from his desk, pulls up a chair and sits closer to Ida. He's on her same wavelength. With arms rotating, he rides merrily back into his boyhood. 'Remember the episode when Jack Cassidy was the murderer? *Murder by the Book*. He wanted to get rid of his untalented writing partner . . .'

Ida jumps in. 'And what about when Anne Baxter plays a famous actress in *Requiem for a Star*?'

Morrie, 'Yeah, Columbo was crazy about Annie; she was his favorite actress . . .'

Ida, 'And she thinks she's killing her blackmailer, but she kills the wrong person . . .'

Morrie sighs blissfully; 'I think my all-time favorite was with Johnny Cash . . .'

Ida, 'And Ida Lupino, my namesake.'

Morrie, 'He plays this gospel singer . . .'

The two of them are in TV memory heaven. Morrie adds, 'And Marty Sheen in *Lovely, But Lethal*. And Rod Steiger in *Strange Bedfellows*!'

'That show was so great. I never wanted to miss one.'

'Me, neither. When my mom asked me why I watched, I told her it was because Columbo was such a shrewd investigator. I wanted to be like him when I grew up.'

They both are laughing so boisterously, they are almost unaware of the young officer who suddenly appears at Morrie's office door, jabbing importantly at his watch. Time to go. This pulls Morrie out of his happy reverie.

He stands up. 'I could go on forever, but speaking of perps, I need to get back to my job. Quick, tell me what you need.'

Ida takes out the jagged piece of newspaper with Hy's cell phone number.

'Hy Binder is missing and I'm on that case of trying to find him. Gladdy said you can track him down.'

'Hy? Of all people. You want us to call an APB or BOLO to find him if he's in trouble?'

Ida grins, 'Nah, I'll bet he's DOM.' She can speak with initials, too.

'DOM? That's a new one to me.'

Ida slyly, 'Dirty Old Man things. I'll bet.'

Morrie grins and nods. 'You think?'

She watches him do something magical on his computer, then goes across the room to where a printer lives, which then prints the information out for her.

As he hands the page to her, 'Looks like this address is in a trailer park. The owner or renter name is Bloom. Good luck, Ida.' Musing, 'Hy Binder, I wonder what mischief that funny little guy is up to.'

Ida heads for the door. 'I intend to soon find out. Thanks, Morrie. It's been fun.'

'Yeah, for me, too.'

Ida makes the dramatic stop at the door, hands on hips, 'Just one more thing . . .'

Both of them burst into laughter at Columbo's signature exit line.

Ida walks out of Morrie's office in a wonderful mood. Hy better watch out. Here she comes. Ready or not. Easy-peasy.

TWENTY-ONE
Ida Hires a Driver, Julio Really?

Ida is suffering a frustrating day. She's having an inner soliloquy: She has an address for Hy. And a name with whom he's staying. A perfect win-win situation. Go down there; drag that *momzer* back home where he belongs. She'll make a pack of money for the team, and she'll carry it out alone; doing it her way. She hums a few bars of the Sinatra favorite, then stops herself, glum at her negative thoughts. Not so easy, after all.

Of course, she can just give Morrie's information to Lola, and let the chips fall where they may. Her job would be done. She can envision a situation where Lola takes a gun, drives down to that Miami address, catches Hy, quivering in his love nest. The two of them, hiding under the sheets, begging for mercy; just don't shoot us. There is no mercy. Lola blasts away at the sinful couple. Bang. Bang. Two dead bodies. With the offended wife, wearing black, crying out, 'I'm glad I did it! I'm glad!'

It would make all the newspapers the next day. All over the Internet for people who have computers. Millions of hits as the teenagers would say. Killer Lola will then get hate mail and equally as much mail congratulating her for giving the devil his due. Ah, sweet daydreams, these are.

But Lola doesn't have a gun, and she doesn't drive either. Besides, Hy has their only car with him. And the truth is, she wouldn't hurt a fly; she's not really the type. So, she'd have to call a cab and go down there, needing to stop to pay the cabby, somehow ruins the whole effect. All in all, unworkable.

Besides, what would she, Ida, get out of that? Nothing. Nada. And anyway, no way; she is not giving up this opportunity. This gift, this opportunity is hers. She will be the one bringing back the cheating husband. The joy it will be to see the terrified face of Hy when he faces her. The soon-to-be famous bounty hunter, Ida Franz; her name in all the newspapers, showing the philandering husband brought to his knees in front of the enraged, suffering wife. Sweet moment that will be for Ida.

Lola will thank her a thousand times. Gladdy will proud of her for doing it all on her own.

And that's her problem. She has no means of getting to Hy, either. She doesn't own a car anymore. Not that she'd ever want to drive again. Traffic has gotten worse, and so have her eyes. And, yeah, maybe her coordination is a little rusty. And, let's face it, she can hardly drag her body in and out of a chair these days, let alone a car. If an accident happened, she'd never get out of a car in time; she'd be toast!

She gave up her license five years ago, when she bumped into another car. Such a little bump, but that touchy Motor Vehicles decided because of her age, her driving days were over. That accident was a nothing! Anyone would call it hitting a tap on his rear end. Not a scratch, well maybe his auto got a tiny dent, a ding, hardly noticeable, and right away, that bum driver was *geshreying*, 'Whiplash! I'm in pain! Call an ambulance!'

She can't take a taxi. What if she needs to spend hours there or more than a day? Way too expensive to go back and forth. And overnight? Hotels cost money. But she needs someone to drive her. Can't ask her neighbors. No way will she ask any one of those cheapskates for a favor. Not in this lifetime.

She's heard about driving companies, Ubers and Lyfts, but she doesn't have an iPhone so she sure doesn't have apps. What is she supposed to do, grow wings and fly? She's so frustrated.

What's left? Hire her own private driver. That's it. Eureka!

The fact that there aren't any private driver listings in the phone book is a surprise. Now that people use computers; she understands that's where most people advertise. No help to her in her chosen tech-free world. No apps available for her.

She has to depend on ads in a local throwaway rag; the cheap shoppers guide, with its get-it-free ads and free coupons. Coupons for nothing she would ever want. After perusing one useless ad after another useless ad – no, she doesn't want to buy a wig or start karate lessons or take a mud massage – she manages to find a listing, at last, in a hard-to-find corner on a back page. '**Private Drivers**' cries out to her in bold letters; trolling for customers:

Seniors; Give up that stone around your neck! **Sell**
your **car**!
No more huge **gas prices**!
No more expensive **insurance**!
Be free! Hire someone honest and reliable!

A lot of bold letters and too many exclamation points! All that
jazz with very few drivers listed. That does not bode well. Crackpots
advertise in this freebee.

The first three calls make her want to tear her hair out.

One guy only drives around Fort Lauderdale. No he won't go
a mile further. Another one speaks what she can only guess is
Chinese. Time wasted trying to understand each other. A nutcase
wants five hundred dollars a day. What the hell!

Only one more phone call and that's the end of the meager
listings. And then she's out of luck.

Blah. Blah. Blah. What's with *this* guy? She thinks he's speaking
Spanish. Then he switches to English; which she hardly understands. Then they do this dance. She says, 'Watta ya charge?' and
he says, 'What'll you pay?' He wants to bargain? He thinks he's
dealing with some dumb dame. He'll be sorry.

She feels him out, her bargaining technique like a slithering eel
– slow and slippery. 'So, sir, what do you usually get per hour?'

'It varies.' It sounds like he says – vareeece.

Wanna play games? He's met his match in Ida Franz. 'What's
the best money you ever were paid per hour?'

'Fifty dollars?' He knows how to say money in perfect English.

Aha, Ida is positive it was meant to be a stupid trap. Here she
goes, setting her own trap. Bite this, mister. 'I'll pay ten.'

'Forty?'

'Ten.'

'Thirty?'

'Ten.' She wants to tell him to wash his ears out so he'll hear
her better. 'I said ten.'

'I suppose twenty won't make you happy?'

'You got that right.'

'*Bueno.* Is good. I give to you, I do it for ten.' His English is
getting better.

'Five.'

'What happened to ten? *Mama mia, es stupido, que pasa?*'

'Your time is up. Five or goodbye. I'm a busy person.'

'All right. Five, *pero* with *una* condition. *Que es* . . . What you call it – unbreakable?'

'You have an unbreakable condition?'

'That I drive my own truck and you give to me a lunch hour every day at noon, for *una hora*, one hour.'

Ida smiles. Gotcha! 'Sounds good to me. How soon can you get here?'

'What is your address?'

Ida fills him in, and he says he'll be there in thirty minutes and she informs him he better be on time. She pats herself on the back. Well, not really. She can't reach her back, but she knows what she means.

Thirty minutes later, packed with what she thinks she'll need, and ready to go; right on time, Ida hears a horn. It's a weird horn. It blows some kind of a fast-musical tune. He is probably Cuban, so maybe it's a Cuban-type song?

She goes downstairs. What the hell? There's a huge white panel truck parked in front of her building. With writing all over it: *Emmanuel's Taqueria en la Rueda-el mejor empenadas en todos Miami. Tacos. Tortillas. Burritos. Chile Rellenos. Arroz y frijoles.* Words, words, words. She stares at the truck, dumbfounded. She doesn't have a clue what they say.

And a short, nice-looking, dark-haired, dark-eyed, cheerful looking man in white shirt and blue jeans, in what might be his early forties, stands in front of it and waves at her. '*Ola, me llamo Julio*, you don't pronounce the J, it's *Hulio* Mendez. You like my theme song? It's very popular – *Don't Worry, Be Happy.*'

Ida is speechless.

'What's this truck doing here?' Ida is horrified to see Lola Binder suddenly standing next to her. Another surprise.

Think fast, think fast whirls through Ida's mind. Don't die here. What would Gladdy do or say? Ida manages a toothy grin. 'Isn't this neat? Something new in the neighborhood. I've never seen one of these kinds of food trucks before; isn't it interesting? I wonder how the food is.' She's blathering, but she can't stop herself. 'I'm going to try it.'

She turns to Julio and pokes Julio hard in his arm. 'So, what's the special today, *Senor*?' (She pronounces it snore.)

Naturally Julio is puzzled; the lady's face is changing by the minute as she looks at him. He recognizes many emotions: fear, the beginning of tears, and then a silly smile. And she keeps poking him. The woman is trying to tell him something.

Ida's eyes are pleading. 'Is it too early to open up and serve some of your delicious food?'

Lola addresses Ida. 'This is weird. I've never seen one of these trucks around here before either.' She smiles, 'Hy and I saw a really good movie once about a guy and his young son riding around the country cooking up a storm along the way. It turned us on to Cuban food.'

Don't mention Hy being missing, Ida prays. In front of a now gathering crowd. 'Yeah, I saw that movie. I liked it, too, and was hungry while watching it.' I point to distract her. Look at the menu, don't think about Hy. Whew, she does just that, mouthing the words, as if that would make her understand them.

Julio is one smart hombre, Ida thinks; feeling hope. He's caught on.

Julio bows to Lola. '*Senora*, it would be my pleasure to cook for you. What would you like?'

He also indicates the side of the truck. 'As you can see, there are many wonderful choices.'

Lola examines the menu as Ida starts to breathe again. She smiles at Julio, her new hero, 'Me, too, *snore*. I feel hunger coming on.' She just had finished a huge breakfast, but what the hell.

Lola, self-appointed connoisseur of foreign food, asks bravely for a taco (pronounced *tack-o*).

'Soft or hard? Flour or corn? Meat or vegetarian?' Julio asks. Ida blesses him; he's struggling to say it in English; he knows he's helping me.

Lola smiles at her new pal. 'Oh, you choose for me.'

'Me, too,' says Ida jumping in. Anything to keep Lola from finding out she is speaking to the man who will drive her to where Hy is hiding.

Julio gets started opening his truck. First he pulls down the side panel, including a shelf, which opens up to his spotless interior tiny kitchen. He busies himself to start his cooking. First he changes the music to peppy Afro-Cuban jazz, and then Julio picks up a huge frying pan and waves it at his two customers, smiling cheerfully.

Lola gushing, calls out to Julio, 'Do tell us what you are cooking for us. Say it in *Cubana*. I'm just crazy about the sound of foreign languages.'

By now a small group of neighbors is forming. They've never seen this kind of truck before, and they are curious. Among them is Tessie.

Ida gasps. Oh, no, not Tessie. She'll blow my cover. She pretends not to see her.

Julio announces, '*Bienvenidos a Emmanuel*. Greeting from the truck of Emmanuel. I now cook for the two beautiful s*enoras*: *tacos, maiz de concha blanda. Carnitos asada.*' He translates, 'Corn tacos, soft shell, with little meats.'

Lola smiles proudly, as if she'd known all along what it meant. She is having a good time. Good, she isn't thinking of Hy.

Julio makes a production out of his cooking skills, waving his knives and doing a little dance to his music. The audience oohs and ahhs. Their feet are moving to the catchy tune.

'Call out what you want,' says Julio. 'I am here to cook for you and make you happy.'

And the voices of her neighbors do call out, reading from the menu on the side of the truck, not realizing that they are butchering the Spanish language:

'*A shrimpo salado*!' Irving from Building R thinks if you add an 'o' or an 'a' to any word, it becomes instantly Spanish.

'One order *flautos*.' Along with a giggle from Lena from Building S. 'I wonder what I just ordered. It sounds . . . musical.'

And from Tessie, unaware of Ida cowering; in a big voice, 'I feel like a large *Chile Colorado Tostada*.'

Phil from Tessie's building, standing next to her can't resist, 'And you look like a large *Chile Colorado Tostada*.'

Tessie swats him playfully. 'I once visited Colorado, so shut up, Phil.'

Julio is a magician, Ida thinks. He is cooking four things at once and humming and dancing along with his music.

The food fest goes on. People eat, spilling salsa and meat juice on themselves, unmindful, uncaring. Throwing money at Julio.

Feet still wiggling. The smells of this food, enticing. Everyone's having a good time.

And then something happens that tells Ida she has met the man of her dreams, business-wise.

Julio calls out to his small group. 'No money today. Whatever you eat is free. A free sample of what Emmanuel's Food Truck cooks. So next time I come around, you come to eat. Then you can pay.'

They cheer. The truck stays put as Julio cleans up his kitchen. The eaters happily take back their money.

Ida watches as the crowd is moving off, happily patting their full stomachs. The street is empty. Ida is relieved. Alone at last. Not quite.

Except for Lola and Tessie. Ida is horrified to watch Lola, wiping the sauce off her blouse with a napkin, and Tessie, eating her second tostada. Both of them waiting to chat with her.

A catastrophe about to happen. The last two people in the world to be chatting with one another. Tessie, with her big mouth, who can't keep a secret. She knows Hy is gone. She suspects hanky-panky. If she blurts this out, better duck when she lets loose the fireworks. Lola with a short-fused temper will hear those words; will attack with the power of a banshee. And Ida will bear the brunt of this disaster.

Ida tries to defuse in advance. 'Nice treat, that truck. Hope it comes around again.'

'Delicious,' agrees Tessie the gourmand, interested in anything called food.

'I thought the tacos were soft enough.' Go away both of you, Ida prays, before it's too late.

'Tasted delicious to me,' Tessie, with gravy on her cheeks, waves her sloppy, wet napkin in response.

'Lola, what else did you have to eat?' Ida asks as if she really gives a damn. Keep them from getting on the wrong topic.

Lola proudly, 'I had a burrito, vegetarian, not with any meat. There goes my diet. I hate to think how many calories were in it.'

They all laugh.

Tessie with stomach rumbling, 'Who cares?' This from a woman who thinks diet is a dirty word.

'So, Ida,' says Lola breaking away from the food subject, with her idea of subtlety, 'I thought you were going out of town with Gladdy.' Translation – why the hell aren't you away from here, looking for my husband?

'Well, I wasn't feeling well, but I'm so much better, so I'll be leaving tomorrow.' Translation. I'm on the job tomorrow. So shut up and scram.

Tessie is about to say something horribly wrong, so Ida quickly derails her. 'Any word from Sol on the safari? I bet by now they've taken pictures of a lot of amazing animals.'

Tessie frowns. 'Not one letter. Wait till he gets back, he'll get a what-for from me!'

Ida forces a cheesy smile. 'I just know they are having a wonderful time. They are so lucky to be on such a great trip. Next year we women should go away on a vacation of our own.'

Ida starts toward her getaway. 'Well, I need to do a few things around the apartment. Toodle-doo.' She waves bye-bye at them. Then stops as if she just thought of something. 'I must thank that truck man for the wonderful food.'

Both women leave, unaware that they've been given the heave-ho; a little disappointed and not knowing why.

Ida waits until the two of them wander off, thankfully in different directions. Then, she quickly races to Julio's truck. His kitchen is immaculate and he is closing the serving door.

Julio grins at her. 'I get the job, *si*?'

Ida hugs him. 'You sure do, Julio with a J, now vanish. No way we leave today. Come back eight a.m. tomorrow and we'll head out for Miami then. Don't play any music, and park around the corner; just show up. I'll meet you there.'

'*Hasta Manana.*' Julio closes up his truck and takes off; with *Don't Worry, Be Happy* playing again in all its ear-splitting grandeur.

Ida feels like she just dodged a bullet.

TWENTY-TWO
The Papa Quiz With Visionary Bella

I give my girls last-minute instructions.

'Remember, we're here to get information if . . .' I choke on it. The reality of this situation still irks me. '. . . the ghost knows something about what really happened to Robert Strand. We'll try kindness first.'

Evvie laughs. 'If Ida could see us now. She'd shriek with laughter and call us idiots.' Mimicking, 'You see ghosts, you are crazy.'

Sophie says, 'What if Papa's in a bad mood?'

I say, 'We deal with it. Whatever it takes. Just follow my lead.'

Sophie, 'I'm afraid of him.'

Evvie laughs again. 'Why? He's dead. What can he do to you? Yell Boo?'

We arrive at Gray Lady and go through the same rigmarole. The Wassingers want to serve tea or coffee. We want none of that tepid liquid, no sidetrack hurricane discussions, and no stops for admiring antiques, straight up the stairs. Do Not Pass Go.

Evvie entertains herself climbing behind Sophie and to torture her, whispering, 'Boo' in her ear.

Bella is silent. I'll bet she's anxious about her next session with the dead guy. Worried whether she'll still see and hear the ghostie. And more troubled about the things he might say to her. And worry about us being mad at her again. The wonderful thing about our sweet Bella is I can always read her thoughts.

'What's the weather up there, mood-wise?' I ask Louie and Sadie, halfway through the climb.

'Cheerful,' says Sadie.

'Grouchy,' says Louie at the same moment.

I'm beginning to pretend climbing these endless stairs is exercise. See how easy it is to think positive when all else fails.

Here we are, on the roof. Same scene. Same empty spaces. Weather a little cloudy. Sun peeks out occasionally.

We call out in chipper mode, 'Hi, there, Papa.'

We get via Louie, 'Lookie here, back again, the girl scout brigade.'

Uh oh. The emotional weather promises dark skies, with stormy weather ahead.

Evvie's mood is playful, sarcastic. I let her loose. Plan A.

'Dong!' she says pretending to be a bell. 'Round Two coming up. In one corner, the Champion, bloody, but not bowed, Papa Ernie. In the other corner, the Challenger. She's the up-and-coming bruiser, favored by the odds to win, Gladdy Gold.'

'Ho ho,' we are told by Louie, 'Papa likes this. He's an expert in boxing.'

I use it. 'A man for all seasons. And for all reasons. A man for all wars. Why, he won a medal for his bravery in the heartbreaking Spanish Civil War.'

Louie again, 'Papa's smiling. He says you got that right.'

'Received that medal,' I say to finish it, 'not as a colonel, nor a sergeant, not even a foot soldier – as an ambulance driver.'

Louie again, 'You're making him angry. He begged the draft board to sign him up. They refused to induct him.'

Sadie adds, trying for peace. 'He did save a man's life.'

'Dong!' rings Evvie again, calling the sport. 'Below the belt accuses the Challenger. The Brawler fights back with angry, aggressive punching.'

Louie is shaking now. 'Don't call him a brawler. He fights fair.'

Bella finally squeaks up, desperate to help, 'We come in peace.'

Evvie and I laugh. Leave it to Bella, doing her best. Nice try, but this is not about greeting tribal Indians.

Now ghostie relates to Bella. She timidly repeats, 'What are you doing back here? I thought I got rid of you.'

I answer. 'We came for the information that you say you have. About Robert Strand's death.'

Bella getting the voice from the beyond again, repeating, 'And why should I give that information to you broads?'

I ignore the anti-feminist put-down. 'Because, you can't act on it, and we can.'

'Bong!' calls out Evvie, announcing, 'Papa has a glass jaw. Gladdy's got him on the ropes. Gladdy goes the distance.'

Louie cries out for Papa, 'Low blow! Low blow! Stop that! Stop that this minute!'

'Palooka,' Evvie whispers loud enough to be heard.

Louie is shouting as Papa. 'Don't you dare call me that! I am not clumsy. I am a winner. How dare you accuse me of lacking ability! I have been called one of the twentieth century's most important and influential writers ever!!!!'

Evvie snarky, 'The bigger they are, the harder they fall.'

Louie as enraged Papa, 'Get out of here, you stupid bimbos!'

My turn. 'Not until you give us what we came for.'

A few minutes of silence. We hold our breaths, then:

Louie repeats, trying for sly, 'Papa says, what will you give me for this information?'

I go for earnestness, pun intended. 'What do you want?'

Sadie takes over, 'He wants a new box of his Cuban cigars; he's run out and he'd like his favorite red bullfighter's cape.'

Louie jumps in quickly, 'And I know where to find them. They're in the mansion. I'll take you there.'

'No thanks. Time to leave,' I say, leading my crew towards the staircase. 'We're out of here.'

'Wait!' Sadie cries out, desperately needing us. 'Don't go.'

Louie and Sadie are beside themselves. Probably thinking, what are we foolish women doing? One mustn't anger their dear Mr Hemingway.

'Wait!' Louie calls out for Papa, 'First, remember, I get to quiz you. Before I'm willing to deal with you.'

We stop, but do not go back. 'Quiz away,' I toss at him, my feet on the first step down.

Sadie, for Papa, 'Question number one: they said my mother dressed me like a little girl until I was eleven. A lie, of course, my dear mother never did that; but what color might those dresses have been?'

I am ready; the library paid off; in a sugary voice, 'They were lacy white and flowery dresses with pink bows. Must have been tough being called your older sister's twin.'

Sadie for Papa, 'And don't you dare say I hated her. I adored my mother. I took care of her all her life.'

Evvie standing on the next step down, 'Sure, you did, Mama's good little girlie.'

Louie doing Papa – drastic, 'You shut up. I'm questioning your leader. Question two. They called me a survivor. What did I survive?'

I call out the list and continue reciting, step by step, as we all go slowly down the staircase, 'Anthrax.' Step. 'Malaria.' Step. 'Dysentery.' Step. And so on. 'Hepatitis, diabetes, two plane crashes. Ruptured kidney, spleen and liver, three car crashes and a fire in a bush somewhere.' And we are downstairs, arriving at the door.

We can hear Louie yelling down the stairs, Papa's final words, 'I'm not finished! You come back! Or you're fired!!!'

It echoes down the staircase. 'You're fired! You're fired!'

We remain standing in the street in front of the Gray Lady, half laughing, half really upset. The nerve of that man.

I hear Sadie calling our names. I know what that means. Begging time.

We wait quite a while, waiting for Sadie and probably Louie, as well, to make their way – oh so slowly – down that tortuous staircase. They finally reach us, breathing hard and sweating. Very worried, poor things.

I try to stop what is coming. 'We've had enough. We're going home.'

Sadie is near tears. 'Please. You're our only hope.'

Louie says, 'We called every private eye from here all the way to Miami. No one would help us.'

I say, 'I've already guessed that we weren't your first choice.' The others wouldn't have jumped in as quickly as we foolishly did without learning about the elephant in the room.

Evvie, 'I assume the word "ghost" was a turnoff.' She smirks.

Sophie, trying to help adds, 'I'm sure you nice people probably also believe in aliens from outer space.'

I say quickly, 'Sophie, don't derail us. Don't get them started on a new topic.'

Louie, 'It's like religion. People believe and others don't believe.'

Oh oh, here we go with another sidebar. Probably on the history of those who fervently believe in Extra Terrestrials. What quickly comes to mind are the famous movie words, 'ET go home'. A good idea for us, too. 'Please Sadie, Louie, give it up.'

Evvie says, 'We're non-believers in ghosts. So, give us one

good reason to stay on this case. We understand your concern for your Papa's living arrangement, but he'll have to find another place to haunt.'

There is a few moments' silence. Good for Evvie. She's said what was needed to be said. I'm already thinking about packing.

Louie and Sadie are as one person. She says, 'Louie, you tell them.'

Louie, of course says, 'No, dear, you're better at expressing valuable essentials.'

Sadie says, 'I bow to your conciseness and astuteness.'

Here we go again. Another version of listing hurricanes. They're going to drive us into a stupor with their who-should-do-the-selling-pitch routine. I pretend to look at my watch. Yes, I still wear them. No iPhones for me. 'Time is marching on.'

A quick back and forth of the Wassinger's 'no, you', and finally Louie steps forward, blocking us from my car.

He puffs out his meager chest, lifts his head high and faces us, a serious man about to emote. 'There is a much larger issue here, besides our dear friend Papa's residence problem. You didn't know Robert Strand. A kind man. A loving husband, though Sheila has already passed away. A good father, though his son Billy has had brief bouts with drugs. He's much better after being in rehab. They've given him back his driver's license. Well-meaning boy, our Billy; so upset about his dad dying.

I sigh. How long will this go on?

'Robert was the kind of lawyer so different from those who think only about their billing hours and fame and fortune. He looked after those who needed help and couldn't pay the exorbitant prices. I mean, who can these days? Have you noticed how the economy has tanked?'

I shake my head at the girls, in warning. Don't get dragged in.

Louie, not getting rebuttals, shouts out, 'The issue here is justice! With a capital J. Robert was murdered. We firmly believe that. Others disagree.'

Yes, that disagreement includes the entire city.

'We hired you to find out the truth. And the truth shall set us free!' Louie bows; he's done. Quite a performance.

'Visit them all. I have a list. Make them tell you the truth!'

I have to say something. 'And if we investigate and absolutely learn that Robert Strand's death was really accidental, will you back off?'

Again Louie and Sadie confer wordlessly with their eyes. They both nod.

Louie, 'Yes, we would abide by your findings.'

Sadie says eagerly, 'Then you'll stay?'

Sophie is about to say yes; I beat her to it. 'We have to think about it. That's the best we can give you.'

Sadie hugs Bella. 'Thank you for your help with Papa.' They are both in tears.

I walk to my car door; take my keys out. 'Come on, girls, get in.' Quick, fast before the Wassingers give us more lawyer-speak for another hour.

We say our goodbyes and I drive off seeing the Wassingers in my rear-view mirror, waving and smiling at us.

Bella and Sophie share a cry fest in the back seat. Evvie won't join them. She stares directly ahead, after a quick wink at me. I will not discuss anything about this case right now. The ghost says we're fired.

The hosts give us a reprieve.

I need a Tylenol. Evvie will want a martini.

I'll count to three and the subject of food will come up. One . . . two . . .

'Where should we eat?' a voice rises from the back seat.

'I'm thinking fish and chips,' this from the other voice.

TWENTY-THREE

Now Playing: Hy, Dolly-Ann, Manny Story

Three agitated people are locked in fierce verbal combat. That is, they are two vs one. They sit in the beat-up, old-style 1950s vintage model Airstream RV, set in a mobile-home park in a low-rent neighborhood of Miami.

An RV, in which the owner, Manny Bloom, has never thrown anything away in the twenty years he's lived here. Pack-rat, as a description, barely touches the level of his crowded junk. Sharing this tight living space are objects like a rusted old tool kit, a lug wrench, an old auto tire, a box of odds and ends containing objects like metal coils, bungee cords and a broken mousetrap, plus an outboard motor leaning against what would ordinarily be the driver's seat.

One can hardly peer out of the grimy, dirty windows in the entire RV.

Hy Binder is trying hard at playing tough. Difficult to pull off, since he'd rushed away from Lanai Gardens to his ex-girlfriend's side wearing a grey suit and tie and highly-polished black Oxfords. An outfit that was his most expensive in his closet. He had no idea what he'd be facing, but for this lady, he wanted to dress nicely. In this dump of a trailer he feels stupid and at a disadvantage being over-dressed.

'Manny, Dolly-Ann is worried about you.' Hy addresses the angry old codger, formerly from their old neighborhood, which at that time was the tough meatpacking, smelly, north-west side of New York City.

Manuel Bloom has bad teeth, and grizzled gray hair; a guy in his late seventies, who looks older. He wears a torn Yankees sweatshirt, paint-covered overalls, rubber boots and a rigid grimace. His hands and teeth are clenched. Hy is pleased to see his homely, old, arch-enemy has not aged well.

Hy is seated on a worn, plastic, padded bench next to Manny's sister, Dolly-Ann Bloom. She is wearing what she refers to as a dirndl skirt and a peasant cotton blouse with a lace ruffled neck. She always looked so lady-like to him.

Divorced recently (she informed Hy), she has reverted back to her maiden name. She may be in her late sixties, but Hy still sees her as she looked when she was his girlfriend, when last he saw her on that fateful prom night in high school so many eons ago. In his eyes, though the blond curls may be gray, with freckles now turned into wrinkles and the early curves thickened, the adorable dimple in her chin is still there. To him she hasn't changed at all and is still a hot babe. At this moment, she is an anxious hot babe.

She is having trouble with a stubborn brother who is determined to self-destruct.

'Manny, please listen to Hy.'

'I've been listening to him jabber since he got here. Who is he to tell me anything? What's he doing here anyway? Sniffing at a divorced babe? Don't he have a place to call home?'

Hy and Dolly-Ann exchange guilty looks.

With an angry pointing of his hand, Manny gripes, 'And you, my faithless sibling; if you mention retirement home to me one more time, I'm gonna spit blood!'

'Brother, please be reasonable. You can't continue on like this.' She waves her hands, pointing, encompassing his trailer. 'You live in chaos; how can you stand it?'

Hy adds, taking, his clue from Dolly-Ann, 'You don't have to live this way. You have choices.'

Dolly-Ann pleads. 'Stubborn fool. At least go and visit some places . . .'

He interrupts, by putting his hand over her mouth. 'Not another word!'

Hy makes a gesture towards Manny. Manny turns and pretends to shadow box him. 'Why should I listen to you? Who are you? I remember you *when*, Hy Binder, you were that pathetic boy from our old street, wearing his stupid heart on his sleeve. That chubby loser, that's who.'

Hy has never forgotten how badly Dolly-Ann's older brother treated him when they were growing up. Her brother saw him in the same negative way he saw himself in those younger days. Always the shortest one in the class; with acne, dandruff and belly fat and totally insecure. With a father who abandoned them and a mother who spent her days drinking and worrying about money, everyone in the Binder family was a loser.

He couldn't believe his luck, when a perfect dream girl like Dolly-Ann was nice to him, when no one else was. Her sweetness was the only thing keeping him from suicide. Not that he would ever kill himself; but he read a lot of poets who achingly, willingly died for love. He understood their pain; he had plenty of his own.

Manny used to beat him up whenever he saw him anywhere near Dolly-Ann. Big and bulky for his age, he was able to keep a lot of boys away from his popular sister. But most of all, Hy, whom he couldn't stand.

For Hy, it was the childhood from hell. Hy clutches his gut

remembering Manny's sing-song, 'Hy, Hy, I made you cry, go away or you will die,' as Manny punched him. If he had to admit it, he was still afraid of her brother.

'Manny, you are so stubborn!' Dolly-Ann keeps trying.

'And you are annoying me. Why don't you go back to New York where you belong! I never asked you to come down here. My nosy neighbors had no right to call you.'

'They were worried about you.'

'Bullshoes. All they worry about is running out of beer and getting to Walmart's before closing.'

'I don't think they sell beer at Walmart.'

'Wherever. Whatever.'

He looks at Hy, then with a smirk, 'This is your Superman, the hero you brought here to save your brother, who doesn't need saving? To me he's still the same dumb *shmuck*.'

Hy is furious. Not the same, oh, no, not a loser anymore. He is a winner, Hy Binder, as he has become over the years, a successful businessman. A confident man. A loyal man. And immediately he guiltily thinks of his wife, Lola, who has been his rock and helpmate through all those years.

Yes, Hy thinks, he could knock his socks off today, Manny, that creep. Easily, in the poor physical condition he's in. But he has to keep his temper in check; not wanting to upset Dolly-Ann.

Manny pulls himself up off of the other end of the ratty, duct-taped bench, climbs over the boxes of junk in his way, and opens up the creaking door. Pointing to both of them. 'Leave. It's time for my cocktail hour. Get back to your own digs. Or better yet, get the hell out of Dodge!'

Dolly-Ann sighs, a long, drawn-out murmur of sadness, as she shrugs and heads out. Hy follows after her. Each of them tiptoe through the trailer's disorderly path of Manny's mountain of useless possessions; being careful not to trip.

When outside, they walk without speaking, the few steps that brings them to another mobile home two doors down. Curious neighbors peer through curtains and watch their progress. A few look sullen and annoyed. Hy senses that these people are exasperated by Manny's behavior. Not a good situation and Hy, who has come to help Dolly-Ann, feels powerless.

They enter her recently rented, furnished RV, clutterless but probably just as old and moldy. It was the only nearby place Dolly-Ann was able to obtain part-time when she came down to Florida.

'Would you like some tea?' she asks Hy.

He nods. 'If you're having, I'll drink, too.'

She fills the kettle, and then turns to him in tears. 'The stubborn old coot! Ever since Sally died, he's been going crazy. When his wife was still alive, things were orderly. Look at the pigpen he lives in. It's disgusting.'

She faces him, fighting tears. 'I never should have called you, and dragged you into my problems, but I was so desperate. I didn't think I could handle it by myself.'

Hy reaches out and pats her hand. He doesn't dare to do much else. If Lola knew where he was, she'd murder him. In-between feeling terror about how he will explain things when he gets home; and secret joy, filled with the pleasure of once again seeing his first and only great love, Dolly-Ann Bloom. He's an emotional mess.

This is the girl he was meant to take to the senior prom. With an engagement ring in his rented tuxedo pocket, which had cost him a year of his saved earnings from mowing lawns and running errands. And the excited expectation of asking for her dainty hand in marriage that night. A girl who then broke his heart and went to the prom instead with Johnny O'Toole, the football hero. What a cliché! Dumped at the last minute for that jerk, just because he was an athlete, and Big-Man-On-Campus. And because it was guaranteed that she'd be crowned prom queen, dancing the magical night away on his muscular arms.

And then, it went from bad to worse; they went and eloped the next week. Hy's thoughts sink blacker and blacker. It was known that they got married because she let Johnny . . . sleep with her on prom night. He won't use the dirty word he was thinking. The pictures in his head make him feel ill.

As if she were reading his mind, Dolly-Ann says, 'I never should have married that dumb cluck. He was so full of his famous self; he had no room for me.'

She doesn't say the next words but both are thinking them. She should have married sweet, kind Hy, who adored her. Hy, who then married plain Lola Epstein, on the rebound. Gave *her* the

ring he'd bought for another girl. And never forgot the girl who
got away.

That girl, that woman he is facing this very minute. Who called
him four days ago, saying she was in trouble. She needed his help,
and because he promised to help, it gave her the courage to come
down to Florida.

Without thinking of what it might cost him, Hy, after showering
and changing his clothes, immediately leapt into his car when she
called him to let him know she'd arrived. Driving as fast as he
could toward his destiny.

Dolly-Ann breaks into his reverie. 'Are you positive you hid
your car where he won't find it?'

'I did it the best I could. I parked it behind a billboard. When
will you be able to get yours out of the shop?'

'The mechanics weren't sure. They never had to deal with a gas
tank filled with sugar before. My crazy brother's handiwork.'

Hy manages a smile. 'I gotta hand it to him. Your brother is
resourceful. He firmly believed you would follow him so had to
put your car out of action.'

'Yeah, he still has a mind like a steel trap. At least we have
your car.'

'That's if we can stay awake tonight. When does he take off?'

'When he's knows I'm asleep.'

'How does he know that?'

She shrugs. 'Maybe he looks through the window. The curtains
in this dump don't completely close. Or maybe he just guesses
and takes off way late at night.'

'That's what we'll do. We'll take turns sleeping. Then catch
him when he leaves.' Hy is satisfied with his plan.

Hy sips at his tea. He continues to wait for her to talk about
what Manny is up to when he disappears each night. The first
night he was there, and after they discovered her car was disabled
and too late to use Hy's, he expected her to tell him. He knew
only that Manny did this kind of thing practically nightly and that
she wanted to find out where he was going.

And he came home the next morning, whistling. Telling her
nothing.

Which made her furious. Which then changed Manny's mood
radically. Arguments escalated.

Hy had rushed to be at her side but she was sharing no information about these night vigils. Hy wondered and worried how long he dared stay.

'I'm so glad you're here,' Dolly-Ann repeats again and again. 'I don't know what I'd do without you.'

'I'm glad, too.' He smiles at her. 'Would you like to talk?'

'What about?'

He hasn't seen this woman in thirty years and she says – what about? 'We could talk about Manny, and what he's doing. Or talk about you or me. We have a lot of years to catch up on.'

She sighs. 'I have a terrible headache. Could we wait until tomorrow? I just need to rest.'

'Anything you want. I'm here for you.'

She said that last night as well and fell immediately to sleep. She has a lot of headaches. He feels . . . used.

They stay dressed, with jackets close by for the cool night. And seat themselves in chairs; in order to not fall asleep.

She reaches over and takes his hand and holds it. Oh boy, worries Hy. Manny is the least of his troubles. He wants to kiss this beautiful woman, so badly he can hardly bear it. It was hell sleeping on that sofa inches away from her bed last night. Aware she was just a caress away. How will he survive another night?

His thoughts are like a gerbil running circles around his cage. He has never cheated on Lola. He would never cheat on Lola. But he wants to cheat on Lola. Lola will kill him if he cheats on her. Is it worth destroying his marriage? It will upset his ideal lifestyle. Is it worth dying for? Is it? He argues with himself; using it to keep awake.

Hoisted with his own petard, he thinks sadly. He vaguely remembers that line came from Shakespeare; something about bombing yourself with your own bombs. Did they have bombs in Shakespeare's time? What did they mean by bombs? Thinking these oddball thoughts until he falls asleep; in spite of himself.

'Wake up, Dolly-Ann. It's three a.m.,' Hy whispers in her ear.

She pulls herself out of dreamland, and sighs. 'We fell asleep again.'

Even though sitting up in chairs, their eyelids betrayed them. So much for their plan. They quickly throw on jackets and shoes.

The lights are off in Manny's trailer, but that doesn't prove anything. They had to get to Hy's car, where he left it.

And sure enough, when they reach behind the billboard, Hy's car is still there. But with four flat tires. Manny had escaped again. On his well-hidden bike. To wherever it is he goes.

And they can't follow him this night either.

Discouraged, they return to Dolly-Ann's trailer. Without making eye contact, they each go to their 'bed'. She, to the single bed against the back wall and he, to the sofa that is way too close.

She lies down. 'I'm too tired to even change my clothes.'

'Me, too.'

'Good night.'

'Good night.' She turns off the light.

There's silence for a while with only the sound of bodies twisting and turning. Hy peers through the crack in the curtain watching the sky slowly get lighter.

Finally she says, 'I can't get back to sleep. I'm overtired.'

'Me, neither.'

She turns the light back on.

They stay where they are, still lying down.

'Hy?'

'I'm here, Dolly-Ann.'

'Did you ever think about me over the years?'

Dangerous question. He never forgot about her. Careful. Be bland. 'Many times. I wondered how you were doing.'

'I was so dumb getting married so young. My folks tried to talk me out of it, but who listens to parents when you're a kid.'

Yeah, how could you possibly resist a dumb football player with a brain like a pea pod? Hy thinks, aggravated, but he wouldn't dare say it. He's surprised that he can still feel the hurt. 'Yeah, kids are like that.'

'Did you and your wife have any children?' she asks.

'We tried, but no luck. After a while we stopped trying.' He doesn't need to tell her about painful, frustrating, negative years until you finally make peace with what cards you're dealt.

'We had a son. Randy,' she whispers.

'Tell me about him.'

'There's nothing much to tell. He was a difficult kid from the git-go. He grew up hard to deal with. He and his father never got along. His father didn't respect me, so my son didn't either. And finally with the help of drugs and bad companions, he walked out of our lives altogether.'

'I'm so sorry.' Poor thing. What a sad life.

More silence, then she speaks again. 'The footballer never got the college success he imagined. There were always bigger and better players. The big time was out of his reach. He never got over it. Then, such a cliché, he turned to booze and other women. Fighting with the son. Fighting with the wife. Fighting himself.'

They are quiet for a while.

She laughs cynically. 'Who was that president who only lusted in his dreams or something like that? My hubby was a full-time lust-er. Anything with big boobs would do.'

Whoa, thinks Hy, that's a lot of pain in there. He feels sorry for her, but surprised, he really doesn't want to hear any more.

'Change of subject,' she says, but not going far afield. 'My brother's life was no piece of cake, either. Injured in the war, WWII. Spent time as a POW. Came home a sick vet. They didn't know about the psychological problems from war experiences back then. Manny never got over his nightmares. One bad marriage after another. Ditto with bad jobs. Then he got lucky and found Sally. Real true companionship. And then she goes and dies too soon. He's been kind of unhinged ever since.'

Hy is feeling something strange, hearing all these tales of woe. He is startled. He'd never really given it any thought before, but he's had a successful life with a good marriage and years of considering himself happy. These tales of woe are depressing him.

Almost as if reading his thoughts, she says, 'Some of us don't win that promise of life, liberty and the pursuit of happiness. May I turn out the light? I think I can fall asleep.'

'Me, too.'

And whether she's able to or not, he falls asleep immediately, with a smile on his face.

TWENTY-FOUR
Manny Bloom the Late Night Crawler

Manny, dressed totally in black, never picks the same street twice. Not a good idea. Too easy to be caught. But there are plenty of streets to choose from. He knows Miami, having lived here twenty years. But in this, his life without Sally, he has learned to stay away from the rich beach areas. Miami Beach and Coral Gables the richest. Another keep-away, expensive South Beach, which stays awake most of the night. Oh, the music, the lights, the food and the dancing. It would be fun, but not in his plan book. Ditto Coconut and North Grove.

Keep out of Little Cuba as well. He tried that once and because he didn't know the language, it caused an incident of awkward communication.

He smiles, remembering the *senorita* who welcomed him into her bed. Was that during the *Calle Ocho* Festival? Lots of rum, lots of laughing. Lots of dancing and soon, to bed. She kept saying *si, si, si*, which he did understand. Until her boyfriend arrived unexpectedly. *No. No. No.* He touches his jaw which still aches when it rains.

Stay away from Valencia. He was caught on that street. Women who own their own guns? Hidden under their pillows? What is this country coming to?

Manny thought his salad days were up; shot while on the hunt? No, thanks. He wasn't ready to meet his maker. He thought about praying, but he forgot how. Thank goodness (or was that God?) the broad managed to keep the weapon steady until the cops came to get him. Brrr, ice cold babe that one.

Tonight he will do one of the numbers streets. SW37? SW42? Okay. Let's try around SW37. No closed garages; carports only so he can count cars at home. Two usually means a husband inside. Or maybe a teenager. Not always right about that; cars get parked on the street as well.

His bike winds its way down the quiet street. He's had much practice. Even though a house is dark, if there's a light on in the house next to it, that's a no go. Don't want any nosy neighbor peeking out a curtain.

This one looks good, four houses in a row unlit and ditto across the street. Pick one. Eenie, meeney miney mo. He parks his bike on the side of the house, out of sight, and tries the door. Triple-locks, darn it.

He ambles across the lawn, heading for the next door, as if he belongs there. Easy. Single lock. One car in carport. Looks like an early model Ford. Needs a paint job. Very dusty. At least a trip to the car wash? Decides it belongs to a woman. Men take better care of their cars.

Yard needs work, too. Wilted flowers, need pruning. That's part of the fun, guessing what delicious lady awaits him upstairs. Guessing a school teacher lives here. Quick instant analysis; yes, school teacher, low salary. Divorced, didn't get alimony. House needs work.

With a last look around; no one walking some dumb dog, no late-night numbskull, jogging. He takes a peek in a few parked cars. No couple doing the dirty in their back seat. All clear.

Manny takes out his handy-dandy credit card and zip, he's in.

First stop. Inside door. Listen, anyone moving around. No.

Second stop, the kitchen. Only light needed; the open fridge. Looks like a great leftover plate of spaghetti with meatballs. He'd be happy to nuke it, but until they invent silent microwaves, he eats his pasta cold. Loaf of bread. Butter. A bonus. No beer, though. Diet Pepsi. Yuk. Beggars can't be choosers.

Yum. Good dinner. Never did learn to cook, though Sally tried to teach him. No interest. Now it's frozen dinners or take-out. Or meals in some other woman's home. Like now.

Ready for dessert, his style. He heads up the dark stairway, helped by ambient light, listening for any sound. Two bedrooms. Both doors open. The smaller one must have been for a kid, lots of old-time band posters; now not living at home.

Bedroom two. A gentle snoring. Ladies don't like it when you tell them they snore. They say only men snore! Bad gambit, he never uses that one. He smiles. He believes in making nice.

A plus. Window shade up. Light from a street lamp.

She's sleeping on one side of the bed. Used to be a man on the other. The night is warm and she's kicked off the covers. Overhead fan blows light breezes.

From what he can tell, she's sixty-ish. Not bad looking. Good. The younger ones squirm at the thought of an old codger touching them. This one's wearing a granny-type nightgown. Been years since she ever wore a negligee. Given up on a man ever being in her bed again. Well, here I am, honey bun, ready to change your luck.

Though she does look a little skimpy. Like our great leader, he's a big bosom kinda guy. But then again ya had to have big chests of money to get a big-chested gal. He laughs to himself. Good joke, he has to remember that one.

Part one. Decrease the fear. He taps her gently on the shoulder. Eyes open. Instant gasp. Terror. Confusion. Wildly looking around for a way out.

'Shhh,' he says. 'I have no weapon. I will not hurt you. Please don't scream.'

The woman couldn't scream even if her life depended on it. And she does think her life depends on it. She's in a state of paralysis.

He waits a moment, in case she has a heart attack. You worry about that with old dames. No, her breathing is shallow, but that's to be expected. That's the part he doesn't like. Frightening them.

He pulls a chair next to the bed and sits down. And smiles a goofy, friendly smile, practiced long and hard in a mirror, to seem non-lethal. 'So what grade did you teach?'

Her lips barely part. Her voice stringy and hoarse. She can barely get the words out. 'Third grade. Do I know you?'

Bingo. Is he good, or is he good! He's got a gift. Sally used to say he could charm any woman with that dopey grin.

'No, we've never met. Would that we could. You're a fine-looking woman.' This tack works only with women over sixty. He should write a book about how to tame women. He's an expert.

Of course, she is biding her time, waiting for a way, thinking to escape. Hoping for some miracle. Yes, looking back and forth to a phone she can't reach.

'Don't hurt me,' she whispers.

They always say that and he feels badly. Though they are

frightened, he's not a man who hurts women. He has to make them understand. Sally used to tease him and call him lover boy, 'cause he never had enough of the bed stuff. Sally, why did you leave me?

'I don't have much money, but my purse is downstairs.'

He shrugs. He knows it before they say anything. Same words. 'I don't want your money.'

Now the ladies are even more frightened. She is thinking rape, even murder. He has to work on finding a better way of getting to the point faster, without the obvious steps they go through.

'I know this will sound strange, but I'm a lonely guy looking for companionship.'

She manages to speak again. She squeaks, 'Why don't you try a church? You could meet lots of nice women that way.'

Manny laughs out loud. That's a new one. 'What's your name, honey?'

'Patricia,' she whispers.

'What would you like?' he asks sweetly. 'I'm guessing it's been a long time since some good man treated you nice in the bed things. I'm here to please you. Any way you want. Straight sex. The missionary position. Doggy style. Kinky sex, though I'm personally not thrilled about that.' He makes a joke. 'I don't even own handcuffs.'

He attempts another goofy smile. But her terror is worsening.

Another joke. 'Foreplay is available, as well.'

Patricia tries to shrivel into something small; as if she can somehow disappear. 'I don't think so,' she whispers.

Like a good salesman who's shown all his wares, he shrugs. Win some, lose some. He learned that years ago when he sold vacuum cleaners door to door. 'Okay with me. No sex, but how about I sleep next to you, no fooling around, just for comfort?'

She manages to nod. Anything, anything to keep herself alive.

With aplomb, he kicks off his shoes and climbs into the vacant side of the bed and turns his back away from her. 'Night, night, don't let the bedbugs bite.' With that, moments later, he falls into a deep sleep.

He misses the sight of the rigid lady, lying there totally flummoxed. Listening to a lunatic, who snores. He misses that fact that she doesn't sleep at all. But is too terrified to try to phone or leave the bed and possibly wake him.

To her amazement, he stays for breakfast. While he eats the bacon and eggs, coffee and toast she managed to cook with shaking hands, she will sneak a cell phone into the bathroom, lock the door and call the police.

TWENTY-FIVE
A Side Trip. Julio the Guide

Day Four

Julio arrives at eight a.m. sharp and parks around the corner near Buildings O and P, with no bells or music as promised; far enough so they won't be seen or heard by her close neighbors. Ida, who is there already, is pleased. So far, so good. Julio gets points for punctuality.

She almost leaps, climbing into the truck. 'Drive,' she says, 'and fast! Get out of here.' She searches for the safety belt and buckles herself in. Her body wobbles from side to side as he quickly pulls out. She is relieved that this beat-up, old panel truck has a belt. That's another good sign.

She is amazed at herself, trusting some total stranger that she only met yesterday. She is proud of her sense of adventure. And her ability to pick a good employee.

Bumping along in this odd food truck, she is excited by all those Spanish words painted on it. Wait 'til she gets to tell the girls about her new helper. And how well she is handling working on her own. A prime player of the Gladdy Gold company.

However, a first thing first; wearing the Columbo raincoat, is problematic. She tugs at it to pull it out from under her. The safety belt is practically strangling her; and she's stuck and can't extricate herself.

Julio wonders why this woman wears a raincoat in such a hot city. But never mind, from yesterday, he already thinks she is strange. Such a remarkable country, this America. So many different kinds of people that is necessary to understand.

Julio does her bidding, '*Buenos Dias, Senora*,' he says as he fairly careens out of the gate and pulls into the front entrance to Lanai Gardens. 'We are going maybe to a fire?'

'I just don't want my nosy neighbors to see us.'

'And why is that a bad thing? You don't like your neighbors?' To Julio, living in the Cuban community, this is unimaginable.

Ida stares sideways at her driver, eyes narrowing with concern, 'Let's set down some rules right now. I hire you. I pay you; therefore I'm your boss. You drive; you don't talk.' There, that's settled. It's important, when doing business to make sure there is clarity. Saves problems later when it becomes a legal matter of 'she said, he said'.

Ida goes back to trying to release her raincoat from under her bottom, with little success. She'll just have to wait until they arrive.

Julio is stopped in the front of the entrance gate. He is held up at the traffic light signal. The light is red.

Ida grins. This will be a memorable journey. I've never driven in a big truck before. And with my own private driver.

The light turns green. Julio doesn't move.

Ida is startled. Julio is staring straight ahead. Nothing is happening. She is confused. 'Why are you standing here? Now the light won't change for one minute and thirty-nine seconds. I know because I once timed it.'

Julio remains still. She pokes him. 'What's the matter with you? Are you deaf? Say something!'

Julio is calm. Julio is almost always calm. Later he might tell her that's how he learned to survive in his adopted country. A country he worships. Julio has learned to speak English literally. 'You said I shouldn't talk.'

The light changes again. 'Oy! Turn left! Turn left, we need to get to the freeway.'

Julio is about to obey. But, he's missed his chance again. The light turns yellow, then red again. He still doesn't look at her.

She's having a conniption. 'Now we have to wait another minute and thirty-nine seconds! Don't you have any idea where we're going?'

Julio shakes his head.

Ida wants to scream. 'Oh, for God's sakes. Talk, already!'

Julio smiles. 'Yes, *senora*?' This strange lady changes her mind many times. How is he supposed to read what is in her mind?

She gives him the address of the trailer park. 'Do you know how to get there?'

He points to his GPS. 'America; such a wonderful place. Filled with such amazing toys, like a computer and iPhones and iPads and this magic thing that gets information on how to get anywhere from a satellite, some kind of space vehicle, up in the sky that flies around in orbit, compliments of the United States government. Definitely magic.

'This GPS . . . it knows the way; it is never wrong. It will take us wherever we want. But *por favor*, first I need to make a stop. Only for a few moments. It is on our way. Also in Miami.'

Ida shrugs. Now that she let him talk he doesn't shut up. Being Ida, she wants to add to her list of rules. No stops! But something in her suggests she ought to go a little easier on her new employee. Grudgingly, 'Only for a few moments.'

Julio groans. *Ay chico*! Wait until she meets his *abuela*. A woman who knows no time.

When they get off the I-95 freeway, Julio tells Ida, 'Welcome to Little Havana. This huge area is an almost eighty-five percent Cuban community.' He assumes, rightly, that she's never been here.

As Julio drives, Ida is startled by the unexpected brilliant splash of colors. Signs everywhere, walls covered with vivid, fascinating murals. And so many stores. Restaurants, people eating. People happily walking in the streets as well as on sidewalks. Loud and exciting music is heard playing on every street corner. She is startled by huge life-size statues of chickens.

Her curiosity gets her to ask, 'Why are there so many statues of chickens?'

Julio grins. 'They are sculptures of roosters. There is much art in this community. I think the roosters are a symbol of something. But what, I don't know.'

'I keep seeing signs that say *Calle Ocho*.' She pronounces it *cawl owcho*.

'*Calle Ocho*,' (calyay ocho, pronounced correctly) 'is a famous long street where every year in March there's a huge Festival. Last year it was said that a million people came. Very exciting.'

He indicates, 'As you can see, I don't open my truck here. Plenty of Cuban food available on any street corner.'

Ida thinks to herself, she will have many new things to tell the girls about this state they live in; so many places they've never seen. But not to visit here in March. She hates crowds.

Julio turns down a quiet street. Small houses, but with many pretty flowers. People sitting on steps in happy groups. Oddly, though, many cars are parked on lawns.

Julio pulls over and parks in a driveway, blocking a garage. 'This is where my grandmother lives. *Abuela* is the word for grandmother. I address her that way out of respect.'

He gets out of the truck, then turns to look at Ida through her window. 'Won't you come inside and meet her?'

'Shouldn't I just wait here?'

'It would not be good manners not to include you.'

Ida is indifferent. She climbs out, not wanting to insult her driver. She is pleased. Add this little stopover to part of her new adventurous life.

Before they enter, Julio gives Ida 'a tour'. He remarks on the windows on all the houses; all with wrought iron bars.

Ida comments, 'A lot of crime here to keep the bad guys away?'

'No, they are not for safety; barred windows are the style that comes with us from Cuba.'

He opens the door; they step inside and Ida's eyes are caught by a little elephant statue leaning against a wall. Julio explains, 'Elephants are for good luck.'

The grandmother's house is small, but it is charming. As Ida looks around, Julio comments that all the walls are painted bright colors. 'Notice mango green and papaya yellow. Also quite Cuban.' He spots her looking at the shelves. 'All for family pictures. I have four brothers and three sisters; so, many, many photos.'

And on one wall a single photo has a place of honor. It is a country scene, a small shed, bare of greenery, and with one scruffy tree. 'That was our home in Cuba many years ago.'

He calls out and tells his grandmother that he is here. A voice answers back. Julio tells Ida his *abuela* will come soon.

Ida peeks into the living room. Julio laughs. The furniture pieces are all covered in plastic. 'Nobody ever goes into the living room. It is for company only. Go into any former Cuban living room. They are all the same.'

He takes her to the kitchen. Along the way, Ida recognizes artifacts that are religious. Julio, reports, 'Those are crypts of favored saints. That one is *Caridad de Cobre*. The patron saint of charity.

His grandmother appears. She is tiny, bird-like and extremely old. Late nineties, Ida guesses. Dressed in a pale, long-sleeved, fragile-looking dress. As fragile as the woman herself.

'*Abuela.*' He bends way down to kiss her forehead. He hands her a package. Julio explains, 'My grandmother has what you call the sweet tooth. Chocolate is her favorite treat.'

'*Gracias, mi hijo,*' she says smiling.

Julio introduces Ida. Ida bows, guessing that is the right thing to do.

In this tiny, immaculate kitchen, the grandmother asks, '*Has desayunado?*'

'Grandmother asks if we're hungry. She always cooks many things expecting one or more of the family will always show up.'

Ida panics. 'No, no, we haven't time for this.'

'*Sientase a comer,*' says Grandmother.

Julio indicates a chair. 'She wants us to sit down and eat.'

Ida starts backing out the door. Eyes in headlights kind of look. Ida is scared that they will be trapped here forever.

The old woman is surprised. Nobody ever turns down food in her house. '*Quien es Ella?*'

'*Abuela, La llemo en algun lugar.*'

'I'm telling grandmother I need to drive you someplace.'

He doesn't mention her query; what's wrong with this woman? '*Ella nunca soneir?*'

Julio doesn't translate that either. His grandmother wonders if this woman ever smiles.

He directs Ida. 'Go outside and wait for me. I will say a few words and then I'll join you.'

Ida hesitates; she understands that respect is very important. She bows again and says, 'I really would love to stay and have a lovely meal, but I have a big problem to solve.'

Julio translates and the grandmother nods.

Ida waves at the old woman and rushes out, calling, 'It was nice to meet you, maybe some other time. A rain check.' To Julio, 'Hurry up!'

Grandma shrugs. She doesn't understand this funny lady in the big raincoat. She wants to come back when it rains?

Sitting in the truck, Ida taps at her watch in annoyance. It's already fifteen minutes and Julio is still inside. All around her children are playing, people are chattering and laughing, music is playing from someone's boom box; but Ida is a woman who knows how to focus. She stares straight ahead, seeing nothing except the hands of her wristwatch going around.

Though she does see that the garage door in front of her opens and a young man steps out. Before the door slides down, she glances at furniture. He walks around Julio's car, paying no attention to it, or her, and gets into a car parked in the street; and drives away.

Julio finally comes out. She is tempted to tell him about her other rules; like you don't keep your boss waiting; but Julio is all she has to get her to Hy.

Julio apologizes, explaining it was all about his grandfather, who no longer lives at home. He lives in an assisted care retirement home. He goes to visit often and he promised his *abuela* he would go again very soon.

Blah blah blah, Ida tunes him out.

Julio resets the GPS and they start out. Ida has one more comment. 'Someone opened the garage door and came out. He walked around your car and drove away in his. The garage looked full of furniture.'

Julio says, 'I'm sorry I missed him. My brother, Jaime; he lives in the garage.'

Ida is shocked. Julio is amused. 'Almost half the families around here have a relative living in their garage. One of these days I'll tell you about how we came from Cuba and how we live.'

Ida, strong, 'But not today.'

'Agreed. It is a long story.'

Ida leans back and smiles. Finally, off to the kill.

TWENTY-SIX
At the Beach for Instant Tan

The girls and I are at a local beach, with our long sundresses and pantsuits rolled up, so we can sit at the water's edge and dangle our toes in its delightful coolness. None of us thought to bring bathing suits, but at least we have sun hats. We are enjoying our ice-cream cones, licking the sides of the cones as the sweet cream drips down, in a race to whether mouth or dress will receive the stain. Perfect weather: hot, but bearable. Not a cloud in the sky. A deep and startling blue all-pervasive sky. And a sun beating down; relentless in its radiance. The air smells like seaweed.

Two busy little kids with parents lying next to them are building sand castles. I'm wondering if the children have been oiled down with sun block. I hope so.

Sailboats passing by, with gentle winds guiding them. The whole effect like a pretty watercolor by Claude Monet.

I think of the Wassingers' hurricanes; when this water would be dark, icy and frenzied. When ninety miles away, Cuba and the other islands would batten down for whatever terror will come.

The beach is half full; probably tourists. Doing the touristy things, writing postcards of the wish-you-were-here cliché. Snapping photos for later memories, eating hot dogs, ice cream and whatever else the beach sellers with their ice chests on wheels are offering. The men can be seen pushing their way through the coarse sand, calling out their wares.

A couple of teenagers stand by the lifeguard stand, holding their surf boards, looking wistful. Wrong day. Wrong beach; no surfing for them here today.

How nice to be doing nothing but enjoying being alive, in a beautiful place. '*Carpe diem*,' I say. Evvie smiles, she knows what it means – seize the day.

I think of my grandchildren. I miss them. One of these days

Jack and I should hop on a plane and visit the family in New York. Both of our families live close to one another and are dear friends. We keep putting it off, and we shouldn't. Time goes by too fast.

My sister can often guess what I'm thinking. We've always had this connection of similar thoughts at the same time. We used to say that we had ESP with one another. Like when I'm just about to pick up the phone to call her, my phone rings, and there's Evvie calling to say she's thinking about me.

'Jack on your mind?' she asks.

I nod. 'Joe on yours?'

'I wonder how the guys are doing on their safari.'

'Shooting photos of amazing animals. They'll be back with dozens of pictures for us to see.'

'Having a better time than we are, I'll bet. This case is a conundrum. I don't see any answers to our problem.'

I sigh. She can't stop thinking of our case, either.

I change the subject. 'Surprising, we haven't heard from Ida today. I wonder how she's doing with Lola. And what on earth can Hy be up to?'

'We can always call her and find out.'

'Nah, let's leave it to her to handle whatever it is. It can't be too complicated.'

Bella sits a foot or two away from us, still feeling like a pariah because of her 'relationship' with the Wassinger ghost. No one speaks to her, and poor thing, she can't stand being left out. I feel sorry for her.

'Ah, this is heavenly,' says Evvie, kicking her feet out in a circular motion.

Sophie agrees splashing water on her face, 'I like this a lot. Why don't we ever do this at home?'

'Why don't we?' whispers Bella from her purgatory.

I say with sarcasm, 'Why not, indeed? Especially since we live a ten-minute drive from our own gorgeous, famous beaches? In twenty-five years has anyone ever visited *our* beach? Anyone ever sat near the water, dangling their toes?'

Evvie laughs. She imitates Sophie in a nagging voice. 'What? And drag sand back into our apartments?'

Sophie sulks. 'I never said that.'

Bella, now feisty, 'Oh, yes you did. I heard you.' And feeling guilty for turning on her best friend, adds, 'And so did Ida. She says she never wants to sweep sand out of her apartment.'

Sophie ignores her and says, 'I'm enjoying our day off, but what next?'

Bella, 'Yeah, what?' She's trying so hard to get back into our good graces.

The so-called 'elephant in the room' is on their minds as well.

Sophie adds, 'Have we got a tan yet, so we can prove we vacationed on the beach?' Plaintive, 'So we can go home.'

Bella jumps on her bandwagon. 'I feel tan.'

I ask, 'So, you're saying you still want us to go home and quit the case?'

Sophie says, 'What else can we do? We have a murder to solve and our only witness is . . . a spirit. A spirit with a temper,' she adds.

Bella speaks softly, 'He's a guy. He's a famous dead guy.'

Evvie is annoyed. 'Yes, A dead guy, Bella, even if you're the only one who can see his ghost, it doesn't help us.'

Bella getting more confident, 'But Louie and Sadie can see him, and besides I liked Louie's speech about justice.'

Evvie agrees, 'Yes, he made a poignant plea about wanting justice for Mr Strand, but there seems no way to get that for him.'

Silence, all deep in their own thoughts.

Evvie pokes me. 'Something's going on over there.'

I look to where she points. At first I don't see anything unusual. I turn. I see what she's staring at. It's the couple with their two children playing in the sand. The parents are now standing up with arms crossed; it seems like they are shouting at each other. I look at the children, with their hands over their ears; they do not want to listen.

'My guess is they're having a fight,' Sophie says, looking also.

Bella agrees. Then gasps. 'He hit her!'

We stare, shocked. This husband has just smacked his wife in the face. She holds her hand over her cheek and is crying.

Bella says, 'That's awful.'

Sophie asks, 'I wonder what's going on.'

Bella asks nervously, 'What should we do?'

Sophie says, 'Nothing. Keep out of it.'

Bella continues, 'But we should do something. What if he

hurts her again or kills her?' Bella can sometimes be quite bloodthirsty.

The mother has dropped down on the sand, looking down and . . . digging? The father is pointing at her and shouting. The children are looking away. They are crying.

Sophie now worried, 'Or maybe we should call the police?'

Evvie wonders, 'I don't know. It feels wrong to just sit here and watch.'

Sophie says, 'Why don't we get one of the lifeguards. Guys to handle a violent guy.'

We look, but no one is at that stand. Lunch hour break? If they were here, would they interfere?

Bella says, 'They'll tell us to mind our own business.'

Evvie agrees, 'I'm sure they will.'

I try to see if anyone else is witnessing this family argument. No. No one else is near them. 'The most ironic thing,' I say to Evvie, 'a quotation just popped into my head. From, of all people, Ernest Hemingway. As corny and illiterate as it sounds. "I know what is moral, it's what you feel good after and what is immoral, you feel bad after".'

Evvie jumps to her feet, patting the sand off her skirt. 'We can't just sit here and do nothing.'

As she heads for the family, slogging across the sand, Evvie turns and calls out to me, 'The quote that pops into *my* head is "We are on this planet to help others".'

'Who said that?' I ask as I get up, toss my napkin that held my ice-cream cone into the trash and follow her.

'I don't remember,' Evvie says back at me, 'but we are in the business of helping people, so here goes nothing.' Now, she's hurrying.

It *is* our business. We *are* in the business of helping people. 'It is the business of anybody who sees a wrong that needs righting.' Another quote. And I am hurrying after her.

'Wait for us,' I hear behind me. Both girls are coming with us.

We reach the scene of the drama. Without anyone suggesting it, we encircle the couple. The couple is surprised to see us.

'May we be of help?' I suggest quietly.

The father fairly snarls. 'We don't need any help.'

The wife turns away, trying to hide her face. 'It's nothing. Really.'

The little boy, about eight years old, I guess, cries out, 'My daddy hit my mommy!' The tiny girl who is younger, cringes in fright.

The father raises his hand, then shouts, 'Shut up, Josh.'

Bella asks sweetly, 'Are you going to hit him, too?'

Right on, Bella, I think. Amazing, she said that in all innocence, not realizing how powerful a statement that is.

The father is startled; his hand drops down to his side.

Evvie asks the mother quietly, 'We really would like to help if we can.'

She shakes her head, in misery. 'I dropped one of my contact lenses.'

For a moment the father forgets we're here. 'You have any idea how much those damn things cost? You're always losing things. You're hopeless.'

She looks up at him, beseechingly. 'It's because you make me feel so useless.'

He is furious. He yells at us. 'Get the hell away from us!'

Evvie drops to her knees. To the mother, 'Where do you think you dropped it?'

'Somewhere near here,' she says timidly. 'I wouldn't bet on finding it.'

As if on cue, Bella and I join her. Sophie, who has knee problems, takes longer, but she manages to plop down. We dig and dig and dig. The two children join us and dig, also. They can't look at their father. Their father glares at all of us.

A few moments later, Bella holds up the missing lens, 'Here it is!' She hands it to the mother, who sobs in gratitude.

Evvie, who pulls no punches, says to the father, 'See how easy that was. Now if you were a *real* man, you would have helped your wife.'

We have put him in a precarious place. We have embarrassed him in front of his family. We wait, I admit nervously, for his next move.

But Evvie is taking no chances. Without any qualms, she tells an outright lie. 'Just to let you know, sir, I have it all on my iPhone. Once I find out your name . . .'

His crying son jumps in, 'It's Larry Fulbrite,' the little boy says bravely. His father's face seems to collapse.

Evvie completes it quietly. 'Thank you, Josh. As I was saying, Facebook will have a party with my video. Oh, and the clicks that pick it up. It'll go viral!'

I am amazed that my sister has a clue what those tech words mean; I hope to God, she got them right. Evvie, an actress all her life.

The children go to their mother and she hugs them. From the look on her face, we have given her the strength she needs.

I come close to her. 'I suggest that your husband should go into Anger Management. If you ever get hit again, you leave the house with the children and get to a women's shelter. And call the police.'

The man is totally shaken. He goes to his wife. 'I'm so sorry.'

Evvie and I know better. That's what they all say. Until they do it again.

I admit to myself, what we did is dangerous. If the man is psycho, he is capable of real damage. Another quote pops into my head. 'Doing the right thing for someone occasionally feels wrong to you.'

We leave the four of them hugging.

We hear Sophie calling to us. 'You gonna leave me here all night?' We didn't realize she can't get up with those bad knees.

To our amazement, the father comes over and lifts her gently to her feet. She thanks him. Wow!

We return to our original place on the sand. My small gang looks to me. What now? 'First I want to congratulate you all for a job well done.'

High-fives all around.

I continue. 'On one hand we have the choice to go home, dragging our failing tails behind us.'

Sophie interrupts, 'And don't forget we're gonna say we came here on a case, which didn't pan out so we stayed for a vacation.'

Evvie, being our treasurer, points out, 'We haven't been paid yet, and I doubt we'll ever see a dime of it. Not that they'll think we did anything to deserve it.'

Sophie comments, 'Big deal. It won't be the first time. We've done plenty of freebies. Think of it as an adventure. How many people get to work for a ghost?' She starts to giggle.

One by one, we all join in. I say, laughing, 'Yes, this famous ghost interviewed us. Thought we were pitiful. Then fired us!' The laughter spreads. 'How dare he!?'

Evvie asks, 'What was that TV show we used to watch with that funny looking guy with floppy yellow hair who used to yell, "You're fired!"?'

Nobody remembers.

Bella, 'I wonder what happened to him.'

Sophie, 'He woulda made a great car salesman down at Alligator Alley Ford Autos.'

I pause to let the laughter die down. Then I go on from where I started, 'On the other hand, we are investigators, and actually we haven't investigated anything.'

Bella interrupts. 'We just did.'

'Rightly so. But in the case that brought us here, we got distracted by an aggressive ghost and the Wassingers and their sidebars. My point being, it has been determined what we are to think and we've not found out anything on our own.'

A couple of minutes go by, then Evvie claps. 'You're right. Absolutely right.'

Sophie is puzzled. 'But we were told that Robert died in an accident.'

'That's right, Teresa said it, as that was the ongoing opinion. The cops said their proof was a photograph of a fish looming over Robert about to kill him. It was an assumption on their part. Ditto, we're told that by his lawyer partners and his pals as well.' I pause. 'But we are taking a lot of opinions at face value. What kind of detecting is that?'

Evvie agrees. 'Too bad they don't have the boat. Maybe there would be some evidence to be found.'

Sophie is concerned, 'What a shame if that boat's gone down in the deep, deep ocean.'

I comment, 'Another supposition. We don't know if that's a fact.' I brush more sand off my sundress. 'So, I say, we get moving and investigate and find our own facts. We interview every one of these experts on our own. If the naysayers can prove they're right, so be it. But we need absolute proof.'

Bella practically whimpers, 'Mr Hemingway says he has the only proof of what really happened.'

Evvie looks at her, eyes flashing, 'But he doesn't share. What good is that? Forget it, Bella.'

'So, we're agreed? We're still on the case?'

'Nobody fires us, right?'

A chorus of 'Right on!'

TWENTY-SEVEN

Jailbird Comes Home. Hy and Dolly-Ann Distraught

Breakfast is about to be served at this same time in Manny's trailer. But first Dolly-Ann and Hy do as much of a clean-up as possible, although it's made difficult surrounded by Manny's junk. They scrub walls, and the floor. They wash every dirty dish, every pot, and all the silverware, though Manny doesn't have much to work with.

Hy worries about getting some horrible infection from the filth in Manny's trailer, but doesn't share that fear with Dolly-Ann.

They sit down to eat.

Hy is curious. She seems calm about Manny's whereabouts, since once again he didn't come home last night. She wouldn't tell him where she thought he was. Though she obviously knew.

'Not to worry,' she says assuredly. 'He'll be showing up soon, with some companions. And all will be revealed.' She smiles, but it isn't a happy one. Her words are said with irony and displeasure.

Why is she being so secretive? Her brother leaves during the night to go where? She wants to follow him, but Manny makes sure her car isn't running, so she is frustrated. And if she found him, what would she do?

Yesterday morning, he showed up on his own. Last night Manny let out the air in his tires, so another night went by. Who is she expecting today, but she won't tell him who or why.

'The scrambled eggs are just perfect,' Hy says, desperate to make conversation. He is a man never comfortable with silence. Or puzzles. Especially here and now with something hanging heavily over Dolly-Ann. A quick guilty thought again of his wife, Lola, who's never too far out of his mind, terrified of what she will do to him when he comes home.

He thinks about early this morning when they woke up in Dolly-Ann's trailer. He was up ahead of her and was in a quandary. They'd fallen asleep with their clothes on; now he needed a shower and change of clothes. The previous nights had been easier. When Dolly-Ann woke up, she'd gone straight to Manny's trailer, so getting dressed wasn't a problem. Today, he did the best he could in that tiny bathroom, washing his body and changing clothes. All in all, this experience was getting bothersome.

'Is your wife a good cook?'

Hy is startled. This is Dolly-Ann's first reference to his marriage; or for that matter mentioning anything personal about him.

Cautiously he answers, 'She's good enough.' He hasn't any idea how to handle this ticklish subject. He thinks twice about mentioning how much effort Lola makes for his meals to be delicious, and looked forward to. Lola has seven specialties and every evening, a different one of them is prepared. And every month, she finds seven new recipes to try. She's been doing this for as long as he can remember. She believes for a marriage to succeed, a couple must work at it. That's how it has stayed fresh for so many years. Is Dolly-Ann hoping he'll say his is an unhappy marriage?

She says, 'I was a good cook. I tried so hard to please my disinterested husband. I even took a Cordon Bleu class on cooking. My house was kept spotless. I was the perfect little homemaker. I met my husband at the door at night with a bottle of his favorite beer. Did he even say thank you?'

She looks so sad; Hy doesn't have the words to say. But his heart feels what he wants to do. He wants to hug her and find a way to make her happy. Stop that! You're a married man!

The doorbell rings. Dolly-Ann peers out the side window and smiles. Smug. That's the expression on her face.

This is obviously what she's been waiting for. Hy stands up, waiting for what will develop next.

Dolly-Ann opens the door to two policemen holding onto brother

Manny by the scruff of his neck. His clothes are rumpled, his hair disheveled. But there's a smirk on his face.

Manny pulls away from them. They let him loose. He shakes his body, like a dog might after an unwanted bath, as if to toss off the odor of cop.

The first cop grins. 'What happened the other night? Did he take a night off? We missed him.'

Dolly-Ann is familiar with these cops. They've been here before. This is a well-beaten path. The cop is referring to the night before – the second night Hy was there. Manny meets his grin and doubles it. 'I got real lucky that night. A babe who knew when she hit the jackpot. Me.'

The second cop, a huge guy, as big as Manny, is not amused, and obviously has no sense of humor. 'The *babe* you picked last night was not pleased.'

Dolly-Ann's face clouds up. Now he understands. She knows what he's been up to and she is embarrassed. And angry.

'I don't know what to do with him anymore,' she says, defeated. 'He won't listen to reason.'

Cop number one says, 'I don't understand those women. None of them will press charges. They call us up, hysterical and frightened about a man who broke into their house. Then, when we suggest filing a report, they slam the door in our faces. Why do we even bother?'

Manny smiles again. 'That's because they like me. You should mind your own business and catch bad guys instead of harassing me.'

Dolly-Ann loses it; she shrieks at her brother, 'That's because those poor women are as embarrassed as I am! They are worried about what people will think! What you're doing is ridiculous! And cruel.'

Cop Two, to Manny, 'You're playing with fire, dum-dum. One of these nights there will be a guy in that bedroom. With a pistol. And he'll use it. Then we won't be bothered dragging you home every morning. You'll be brought home in a black bag.'

The other cop is disgusted, 'And that will be the end of wasting taxpayers' money. And wasting our time.'

Dolly-Ann apologizes over and over again. They can only shrug. The cops leave.

She turns to her brother. Manny stands there, hands outstretched, as if to say, 'I told you so. See, you're worrying for nothing.'

Manny looks at the remains of breakfast on the kitchen table. He shakes his head. 'I'll bet Patty is a better cook than you are.'

Dolly-Ann starts to cry. 'Patty, you know her name . . . Omigod! You're hopeless!'

'Actually it's Patricia. But I like to call her by my nickname for her.'

Hy can't stand the suspense anymore. 'What's going on here?'

Manny is annoyed. 'I ain't no criminal! And what are you still doing around here?'

Hy, under his breath, 'Yeah, like I can leave with four dead tires.'

Manny, with an expression like a little boy, who's just been caught, fingers in the cookie jar says, 'That was kinda fun. So sorry. But my silly sister would drag you around town for no good reason.'

Dolly-Ann, through tears, 'My moron brother breaks into women's houses, raids their fridge, eats their food, then climbs into bed with them! And expects them to want him there. How's that for idiocy?'

Manny grins. 'What's so terrible; I bring a little love into their lives.'

Hy has to prevent himself from laughing. This is the problem he was brought here to solve? Manny eats a meal first? Then sleeps with them? They let him into their beds? They cook him breakfast? Un-freakin'-believable.

Dolly-Ann is still furious, 'One of these days a woman *will* press charges; and between breaking and entering and attempted rape, you'll spend what's left of your useless life in prison!'

'You're over-reacting. The gals like me. I never have to rape anybody. Though I do admit, sometimes it takes some of them a few minutes to get used to my technique.'

She shakes her head; her brother is impossible. Maybe crazy. 'Oh, do they? They're sound asleep, thinking they are safe in their homes and suddenly some monster is standing over them, ready to pounce. I'm surprised no one has had a heart attack!'

Proudly, 'So far, they've all been healthy.'

'But you terrify them! What you do is nasty!'

'If you heard my relaxing speech, you wouldn't say that.'

Dolly-Ann beside herself, 'An old man in dirty clothes and smelling bad inspires confidence?'

He is insulted. 'I shower. I dress nice for the occasion.'

'God help us.'

Hy is astonished. This is one of the funniest things he's ever heard. But being a male, he almost feels respect, and yes, maybe a little jealousy for Manny enjoying an exciting existence. Living on the edge like that. Wow! When does he, Hy, ever get to do anything that's thrilling? A daily swim in the pool at the exact same time each day; surrounded by a bunch of boring old women? He answers his own question; his excitement is now. Not telling Lola where he is and with whom. Being with a woman who can still turn his juices on. Yes, he feels empathy for the big slob.

As Dolly-Ann and Manny continue to scream at each another, Hy leans back in his chair and imagines another scenario. Playing the same scene with him as the actor. Picking his quarry carefully; making sure a woman is alone. Breaking into a dark house. Stopping to eat first. He stifles a giggle – what *chutzpah*! Then climbing the stairs to a stranger's bedroom. He shivers at the image of himself as a predator. And what will be waiting for him: a woman with open arms, or a gun?

What's that line? Manny believes in going out with a bang, not a whimper.

There is another pinging of the doorbell. Hy tries for a joke. 'It's like Grand Central station around here.'

Dolly-Ann, still enraged, trounces angrily to the door and pulls it open. And says to the stranger, 'Who the hell are you?'

Still wearing her Columbo raincoat, she walks inside introducing herself. 'Hello, I'm Ida Franz. Hey, there, Hy. How are you?'

Hy wishes he knew how to faint.

TWENTY-EIGHT

Back to Wassingers. For a List

We drop by the Wassingers. They eagerly open the door and we are standing in the dimly-lit entrance hall, which I suppose they would call a vestibule. They are thrilled to see us again and to be told we're still on the job. They just knew the visits to Papa were a success. And especially helpful was Louie's speech on justice. Yeah. Amazing how people can go through the same set of circumstances and see it exactly the opposite. As far as I'm concerned, ghost-visiting was a lot of non-help. Lectures on justice, we didn't really need. We're on our own.

They want to serve us tea. We decline. Been there, done that.

'And no cookies,' Bella whispers, reminding me.

Next, they are ready to *shlepp* us up that horrid staircase again, to see you-know-who. But not this time, oh no. Get thee behind me, oh ghost.

I inform them, 'We came here because we recall you have a list of the people involved in the case; the one's we ought to personally talk to. We would like that list.' Surely a simple request.

Louie says, 'Of course, you should see all those people. You will learn all you need to.'

Evvie agrees, 'That's what we're hoping.'

To avoid a lengthy visit filled with another session of Wassinger memorabilia, I try to hurry them along. 'Louie, the list – right this minute, please?'

Louie to Sadie, 'Dearest one, bring out the Robert Strand file for the ladies. They do need to be on their way.'

Sadie looks puzzled. 'But angel of my life, you were the one who put it away.'

Louie shows us his baffled face. 'Definitely, it was you, love. Remember we were reorganizing my desk and you said you would take care of it? You said we should put it in a special place, so it won't get lost?'

Inwardly I groan. This could take hours.

Sadie thinks aloud. 'Sweet hubby, I don't remember that conversation but let me take a look.' She disappears, I assume to a home office.

Sophie and Bella decide to wait by sitting down on the staircase steps; first they wipe the steps with tissues, as if that would clean decades of dirty shoes. Then they set about fanning themselves with their hands. It is warm and stuffy in this hallway. I doubt the Wassingers have air-conditioning. Or theirs isn't working. Or it's against their religion; heaven only can imagine why we must nearly suffocate.

Evvie leans against a wall, and then changes her mind. She doesn't want the dust on her clothes again.

'Nice day,' Louie says making polite conversation.

'Very nice,' Sophie replies.

'How's Mr Hemingway?' Bella sweetly asks, adding to the socializing.

Oh, no, not that. Do not go there.

I hear a low groan from Evvie.

Louie perks up. 'He is in fine fettle, having visitation days with friends coming and going all week. Quite exciting.'

Don't ask, I beg in my mind.

Bella grins, unaware of our grief. 'Oh, that's so nice. Who's been coming?'

One fantasist to another, Louie shares her enthusiasm. We are now entering coo-coo land again.

Louie counts on his fingers, 'Let's see; yesterday it was Gertrude Stein, of course with her dear, dear friend, Alice B. Toklas. She was the one who ran that famous *salon* in Paris, where so many expatriate *artistes* visited. There was much laughter and gossiping.'

Bella, who hasn't a clue to who these people are, nods enthusiastically.

Louie chatters on, 'Last Tuesday, F. Scott Fitzgerald dropped in and they talked for hours about their famous books.'

He gives a funny little laugh which reminds me of a donkey bray, 'Hee haw, hee haw.' Nobody will ever believe this conversation. Nobody. Evvie smiles, reading my mind.

Louie keeps going, 'And how the critics all over the world valued their each and every volume and how much money they made.'

Bella claps her hands to show her delight.

Louie brays on. 'I could go on forever . . .'

Please don't, I pray.

But Louie does, 'Then, Pablo Picasso, the famous artist was here on Wednesday afternoon. He's such a funny man, though I don't understand much of his Spanish; he speaks so rapidly. But they always talk about the art scene. Ezra Pound the poet, arrived that same evening. Mr Hemingway doesn't like his politics! They're forever arguing. And Max Perkins, his devoted Scribner's editor was there. They almost came to blows. Mr Perkins needed to pull them apart.'

Dead people visiting dead people! Oy! Save us from this *folie a deux,* now five. Louie, still gurgling, 'And all those women he had, what a parade of beauties; don't ask.'

Believe me, I won't ask. I break in, or else I'll scream. 'Speaking of lists, where is Sadie? Did she get lost?'

Louie looks perturbed. 'I shall find her.'

This time I decide to follow him, in case I have to urge him to hurry. Naturally the girls follow me . . .

Into the kitchen. The kitchen is also their office? This ginger-bread Victorian mansion must have at least ten rooms, and this is where their office is? And this is their idea of being organized? I would hate to see their idea of messy.

We find Sadie hovering in front of an open pantry door, papers and file covers are spilled on every shelf and scattered all around her on the floor. The cupboard is filled with who-knows what! Next to her is a small wooden table – their desk? Also crowded with pages.

'Still searching,' she calls out to us cheerfully.

Louie rushes over to her. 'I just remembered it was in a lavender file cover.' He reports to us, 'Lavender is Sadie's favorite color and scent.'

Sadie blushes. 'He brings me lavender bouquets on my birthday. Did you know if you put lavender on your pillow at night you will sleep better?'

This is what hell will be like. This scene, these people saying and doing what they do. Over and over into eternity. 'The Strand file,' I say, weakly.

Louie points, excitedly. 'There it is. On the top shelf. See the lavender thingy?'

Sadie hurries (if you can call it that) to the kitchen table and pushes one of the chairs inch by agonizing inch toward the cupboard.

Oh, no, he's going to climb on that rickety chair.

I nudge Evvie; she is our tallest. 'Reach up, for heaven's sakes, before Louie climbs up and kills himself.' I shudder to think how he got it up there in the first place.

With a bit of stretching, Evvie pulls the file down, along with a stack of other pieces of paper that were leaning against it.

Louie hands me the file, as if it were a piece of fine jewelry, and I was expected to bow in pleasure. To me, it's a plastic mess, with coffee or tea stains. I look inside. There is one sheet of paper with four names penciled in. That's it?

With the one page gripped in my hand, I rustle my gang out of this loony bin. With the bin residents giving advice as we go.

'Watch out for that lady police person,' Sadie advises. 'She's meaner than a bee sting.'

Louie, always up for a cheerful announcement says, 'Robert's law partners are worse than she is. Shakespeare was right. Kill all the lawyers.'

'And those lazy boys Robert fishes with and also drinks and plays cards with,' warns Sadie, 'they're a rowdy bunch and useless.'

I'm waiting for their take on number four, Mr Pebbles, the coroner. They don't give out any advice about him, I won't ask. It will cost at least another lost hour.

The Wassingers giggle, pleased at their art of reference-giving.

Louie waves at that list happily. On his soap box again, 'Then you'll know the truth and the truth will set us free. Justice for Robert Strand!'

Sadie warns us in her sweet little way, 'Many people around here are so negative. Don't let them get you down.'

Evvie calms her. 'We have minds of our own. Not to worry, Sadie dear.'

Sadie is proud as she announces, 'We thank you for all you are doing and Papa thanks you, too.'

Yeah, in your dreams. But I don't tell her that.

Louie asks, 'What about Papa's cape and cigars? Mr Hemingway has asked about them a number of times. I'll be glad to take you to retrieve them.'

I shake his trembling hand. 'Not now, Louie, maybe later.' Maybe never I hope.

TWENTY-NINE
To Cop Shop. First on List

I compare our escape from the Wassingers to an escape from Alcatraz; swimming in dark waters with sharks nipping at our heels. Only in our case, it's more like minnows nibbling at us. With their lack of cool air, we are outside scratching sweaty bodies and sticky hair. It was voted that we need a hearty lunch to give us the strength to go on. I would rather have returned to the B&B to shower and nap. As usual the vote is tied, Bella and Sophie and food vs Evvie and me, but I give in.

The outdoor cafe we are in specializes in hominy grits. Bella and Sophie won't try them, but Evvie and I are game; we're always willing to attempt something new. However, we're disappointed; it tastes like Cream of Wheat breakfast cereal with sugar and some items we don't recognize.

Of course, our curious one, Evvie needs to look it up. She calls Google up on her laptop, which she always has with her. Those grits are especially popular in the south (but not South Florida) especially in New Orleans. She reads to me: '"Grits is a porridge made from corn (maize) that is ground into a coarse meal. Hominy grits are treated with an alkali process called nixtamalization with cereal germ removed".' She pauses as I react to the incredibly long, worrisome word.

'Wait, there's more. That big word means how they make the original hominy; the corn is dried and treated by soaking the mature grain in a dilute solution of lye or slaked lime. Then the maize is thoroughly washed. In Italy grits are also named polenta.'

Lye? Really? They have to thoroughly wash it to get the lye out? *Oy*. TMI as the kids would say. Way too much information. I push my plate as far away as I can. An odd name for a kind of cereal. I've lost my appetite, but Evvie talks me into a small house salad.

Sophie and Bella laugh with glee as they thoroughly enjoy their double-size hot dog special with raw onions, sauerkraut, mustard and whatever else possible on it.

Snarky Evvie asks the girls, 'Would you like me to tell you what's really in your hot dogs?'

Sophie and Bella nervously, at the same time, 'No, thanks.' They keep eating, but with less enthusiasm.

Oh well. What I really need is a stiff drink, after another bout with the maddening Wassingers. But this hamburger joint does not carry booze.

I suggest we check in with Ida. However, the last two times I phoned her, I had to leave a message. I try again this minute with same result. And when she'd try to reach us, we were occupied. We keep missing each other.

Evvie comments. 'She must be awfully busy with her case. I wonder what mischief Hy is involved in.'

Sophie adds, 'I haven't forgotten that rotten thing he did with us at the pool. I still want revenge. Just you wait, Hy Binder, when we get home . . .'

Bella, of course says, 'Ditto.'

Lunch is over. I get up. 'Onward to visit the police. Let's see what they have to tell us.'

The police station was at the top of Louie's list. So we decided that should be our first stop. We called ahead for an appointment to let the station staff learn we are Private Investigators.

Evvie, 'I can't wait 'til we hear their definite opinion.'

'We need to hear it for ourselves.'

The local police station is smallish. The half-a-dozen cops in the plain office seem relaxed. Only one cop is on the phone. Others are reading reports and or newspapers. A large ceiling fan spreads the cool air around. Maybe a slow crime day?

And here comes Sergeant Barbara Ella Robbson, according to her name tag. Oh, oh, I think, as she marches toward us, she's big. Over six-foot tall, rather hefty, with bulging shoulders and brillo-type black hair squashed under her cop hat. She seems like one tough cookie and is naturally carrying a rather scary large-looking gun.

When the female cop reaches us, she walks past us and says,

'Where are those detectives who wanted to meet with me?' Her voice is tough, reminding me of the sound of a cement mixer. 'If they wasted my time . . .'

The girls are immediately panic-stricken. This isn't going to be easy. Sadie's bee sting may be right.

I walk over to her and hand her our card. 'Gladdy Gold. And my associates. At your service.'

She turns to us, as if peering down at something unpleasant, then skims quickly at the card, plays with it, turns it up and down and around; smirks, as if it were some kind of joke. Then she glares at us, treating us with the same scorn she treated our card. She laughs. 'You're kidding. Right. This is some trick or treat?' She looks to her audience of two policemen who sit nearby at their desks, and says ever-so-cutely, 'Is it Halloween already?'

The cops grin, clapping at her humor.

Halloween, ha ha, big joke. Another insult. Here we go again. Teresa was surprised at our vocation, because we were females and seniors. Our 'famous' ghost thought we were pitiful and laughed hysterically, or so we learned from our spirit-communicator, Bella. Now this mean-looking piece of work is demeaning us, and giving us a hard time.

I ignore the affront, and stiffen my body into a sturdy business position. And with an equally strong voice to hers, I let her find out we are to be reckoned with. 'We work out of Fort Lauderdale and we're here hired by the Wassingers . . .'

The sergeant's hand shoots up. She stops me. 'Not them, again! Mercy me. Look, ladies, you are out of your depth. We've already informed the Wassingers that Robert Strand died in a boating accident. And we have definitive proof.'

Evvie jumps in, furious with this hard-nosed cop, 'You must not have found the boat; it might have given you much-needed information.'

Callous smile from Barbara, 'Not that we needed it. Strand's drowned body was washed up on shore. The autopsy definitely showed that he was gored by a fish. I wish all of our cases were this easy. The victim did us the favor by taking a photo of himself being gored by that fish.' She stifles a laugh. 'Sorry, but it does sound funny. Proof positive. Death by selfie. This case is open and shut!'

Wow! I'm impressed. She blew all that 'definite' information out, without taking a breath.

The cops, at the nearby desks, chuckle along with her. One calls out, 'A great fish story.' The other mimics, 'Something's fishy here.'

Barbara gets into the act. 'Good things come to those who *bait*!'

Cop one is next, and says winking at her, 'I like that gal. She's a *hooker*!'

Big laughs all around. but they're not through. We watch with pursed lips.

Cop number two, 'Happiness is a big fish and a witness to prove it.'

Barbara again, 'Couples that fish together, stay together.'

That gets a small woo! Barbara isn't finished, 'Here fishy, fishy, fishy . . .'

Cop one tops her, 'The way to a man's heart is through his fly.'

Big laughs at that. Sophie blushes and covers Bella's ears with her hands.

Cop humor.

Evvie comments angrily. 'A man died. It isn't funny.'

That quiets them down. The guys go back to what they were doing. Barbara stands firm. She's waiting for us to leave.

Cop-lady sure is full of a lot of assumptions. I say, 'About that photo, may we see it?'

Sergeant Barbara Ella cuts me off and practically shoves us toward the door. 'Time to leave. We have real cases to deal with. With real cops, not little old ladies playing at being cops. And do tell the annoying Wassingers to please stop – no more phone calls.'

Talk about being insulted!

Outside, dumped like trash, we stand there for a few minutes, waiting to get over that 'bums rush'. We are seething. Bella is confused. 'I didn't get those fish jokes. Especially that last one. It sounded dirty.'

Sophie says, 'It was, forget you ever heard them. They were mean.'

Bella also wants to know what a selfie is.

Evvie explains it. Bella doesn't get it. Evvie tries again, 'You have a phone that is also a camera . . .'

Bella is confused. 'How can a phone be a camera?'

Evvie quits. Bella will never get it.

Sophie takes over and also tries her hand at explaining it. 'It just is. You hold the phone up and it takes a picture of you holding up your camera. And it's called a selfie, because you take your own self's picture. Get it?'

Bella is near tears. 'It doesn't make sense. A selfie? Is that really a word?' She says low, 'My phone doesn't do that.'

Sophie pats her on the back, as if to say it's all right, never mind. What she usually does when Bella is confused. Bella smiles; she has her best friend back.

No hope back in there with Ms Hard-as-nails cop. 'And she never showed us the photo. She tells jokes? We wasted *her* time? The witch!'

Once again, we're seen as just little old ladies playing at being cops. Indeed!

I promise that soon you will eat those words, Barbara, babe.

THIRTY

A Busy Tale of Three Lawyers

Next stop, STRAND, SMYTHE and LOVE lawyers. We find a posh office on an expensive street. Lots of glass and shiny wood in all the buildings.

In their office, we are aware of the many plaques on the wall showing us how famous the trio is and what city and state awards they've won. And of all the important organizations they belong to. There's also a photo of their pre-teen baseball team, with the winning name, Dolphins, printed at the bottom. Robert Strand is in the photo as their manager. The kids are all smiling and happy. Part of public service.

And even a photo of – I guess his partners – Smythe and Love, proudly showing off a huge caught marlin. This town is fish crazy. But, never having seen a monster like this, I shudder at its long, lethal, spear-shaped dangerous snout.

We inform the receptionist, a gum-chewing, flabby blond with black roots showing, that we have an appointment. She is busily fanning herself with a Japanese type of fan as she reads an issue of *People* magazine. She wears a sleeveless thin blouse in this exceedingly warm office.

With her nose up in the atmosphere, she advises us that only Mr Parkhurst J. Smythe is here today. Mr Albert Love is out of the office. And we are informed that Mr Smythe is extremely busy.

I respond to huffy with huffy, 'We're busy, too, but we'll wait.'

To show how active and important he is, we're kept waiting forty minutes. We show how busy we are by looking around the room a lot. After a closer glance at the awards and such, we become aware that the air-conditioning is on dreadfully low, and we are getting awfully warm. Cheapskates obviously don't want to spend their money. Without the air to recycle it, the room smells of dead cigar.

And everything is so brown! Brown furniture. Brown walls. Brown bookcases; even all the law books look brown. Brown photos of early Key West, sometime in the eighteenth century, in what is called sepia brown.

We wiggle in our seat cushions (brown also) and attempt to read the magazines on the coffee table, but they're all are about yachting. Along with company pamphlets with the title, 'Ten Reasons Why You Need a Lawyer'. The cover is . . . brown.

When Smythe finally comes out, he's a skinny, fifty-ish, five-foot-high man in a shiny black suit. He takes one look at us, and he immediately looks at his watch, to indicate that his time is precious and he is annoyed at being bothered. He asks the blond with black roots receptionist, as if wondering aloud, 'Where are the private investigators?'

She shrugs and goes back to her *People* magazine.

Here we go again. I look down – Smythe's shoes are brown.

I sigh, and then go through my dog and pony act again, quickly explaining: 'Incredible as it may seem to you, yes, we are private investigators; my associates are Evelyn Markowitz, Sophie Myerbeer and Bella Fox. We were hired by Louie and Sadie Wassinger to find out what happened to your partner, Mr Strand and we wish to discuss this case with you.'

All said without taking a breath. I can do that, too.

Bella and Sophie are trying to hide their giggles because they think Smythe's (brown) toupee is crooked. I can tell Sophie already dislikes him because he seems cranky and uppity. Bella also looks askance on this unpleasant man.

After he gets over the shock of our really, truly insisting we are PIs; being a man of the law, and probably paranoid, he immediately wants to see our credentials and license.

Shucks, I was afraid of that. This only comes up once in a great while. Needing to downright lie, I say, playing my role as impractical woman, 'Oh goodness me, I left them at home.'

One of these days, we must get around to applying for a license. My son-in-law, Morrie, has warned me time and time again that this paperwork was a necessity. But at our age, it seems silly to bother. Naturally, when we get back, I won't report that Morrie was right once more.

Being the stuffy lawyer he is, Smythe rightly feels he shouldn't discuss personal information with the likes of us. And because we had no proof of our business, he is unwilling to treat us as equals. He says in his smarmy way, 'Thank you for dropping in.'

He waits for us to leave. I don't move, so neither do my girls. Not so fast, Smythey. It's not about our not having a license. It's the same rigmarole. Women. Old. Couldn't possibly believe we should be taken seriously. We're not bowing to his obvious disrespect of women. I imagine pasting onto the plaque on the front door, 'Misogynist-at-Law'.

Bella whispers to Sophie, 'Do we need to tell him fish jokes?'

Sophie shushes her.

Here I go again, 'About the Robert Strand case . . .'

We hear the expected groan. Translation: them again, those annoying Wassingers.

'All right,' he says caving in like the coward he is, 'but I will tell you only this much.'

He tosses words at us, a lot of legal mumbo jumbo into the air, that he and his partner, Albert Love, have taken over Mr Robert Strand's clients and he can assure us they will do what is right for the Wassingers, and . . . please ask them to stop calling. It is very bothersome.'

Speaking for our clients I say, 'But the Wassingers are concerned that their property won't go to the Historical Society when they are gone.'

Smythe looks as if smoke will come out of his ears. One look at his guilty face and I am positive he does not have the interests of the Wassingers at heart. No siree.

He manages to control himself. 'That is no business of yours.'

'We've heard that there is a photo that allegedly proves Mr Strand's death was accidental—'

Stiff as an ironing board, he interrupts, 'So sorry. I cannot show it to you: it's privileged.'

This is getting repetitious. He walks us quickly to the door. Mr Smarmy sneers, needing to get in the last word, 'Not your concern. Ours.'

The receptionist throws us a little wave goodbye.

But just before the door closes, my eye is caught by Smythe taking a quick glance at his photo of his big fish. Then immediately turns away.

Outside, once again dumped, the girls rate him and with giggles, rename his fancy lawyer sign outside, 'SLIMY, SLIPPERY & ONE DEAD GUY.' I preferred my misogynist title.

We don't like him. We don't trust him.

Strike Two.

THIRTY-ONE
Ida Takes Over. Hy in Shock

Ida places her hands on her hips and is smiling; obviously pleased with herself. Like some ice statue, frozen in time, Dolly-Ann, Manny and Hy stare at the woman in the doorway who is removing a raincoat.

'Gotcha!' smirks Ida Franz, private investigator *extraordinaire*. She looks around, noticing as to how her entrance has crowded this trailer. She can barely find standing room, as she takes it all in. What she sees in front of her is litter. She doesn't want to touch anything. It seems so . . . unclean. What on earth has brought Hy to this depressing place so unlikely, so . . . beneath Hy's sense of self?

The big guy (she will find out soon is Manny) breaks the silence and asks in his usual charming manner, 'Who the hell are you?'

Ida giggles as Hy pulls himself out of his stupor, and waves his arms at her; eyes popping, as if what? To tell her to get out of here? To not say that she knows him? To not admit why she's here? To beg for mercy? Hy speechless? So not like him.

He will find no compassion in Ida. Hy knows what his neighbor thinks of him. She can guess at his terrified thoughts. He will dejectedly recall his recent mean trick at the pool back home, where he took their photo, put it on Facebook, and made fools of Gladdy's girls. He will wonder how she found him, and who sent her?

Ida registers his groan. He's figured it out. There's only one answer. Lola. But Lola doesn't like Ida. But she is one of Gladdy's girls. Lola hired Ida! Heaven help him. He's a dead duck.

Now he worries. Is Lola with her? Where's Gladdy? Waiting outside? In a state of panic he peers out the dirty window, through the dirt stains, but sees no furious women pacing.

Hy desperately makes a stab at an explanation of some kind. He has no idea what words will come out of his mouth. His mind is on remote. 'Ida, hi. Meet Manny and Dolly-Ann Bloom former childhood friends. From my old neighborhood in New York.' He ties their names together; would it fool Ida into thinking they are a married couple?

Manny chortles; unable to resist, 'Yeah, our good pal, Hy, from the 'hood. Haha.'

Hy throws him a dirty look. Manny comes up with a fake choking act.

Trying to ignore him doesn't work. Hy can only manage a weak smile. No choice, but to babble on. 'And this is Ida Franz, my neighbor in Fort Lauderdale.' Knowing that he is digging his grave deeper.

'Who just happens to be in Miami today,' says Manny at his nastiest. 'And this total stranger shows up at my specific address. Amazing she happens to know our unwelcome visitor. What a coincidence.' Manny is thrilled; Hy is about to get nailed.

The woman, Dolly-Ann, watches, bewildered, and braces for

trouble. Ida guesses her thoughts. Why is this woman here? Who is she? Hy is scared silly of her. This is not good.

Ida almost feels sorry for Hy. What a pathetic cover-up. She studies the woman with the frilly dress and the cutesy curls. Even with the chubby face, there is a dimple hidden there. Ohmigod! *She* is what this is all about. He is involved with this woman somehow. Dolly-Ann; what a silly name. Nice try, Hy, entwining the guy's name with hers. He better be her husband or else.

Dolly-Ann speaks. She, of the school of I-cannot-tell-a-lie, 'Manny is my brother. I came down from New York to visit him and help him make a big decision in his life. Our old school friend, Hy, came to help me . . . help him.'

Wrong, kiddo. She can read guilt in Hy's eyes. Can't fool Ida. 'What a coincidence. I also came, to help out a friend.'

Hy is sweating. She bets his male deodorant is failing him.

Ida continues, with relish. 'My dear friend, Lola Binder, wanted me to help find her husband. Since he didn't tell her where he was going, nor did he call or text, what was the poor lady to think? She thought he was a missing person. Isn't that funny?'

Hy collapses down onto the crummy bench. Outed!

Ida adds, with a touch of evil, 'His worried wife didn't want to call the police, so she called me instead.'

Ida smiles. Hy is doomed. His life as he's lived it so far is over.

Although Manny is enjoying the downfall of his childhood enemy, he's bored. He doesn't need to see the chump being led out of here with a ring in his nose. Just let him leave, already. He zigzags through his junk, heads for the door and calls out gaily, 'Gonna head out for a cigarette, and fill my lungs with cancerous smoke.' He waves, 'Later.' He knows how much his sister hates his smoking. He enjoys rubbing it in that he will not quit.

With that, Manny maneuvers his way around Ida, exchanging lethal expressions, and closes the door.

Dolly-Ann barely notices, since her eyes are fastened on Hy.

Outside, Manny spots an unfamiliar white truck on the street in front of the RV park entrance. He lights up and strolls over, curious. There is a man seated behind the wheel reading a book.

Manny knocks on the door; his stomach is reminding him he is hungry. 'You open for business?'

The guy shrugs. 'No, the hour of lunch is over.'

'So why are you still parked here?'

'I wait for someone.'

Manny reads the Spanish words on the truck side. He says aloud, 'Emmanuel? That your name?'

Julio puts down the book. 'No. I am Julio. It is name of my grandfather. He was the original owner of this meal on wheels. I inherit from him.'

Julio climbs out of the truck and stands next to Manny. They shake hands.

'Well, my name is Manny, named Manuel at birth. Close, huh?' Manny offers Julio a cigarette. He shakes his head no.

'*Si*. Same name is in Spanish.'

'Mine, I think came from the Bible. I inherited my gramp's biz. He was in linoleum and rugs. My father took over, and then he expected me to keep it in the family. I was a failure as a salesman. I got to hate all those damn samples. And the people who came in to buy were so picky, so annoying. The business ended with foreclosure.' He lights another cigarette. 'You like what you do?'

'*Si*, I am happy in my work. I enjoy being outdoors and I like the people and cooking. In Cuba, I was chef. In America, I am immigrant. I am chef in my truck.'

'Not able to get a chef job in American restaurants, huh? That piss you off?'

'No. Living in free country is worth it.'

Both are quiet for a few moments.

Julio continues. 'They called us *Maralitos*. We left through that Cuban port. My family arrives in U.S. May of 1980. We escape Cuba on raft. I am five years old.'

'Tough, huh?'

'*Si*, very bad. But I am happy in America, place where no one putting you in jail for reason of politics.'

'Wanna hear about bad times? Mine. Where I was in December, 1944. They called it the Battle of the Bulge. Fought for my country. I parachuted into a nest of Nazis and ended up in a POW camp.'

'What is POW?'

'Prison of War. Treated very, very bad.'

'*Si, yo comprendo*. Understand. Holding onto raft in terrible, rough sea. Followed by hungry sharks hoping that family might drown at any moment. Or, if caught, sent back. To poverty and no happiness.'

Manny is interested. He really wants to hear about it. 'Was it worth it, such a hard way to get here?'

'*Si*. Yes, very worth it. For you to fight?'

'I came home, barely alive. Sick with years of bad nightmares. Not able to work. Depended on my wife to take care of us. Made me bitter.' He pauses, thinking. 'Yes, it was worth it. This is my country. I wouldn't want to live anywhere else in the world.'

Manny is suddenly startled. 'Hey, this is some heavy conversation for two strangers. Who are you waiting for, anyway?'

'A woman, a most strange one. She tells me she is looking for her friend's husband, to take him home where he belongs.'

Manny gets it. 'She's in my trailer. This *buttinsky* husband came here to help my sister force me into some dump of a retirement home.'

Julio doesn't recognize what a *buttinski* is, but he is curious about the man's sudden anger. 'You don't like retirement home?'

'You ever visited one? I did. A good pal of mine, a buddy I fought with side-by-side, ended up in this Happy Trails Retirement Home for the Aged and I went to see him.

'I thought being a prisoner in the war was the pits. This "retirement home" was worse; my idea of hell on earth. Men in dreary hallways sitting in wheelchairs, drooling. Filthy nightshirts for clothing. The residents being ignored. Grown men sobbing. The place smelled of . . . I can hardly tell you how bad it was. Totally dark and depressing, patients just lying there, doing nothing waiting for Death in every corner. I'd rather drop dead in a gutter then go into one of them dives.'

He lights another cigarette with the end of the one he's been smoking.

They are quiet for a few moments. Julio says, 'Manuel, I need to run an errand. Will you ride with me? It won't take long. And besides, I have one warm burrito for you if you are still hungry.'

'You're on,' says Manny as he jumps into the passenger seat. Anything rather than go back to the group in his trailer.

Julio is about to get in also. 'But we should tell them . . .?'

Manny interrupts. 'Nah, they'll be at it for hours. Let's just go.'
Julio gets into the truck and starts the motor.

Manny asks, 'About that burrito?'

THIRTY-TWO

Friends of Robert. Fishing Pals Forever

We are not deterred. Next stop on our list, The Italian Guys Fishing and Gun Club, out near some pier, near what is called 'Old Town'. We were told Robert's buddies play cards here.

We enter a dimly lit seedy bar, smelling of rancid beer and macho sweat. The floor is covered with pistachio peanut shells, as if these were the days of the early 90s when that was considered hip for bars. It looks dirty and unhealthy. And slippery. The bar stools are half full, with obvious boozers, half of them leaning on the bar itself, to hold themselves up.

The bartender, forty-ish, who looks like a boxer who went too many rounds, takes one squinty look at us and guesses we are not drinkers. He winks at his clients, indicating that we're a funny sight. See the old ladies? What are they doing here? Why do I think this lug never liked his parents? The kind of kid who ran away from home?

Sophie and Bella behave as if they want to flee. The guy looks ferocious and they cower.

'Can I help you gals?' he asks, with a cheerful smirk, making a joke to entertain his barflies. 'Lost your way? This is not the Elderly Ladies Knitting Club.'

He gets a few soggy laughs, as he towels dry his liquor glasses.

'Ha ha.' I give him sarcasm in return. 'Oh, so clever. You should get a career as a stand-up comic.' Not a great comeback, but the beer smell is making me nauseous.

He growls, 'Wadda ya looking for?' He no longer hides his attitude.

'We're looking for the fishing and gun club.'

'Back room,' he points. 'Hunters and fishermen are you? Or should I say fish dames.' Some more weak laughter from the imbibers, or maybe they should be called drunks.

Evvie is about to take him on. My sister likes a good verbal battle. I grab her arm and motion for her not to bother. Not worth the effort.

We walk through the bar, our feet smooshing nuts, trying to ignore the hideous collection of huge stuffed animals on every wall, from wretched deer to humongous bear, and dozens of photos of gigantic fish being weighed by smiling fishermen. The stagnant odor of beer follows along with us, choking us with its fumes.

I stop suddenly as I am drawn to a framed photograph on the wall. It reminds me of the one at Strand, Smythe and Love. Three different fishermen near a boat, each holding up a large caught fish. The photo is much older than the one in the lawyer's office.

I turn to our unfriendly bartender. 'Isn't that . . .?'

'Yup,' he says, as he adds a shot of liquor into someone's beer. 'That's my old buddy, Ernie Hemingway and two of his fishing buddies. A good client years ago.'

I bet he's lying. Hemingway died in 1961. This guy probably wasn't even born yet.

The girls rush over to look at the photo. I recognize Hemingway from pictures I've seen in magazines over the years, but Bella speaks from recent experience.

Bella points eagerly to the rugged white-haired, white-bearded man standing in the middle between two other men, wearing his famous fishing outfit. 'See, he looks just like I said.'

Sophie shushes her. This is definitely not a place to discuss ghosts.

We walk on quickly. Sophie can't resist her idea of a joke. She calls out to the mean bartender, 'You ought to pick up those nuts off the floor.' She points at the guys at the bar. 'Those *nuts* will be on the floor soon, too.'

With that silly attempt at sarcasm ignored, we lead delicate Bella holding her nose to the smell and shutting her eyes to the dead animals, as we hurry her into the back room.

It's a smallish nondescript room. Here we find four men playing pinochle. The guys, who might be in their fifties or older, look like billboard ads of men who are outdoorsmen. They are as rugged-looking as their clothes. Each one wears a red flannel shirt, navy blue down vest, navy blue jeans and black rubber boots.

Chips and dips, beers and smokes are at their elbows. The odor of stale beer has followed us.

I quickly fill them in; how we got their names as friends of Robert Strand. They introduce themselves as Tony, Clipper, Vito and Donny; and yes, Robby was their best friend.

We brace ourselves for the usual, 'So, you old ladies are PIs, wow, you gotta be kidding,' routine when I go through the rigmarole of who we are and why we're here. But to our surprise, the guys are delighted to meet us. Perhaps their being slightly drunk and totally involved in their card game helped ease the intros. We're met with: 'Any friends of Robby's, and the nice Wassingers,' etc.

Then I have to explain what we've heard so far about Robby's death: words, words, words . . . They half listen, half pay attention, mostly they're intent on their game. And their smokes and beer.

Then I say the usual thing, only because that's what people say, and I mean it, 'We're sorry about your loss.'

The game slows down a bit with, 'Yeah, Robby was a great guy, good pinochle player and most of all a super fishing buddy. Especially when it comes to marlins.'

That was the opening I was looking for. Do they believe his death was an accident?

Tony comments. 'Hard not to believe with the marlin ready to attack. Poor guy, trying to win an award, and the award kills him!'

Vito says, 'I ask myself, would it have happened if we had been with him?'

Clipper adds, 'Weird thing, that. We were supposed to be with him that day.'

I suddenly get a chill. This is something that grabs my attention. 'What do you mean? You were meant to be fishing with him?'

These guys take turns talking, but their eyes and hands never leave their cards.

Donny starts, 'Darn tootin' – we were all supposed to go, planned for it for weeks, packed our gear the night before, already shoved it in the rear of our truck and we were ready to pile in as well . . .'

Clipper takes over, 'Then, we all get the same texts right that minute, from our buddy, Robby: "Sorry guys, fishing trip is cancelled . . ."'

Tony is next, '"Something came up . . .".'

Vito continues it, '"Maybe we can try again another week . . ."?'

Donny completes it, '"I'm awfully sorry, guys. Better luck, next time . . ."'

Clipper sums up, 'So we played cards, instead.'

Something is ringing in my head. Something important. I finally dig it out of my mind and I ask, 'Why do you think Robert sent that text and canceled all of you? After all, he did go out fishing that day?'

The guys ponder that for a moment or two.

Donny suggests, 'Maybe he felt lucky and wanted to catch the big one, himself.'

Evvie asks, 'Would he do that? Was that typical of him? It seems selfish.'

A chorus of four shakes their heads. 'Nah. Never,' says Vito. 'We were surprised he did that. We've all been trying for the big prize for the largest fish and, for us, it was all in fun. We placed bets to see who'd win. Hey, we knew none of us would get it. Too bloody much competition.'

Bella tries to get in a word. 'We were talking to . . .' Sophie's hand closes over her mouth. There will be no mention of ghosts with these guys.

I say over her head, 'We were told there was a selfie.'

The men think about it for a moment, and then their hands reach into their pockets. Four phones are brought out. At last. One by one they are handed to us.

Donny says, 'I wish it never happened, but there's no doubt, it was a hell of a weird accident.'

They all show the same photo and now we finally look at what everyone has seen. The image no one wanted us to see. The 'selfie'. A gigantic marlin attacking Robert with its terrifying deadly snout bearing down on him. At the moment of his death.

Evvie and I are upset. It seems like it happened the way everyone has said.

Vito is in awe. 'He took a pic of himself getting killed. That's really something!'

Tony adds, 'It went viral on the Internet.'

They guys allow tears to fall.

Bella, puzzled as usual, 'Besides, dead, he was sick, too? What's viral?' She's asked this question before.

Sophie, forever patient, 'Later Bella, honey, later when we get back to the hotel. I'll tell you about selfies and viral, too.' Bella smiles gratefully.

Clipper has the final words, 'What a freaky way to go.'

Silence. The cards are ignored. These guys are thinking of their lost friend. And so are we.

I'm almost letting myself get excited. I say it slowly; almost it's as if I'm working it through while I say it. 'Maybe Robby was surprised that you didn't show up.'

Clipper speaks for all of them. 'Huh? We were surprised when he went alone. He almost always fished with us. He didn't like to fish alone. We were good buddies; we liked fishing together.'

I'm positive now. 'Maybe he didn't send those texts. Maybe someone else did?'

Evvie is getting excited also, 'Someone who wanted him dead.'

The men stare at us, in shock.

Sophie adds, 'Someone who had a motive.'

They sit there, stunned, these mourning guys, wondering at the possibility.

Maybe this case is not so open and shut.

Maybe some doubt, after all.

THIRTY-THREE

The Mortuary and a Scared Otis

One more stop to make. We're getting tired, but the girls are excited. They feel we may be getting somewhere after all. I'm cautious. We have a long way to go toward proof.

'I bet we're on the right track,' says Sophie.

I want to share their enthusiasm, but it's a long shot.

Last stop. At the mortuary in the basement of a local hospital where we meet Otis Pebbles, the coroner. He did the autopsy. The room gives the girls the creeps; we've never been in one of these places. It's an unusual experience for us. Never, in any of our past cases, did this kind of visitation come up. And though the girls are curious how things happen in here, they're a little fearful. So they tiptoe into the refrigerated all-white, highly lit room with its tiled floor, aware of its strange, unpleasant odor. They cross their arms to their shoulders because of the cold temperature.

Sophie whispers, 'It's just like in the movies. I wonder who's in those drawers. Brr.' She glances quickly at the shut built-in drawers, and just as quickly looks away.

Bella adds, 'Reminds me of horror movies. I like horror movies, but I look away at the bloody parts.'

I would color Otis Pebbles pale gray. Wispy. Shaky. Scrawny. With a bent back, I guess from all that leaning over dead bodies. A slight wind could blow him over.

Thank goodness he's in-between corpses; none are to be seen, and we find him eating lunch. His peanut butter and jelly sandwich and takeaway cardboard cup of coffee sits on one of the stainless-steel operating tables. Who could eat lunch on that?

'Don't touch anything,' he tells us.

As if any of us would in this creepy place.

I do my usual introductions. Immediately we are informed he doesn't want to talk to us, whoever we are, or whoever sent us. At least we don't have to go through the usual song and dance about old ladies being investigators, etc.

He cuts to the chase. 'Ladies, I'm positive you mean well, but the guy was killed by a fish. You should let it alone. I really mean it. So, leave it alone.'

A famous line pops into my head. 'The lady *protesteth* too much, methinks.' Methinks Shakespeare was right. That was Hamlet speaking; but in this case it's Otis doing the protesting.

He waves his hand, and points us back out the door. I'm curious to why he is so nervous.

I closely peer at his face. He's got a tic dancing in one eye. 'Please leave. I'm a busy person.'

Yeah. No dead body. Eating lunch. Busy?

The girls obey, starting out, glad to leave this cold and scary place, but not me. I have a hunch and I decide to act on it.

'Otis,' I say ever so kindly, 'you have doubts, don't you?'

He stops mid-bite, rigid and fearful. 'Please go away, lady.' He cannot look me in the eye.

'What if a fish wasn't the culprit?' I keep it up, speaking, ever so gently. The girls stop, surprised. Evvie can guess what I'm doing.

'Hard to believe a fish dives out of the water, leans down and stabs him. Stretches the imagination. But something did stab him. With something like a snout. Or maybe somebody.'

He is actually stuttering. 'I'm s-s-six weeks away from m-my retirement. You kn-now how bad I want to get out? I h-h-have a sick wife. We've n-n-never had a vacation. N-n-never . . .'

Very softly, I repeat, 'Not a fish, but a human with a weapon? Say it, Mr Pebbles. Please.'

He is near tears. 'I tried to tell them. They didn't want to know.'

I won't let go. I'm so close. 'Maybe a weapon that looked similar to a spear-like snout?' And my mind skips to a photo in Robert's office. What did those lawyers do with their caught fish?

He stands rigidly, like some tin soldier. He pulls himself together. He stops stuttering. 'They reminded me of my retirement date. How good my pension is. Maybe they'll move it up sooner. I shouldn't make waves.'

Evvie wants to ask the obvious question. Who's the 'they?' I stop her. We got what we need.

I pat Otis on his skinny, shaking hand. Then I put my finger to my lips. 'We were never here, Mr Pebbles. We never met you. Never. Good luck on your retirement.'

He sobs his thanks as we make our way out.

Evvie beams. 'I thought of the photo also. Reasonable doubt.'

'Yes, but what do we do now to prove it?'

We stare at each other, knowing. The ball is in our court.

THIRTY-FOUR

Manny and Julio Unexpected Surprise Visit

The food truck pulls into a parking place near the front of an impressive building. Two storeys high, almost one street long. Palatial, elegant, all whiteness and gold trim. Huge windows. Beautiful lawn and garden. They walk along an adjacent row of palm trees seeming as if they are meant to be a formal line of green statues, their fronds, bending in the breeze toward the beautiful building. All nice and peaceful.

During their ride over here, Manny insisted on asking where Julio was taking him. But Julio kept saying to wait, it is a surprise.

And he is surprised at the building. 'Wow,' says Manny, 'reminds me of a Disney movie set. Somebody rich must live here.'

'What is a movie set of Disney?' Julio asks.

Manny is surprised. 'You never been?'

Julio shakes his head. He hasn't a clue.

They start walking toward the entrance. 'Never saw *The Lion King*? *Finding Nemo*? *Bambi*? The most wonderful kid movies ever.'

More head shakes. Julio opens the huge impressive, polished oak door.

'Not even *Mary Poppins* or *Dumbo*?' Manny is still mumbling.

Julio thinks this man wants to be so tough, he, who speaks so softly of this thing of children.

Inside the spacious lobby, the décor continues in white and gold. A bouquet of exotic flowers greets them on a front desk.

Julio walks over to the desk, Manny right with him.

Manny smiles. 'I get it; this is a hotel.'

A pretty lady of indeterminate age stands in front of a sign that says, 'Please check in here'. On the telephone, she answers, 'Good afternoon. Twenty Palms Retirement Community, One moment.'

She covers the phone with her hand and smiles at Julio. 'Hello Julio. You've brought a friend.'

He signs in, Julio speaking Spanish. The woman answers him in his language. Then she goes back to her call.

Julio starts to walk down the hall. Manny, at his side, is stunned. 'This fancy place is a retirement joint? But there wasn't a sign on the outside.'

Julio has been here before.

He taps Manny on the shoulder. 'Come. We stop and visit *mi abuelo*. My grandfather, Emmanuel. He is ninety-nine years in age. My grandmother wanted to keep him at home, but he needs too much care and she is too fragile.'

Manny watches for signs of disrepair or ugliness or bad smell – there's none. The building sparkles with cleanliness. Nurses and others walk by, smiling and nodding. Manny is amazed.

Some wheelchair people in the hall are about to pass them. He stiffens, expecting the worst. Six of them. Men and women. They are wheeling themselves or being wheeled at a good pace to some location down the hall. They are clean, well-dressed and happy. They chat back and forth, cheerfully.

Julio recognizes one of them. 'Max, where are you off to?'

The smiling man, Max, calls out, 'Bingo in the big auditorium. Wish me luck.'

'*Buena suerte*,' Julio calls back.

Max answers, 'Thanks.'

As they walk further along, Manny stops at a huge type of billboard. It lists the week's activities. Manny is stunned. Besides bingo, there are so many items including: chess, poker, sewing, photography, gym and exercise classes. There's a library, an indoor pool, a theater; it goes on and on, so many choices. It makes his head spin.

'Nice,' says Julio. 'A home of happy people.'

They reach his destination. Julio says, 'This is what they call the rec room. We will find grandfather here.'

The room is spacious. Light. Airy. Much is going on. Someone plays the piano, with a few people singing along. Residents are doing many different things. Some reading. Some playing board games. Some working on computers. Lots of jolly talk.

Julio finds his *abuelo* playing checkers with a pretty woman.

Manny would guess she is in her seventies. He admires her, she sure looks younger.

'*Ola, mi hijo,*' says Emmanuel, greeting his grandson warmly, 'give me a few moments and I will put Annabella out of her misery.' Manny studies Julio's grandfather. For a man as old as he is and who seems breakable, the old guy is chipper. Emmanuel makes two quick moves with his red checkers and the game is over.

Annabella laughs. 'You should let me win once in a while.'

He pinches her cheek playfully. 'Tomorrow, Princess, maybe you will let me beat you at chess?'

She giggles, and then gets up. 'I shall leave you to your guests. Nice seeing you, Julio.' She gives Manny a big smile. Manny, elated, follows her with his eyes as she glides across the room.

Julio introduces Manny. 'Poppa, here is a man with your same name. Emmanuel, meet Manuel.' The older man reaches out and they shake hands. Emmanuel's hand is shriveled, and spotted, but the grasp is hard.

For a few minutes, the grandpa and Julio jabber away in Spanish. Julio informs Manny that they are exchanging family reports. His other siblings have visited this week, and he is catching up on their news.

Manny makes good use of his time waiting. He glances around the room, eyes seeking out all the women, and liking a whole lot of what he sees.

Julio notices. 'Tell him, Poppa.'

Emmanuel smiles. 'There are ten women to every man here. Although I am a married man, and I stay faithful to my wife, it is a temptation. *Madre* comes here for what is it they call it?' He asks Julio to remind him of the word.

Julio grins. 'Conjugal visits. Just like they do in jail.' Both men laugh.

Emmanuel adds, 'The younger generation; they think old age means no more romance. They are so wrong. This is how you call it, a hot bed of love.' He laughs.

They visit for a while with much smiling and chatting; then Julio explains that he is on a job and must get back to it.

Many hugs between grandfather and grandson and they leave. People call out greetings to Julio who stops for quick words. Once outside, in front of the food truck, Manny repeats happily,

'Ten women to every man. Heaven on earth.' (He's thinking strip poker at midnight, but first in the kitchen snacking on food.) Those lucky ladies . . .

Julio smiles. As his peculiar lady client likes to say, he thinks – gotcha.

THIRTY-FIVE
Ida and Hy Make a Plan

They've ordered takeout. It's already evening and Manny and Julio haven't returned yet. They are waiting for them in Manny's trailer. Ida, Hy and Dolly-Ann are enjoying the takeout meal of Indian food and a few bottles of Kingfisher Indian beer. They are crowded together at the tiny table with its two skinny pads for seats. By now they are getting along and are feeling mellow.

Hy has told Dolly-Ann that he must go home. She agrees that it's necessary.

Ida is content; she's done her job. The women actually like each other.

Hy says to Dolly-Ann, while chewing on naan bread, 'I'm sorry I didn't help with your problem.'

'But your being here gave me the courage to take on my stubborn brother. And I thank you for that.'

Ida sympathizes. 'Men are such trouble.'

Dolly-Ann agrees. 'Toil and misery, that's all we get from them.' She indicates the mess that is this RV.

Hy pounds lightly at his chest. 'Hey, wait a minute, a *man is* sitting here.'

The two women giggle. 'We know,' says Ida. 'We are very aware of you.'

Hy smiles; they are having fun. He's almost relaxed. 'Pass me more naan,' he says pretending he is insulted. 'I'm outnumbered here.'

Dolly-Ann passes him the spicy bread. 'What will you tell Lola?' By this time they've discussed Lola quite a bit.

Hy shakes his head. 'I'm in big trouble. I admit I'm afraid to go home and face her. She will never forgive me.'

Dolly-Ann tries to be helpful. 'But you were a perfect gentleman. You should have a clear conscience.'

Hy thinks, like hell he does.

Ida thinks, like hell he does.

Hy has a question for Ida. 'What's with the stupid raincoat?'

'None of your business.' Hy looks at her slyly. This annoys Ida.

They eat cheerfully for a while, reaching over one another's arms to get at the food plates that have covered every small inch of that table. One false move and any plate will upend on the floor.

Dolly-Ann, 'Isn't the lamb samosa wonderful?'

Ida agrees, 'I'm a big fan of the chicken tandoori.'

Hy says, with gallows humor, 'A perfect meal for a guy on death row.'

Dolly-Ann pats his arm. 'Poor baby.'

Ida is jolly. 'I've just thought of an idea that might save your skin. Kind of hard to believe. It will take super good acting.'

Hy peers at her with amazement. Ida wants to help him? 'I can act, what's your idea?'

'You go home and tell Lola you had amnesia. For two days.'

'What!' Hy and Dolly-Ann both cry out, astonished.

'I mean it. It can work. You went out for a drive. You had a slight accident with your car . . .'

Hy jumps out of his chair, almost knocking over his samosa. 'I should bang up my beautiful Mazda! You know how I keep that car in perfect condition. You always see me scrubbing it down on Sundays!'

'Hey, you want to live your life again? Shut up and listen. You give the car a slight tap.' Ida is remembering her own car 'accident'.

'Then you tell her you hit your head . . .'

Hy shocked, 'I have to hit my head?'

'Also a small tap. You go home. You tell her you climbed out of the damaged car with amnesia. You didn't have a clue who you were or where you were. And also, by the way, lose the cell phone.'

'I love it,' says Dolly-Ann.

Hy shakes his head. 'Nah! She'll never believe it.'

Ida explains, as if to a dull child, 'Yes she will. You'll cry. She'll

cry. You tell her a pathetic story about wandering around and
sleeping on a beach somewhere. By the way, on your way home,
stop at a beach and roll in the sand. And then suddenly; thank
you, God, you snap out of your amnesia and you're Hy again. You
can't wait 'til you get back home to your sweet wife. *Voilà.*'

For a moment, Hy thinks about it. Then, 'She'll drag me to my
doctor, worried about me. He won't find any kind of concussion.'

Ida, kidding, 'I'll be glad to hit you and give you one.'

For a moment, he actually believes her. Then the three of them
burst into laughter.

Ida again, 'You friendly with your doctor? Didn't I once hear
about a guys' night out poker game?'

Hy remembers. 'Yeah, Ralph is one of the players. My proctologist. I can go to him.'

Dolly-Ann giggles. 'So funny! You go to a proctologist for a
concussion?'

Hy is surprised at her surprise. 'Yeah, we consider him our
family doctor.'

Ida claps her hands. A done deal. 'Perfect, you go to Ralph for
your exam and you tell Ralph to save your ass.' She laughs at
how funny that sounds.

Hy, the pessimist, 'But what if he doesn't want to help me?
Physicians' code?'

Ida grins. 'Come on! You guys stick together when it comes to
deceiving wives.'

Hy thinks, 'There was that time with Ralph and a stripper in
Reno . . .'

Ida, 'I rest my case.'

Hy tries to pace, not easy with all the junk around him. He
accidentally knocks over a box of used batteries. 'I can imagine
how the whole thing goes down. I open the door and she screams,
"Thank God, you're alive" and then she'll say, "Where the hell
have you been?" Then I tell her the amnesia story and the first
thing she'll say then, "I'm taking you to the doctor" . . .'

They examine for any pitfalls in the story. Dolly-Ann says,
'She'll ask why you didn't go to the police or to a hospital. You
might have died with a concussion.'

Ida says easily, 'All he thought about was getting home to his
darling.'

Dolly-Ann comes up with something to help. 'You blew out your tires when you had your "accident". That will explain why you bought four new tires.'

Ida says, 'Good catch, Dolly-girl. Hmm. Of course, you have papers in your glove compartment that would identify you.'

Hy contributes to his story. 'I was too confused to even look.'

Ida thinks it, but doesn't say it; that blows the whole story, but maybe he'll get away with it. If he cries enough.

'Hold on a minute,' Ida found another loophole. 'Your wallet. You gotta lose it.'

Hy shrinks, 'No way. I got my life story in that wallet!'

Ida smiles. '*No problema.* Give it to me to hold. I'll sneak it to you at home later.'

Hy also smiles, but his is crafty. 'Like I should trust *you*? Never.'

Ida holds out her hand. Hy shrugs and tosses the wallet to her. He has no other choice.

They are eating their delicious flan dessert. Dolly-Ann has gone to the bathroom.

Hy whispers, 'Ida, what about you?'

Ida startled, 'What about me?'

'You were sent by Lola to find me. What will you tell her?'

Dolly returns.

Ida, 'I didn't find you. Listen carefully. I never found you. I never went into some crummy trailer. Sorry about that, Dolly; I don't want to insult you.'

Dolly-Ann listens to this banter, fascinated. 'No insult taken.'

Ida continues, 'I never went to Miami. I ended up in Homestead.'

Hy is curious, 'What's in Homestead?'

Ida grins, 'Dummy, nothing is in Homestead. That's where I'll say I went running down a wrong clue.'

Hy is touched, 'You would do that for me?'

Ida is back to her grumpy self. 'Yes, but don't ask me why. I have no idea why.' She helps gather up the food plates. 'You go home. I go home. And don't bring any flowers. Guilty men bring flowers. And you never, never mention my raincoat. Just remember this forever: you owe me. Big time.'

Hy grins. 'Agreed. I would hug you, but I can't reach you in all this chaos.'

Dolly-Ann points, 'Speaking of chaos . . .'

The door swings open. Manny stands there, arms outstretched. Drunk as a skunk.

Dolly-Ann is mad at him. 'Where were you? You were gone for hours! And you've been drinking!'

'I was out celebrating with my new buddy, Julio. (He doesn't know from Hulio). Hi, gang. I've got great news. I'm selling this piece of junk and taking out all my bank savings. I've signed on at the Twenty Palms Retirement Community! I move in next week.'

He spots what they're eating. 'Hey, Indian food. And beer. Any left for me?'

Who's Julio? Dolly-Ann wonders. At the same time thrilled; her problem is solved.

My Julio? Ida wonders.

Julio? Hy wonders. Who's he? Who cares? I'm outta here. But by now it's midnight. Think sleepover.

THIRTY-SIX

A Mystery Call from Far Away

My cell phone is ringing. I squeeze my eyes open to peer at my watch. One a.m.! Is that Ida waking me again? In the middle of the night. I glance over to Evvie. Good. She's still asleep.

Before my caller can speak, I say, 'Ida, couldn't you wait until morning?'

'Good morning, my darling.'

I fairly leap out of bed and hurry into the bathroom, shutting the door, so I won't wake Evvie. I am smiling so hard, my teeth hurt. I sputter, 'Jack, is it really you? Where are you? You're still in Africa, aren't you? What time is it?'

I can hear him laughing through his words. 'Sorry I woke you. But you called me, sweetheart. You needed me, so I got to a satellite phone and here I am, at your service. And since you asked, it's eight a.m. here. We've just had breakfast.'

I smile, 'I hope not bugs. Tessie was sure you were eating insects.'

We both laugh. 'Actually I ate hard-boiled eggs, sans bugs. And so did Joe and Sol. What's new back home?'

I sigh. 'We're not at home. The girls and I caught a case in Key West and here we are in a lovely bed and breakfast. Wait a minute. You said I called you? I didn't call you! I said I needed you? I wouldn't even know about . . . satellite phones. How odd.'

'I heard you in my head. As if you were sending me a message. ESP, maybe?'

'That's amazing. I *was* actually dreaming about you. Wishing you were here.'

'And I heard your dream, obviously. So, what's the problem, sweets?'

'Well, it's a very long story, my dear, and I'm sure this call is expensive, so I'll toss out a quick summary. The girls were bored, no new case. Woman calls from Key West, wants us to solve a murder. So I say yes, too quickly. Ida can't go, but that's a different story, so I won't digress.'

I grab for my bathrobe and struggle into it, then I pace.

'Never mind the cost, tell me.'

'We get to Key West and we meet this odd couple and they take us to their boarder, who says he is the only witness to the murder. A murder that no one else in the entire city thinks is a murder. The cops, townspeople have their own proof; they *insist*, they *know* it's an accident!'

Jack jumps in. 'But you have this witness . . .?'

I sigh again. Wait 'til he hears this craziness. 'Are you sitting down?'

'No,' he says, 'do I have to? Right now I'm standing next to our jeep watching gazelles galloping by. Waiting for the others to finish eating. Why do I need to sit?'

'How lovely. Because I'm about to take you into fantasy land. The one and only witness, the person who can solve this crime is annoying . . . no, he's cantankerous, stubborn, impossible . . . and dead.'

There is silence. I'm not surprised.

'Run that by me again, dear. Dead?'

'Are you ready for this? He's a ghost. A very famous ghost, the very dead Ernest Hemingway.'

A bit more silence. 'Really?'

'The couple who hired us can see and hear him. And, brace yourself, so can Bella.'

'Bella? That's interesting.'

'We've been debating going home and leaving this nonsense but . . . somehow we feel we would be letting that fragile couple down. The Wassingers, and our ghost, Mr Hemingway, are upset that justice won't be done. They want us to believe: a) that there is a ghost; and b) that we believe that the ghost knows exactly how the murder took place.

'So, we who don't believe in ghosts, are stymied.'

I can almost feel my Jack taking this all in. Finally he speaks.

He says surprisingly, 'You know, in the many years I was a cop I had cases that felt strange. I'd get a feeling there were unusual goings on. Finally, I had to open my mind to the possibility that something maybe other-worldly was involved.'

'Really? You? Mr Rational?'

'Think about it. There are people who believe in UFOs. Big Foot. The Lochness Monster. Even earlier alien invasions.'

'Even ESP, darling. You say I called you in my dreams. I needed your advice. And here you are.'

'Right. Now you say that Bella can see the ghost. That actually makes sense to me. She has always been the innocent, naive one of your group. I can believe she is open to seeing a ghost.'

I smile. 'Or a Loch Ness monster.'

'Why not?' Jack starts to laugh. 'Shall I tell you what I am looking at right now? I am sitting under the very shadow of the snows of Kilimanjaro!'

'Omigod! I can't believe it!'

He is delighted. 'Think back, former librarian and devourer of gazillions of books . . .'

'That very famous short story by . . . Ernest Hemingway!'

'Even made into a movie with Gregory Peck and that sexy Ava Gardner.'

'What an amazing coincidence!'

'Is it? Is it a coincidence, my dear Gladdy? Remember

Shakespeare's Hamlet? "There are more things in heaven and earth, Horatio, than are dreamt of in your philosophy".'

I sigh again.

'There you are. Enjoy your sleep.'

'Enjoy your day.'

'I love you.'

'I love you more.'

For a moment, I lie there. My mind computing everything we now know. Then I jump out of bed and make a quiet phone call. Evvie starts to stir. 'What's up,' she says sleepily.

I am excited now. 'Get up, get dressed and get the girls. We're going on a night-time tour!'

THIRTY-SEVEN

A Tour. Thieves in the Night

Black and murky as the night is, at least the air is pleasant. The girls are surprised, waking up and going out again way past our bedtime. But this hurried meeting was deemed necessary by me and our guide and 'new best friend' Louie Wassinger. Therefore, here we are out walking at crazy three a.m. We are not surprised that there are still people wandering the streets.

It's only a few blocks until we reach 907 Whitehead Street, the important tourist site that Evvie had intended to read to us from her travel book. The Ernest Hemingway Mansion.

The girls still can't believe I woke up Louie and he was willing to do this immediately. But I insist I have a plan and I think it's a good one.

I say, 'We have to ignore reality and assume, for a while, that ghosts really exist.'

Evvie jumps in, 'In for a penny, in for a pound.'

Sophie asks, 'What does that mean?'

She answers, 'If you have a penny, you might as well have a pound. Odd expression; the penny is American money, the pound is English.'

Sophie, 'I still don't get it.'

'Me, neither,' choruses her buddy, Bella. She, mistress of confusion.

We are getting close to the address and I'm searching for Louie. 'We are going to give Mr Hemingway what he wants and he is going to give us what we want.'

Evvie nods, as she patiently explains the saying. 'It means if you are involved in doing something, you should complete it, though it might be more complicated than you expected.'

I agree, 'What can be more complicated than having to continue to deal with a ghost we don't believe exists, in order to solve a crime?'

'Good question,' Sophie adds.

We're here, and there's Louie, waiting for us; another 'complication'.

I feel like bursting into song out of the Gilbert and Sullivan's songbook, *H.M.S. Pinafore*: 'Carefully, we tiptoe stealing, breathing gently as we may.' Here we are being led by ninety-ish, frail Louie, inch by elderly inch, carrying a huge flashlight, through the closed, getting darker-by-the minute grounds of the Hemingway Mansion estate.

We are moving in a conga-type line, behind him, each holding onto the shoulder of the person in front of us. We can barely make out the building ahead of us, as Louie informs us in a tour guide voice, 'The French Colonial Hemingway Mansion. Built in 1851. Hemingway only lived there from 1931 to 1939.'

With her free hand Sophie keeps poking at me. I ignore her because I'm busy watching my step, so I don't fall and break my neck while following and listening to Louie's lecture. Finally, she shoves me hard.

'Rats,' she hisses hysterically, 'rats running all over the lawn! Rats running over my feet! I'm gonna scream!'

Louie hears her and is amused. 'Those are cats. The mansion is famous for them. Polydactyl, six and seven toe cats. There are approximately forty to fifty of this breed living on Mr Hemingway's property.'

Sophie clutches my arm, screeching in my ear. 'Fifty *cats*! That's supposed to make feel better? I'm allergic! I wanna go back to the car.' She's ready to cry.

Evvie, behind her, reaches over her shoulder and puts her hand over Sophie's mouth for a moment. 'You are not allergic, so shut up and keep moving.'

'Okay.'

Louie drones on. 'The gardens are magnificent.'

Evvie agrees, sarcastically, 'Especially in the dark.'

Louie unlocks the front door. It squeaks. We stop, standing still, expecting guards to throw us out, but Louie is not perturbed.

We enter the building. 'I *dassent* turn on the lights, but if you look up, you'll see one example of the amazing chandelier collection. Well, you actually won't see them too well.' Louie wiggles the flashlight beam from right to left. Yes, one could guess there's something on the ceiling that looks glittery.

Bella says, 'I'm not looking up. There could be spiders.'

Louie and I decide to leave the two nervous girls near the front door with one tiny light turned on and instructions not to touch anything. Hah, they'll hardly breathe, let alone touch.

Louie, Evvie and I climb upstairs, and down a hallway to a special locked closet that Louie is familiar with. His key is whipped out, and in moments, we have a box of Cuban cigars and a red bullfighter cape.

Before going back downstairs, he touches my arm. 'You should know Mr Hemingway cannot leave us. He must stay until his mission is completed.'

Evvie blurts, 'And what mission is that?'

Louie smiles at her. 'He is trapped in purgatory until his soul is cleansed; which will only happen if justice is served for Mr Strand. And we hope that you succeed in getting that justice for him.'

Evvie still on it, 'And if we don't succeed?'

Louie shakes his head mournfully. 'He is stuck in purgatory forever.'

And the Wassingers are stuck with a guest who can't leave. Well, thanks a lot for letting us know how heavy our burden is.

The girls can't get out of the mansion fast enough.

I'm amused. I decide to say, 'Well, we can tell people we were in the Ernest Hemingway mansion, when there was a sudden eclipse of the sun. That's why we never saw anything. Sounds believable?'

The girls do a quick happy hop. Now that they're safely off the grounds.

Louie promises to get the two items to Papa as I try to imagine how an invisible man will wear a cape and smoke a cigar.

'I hope you enjoyed the tour, ladies,' he says cheerfully. 'See you later.'

He races off; thrilled at being able to tell Sadie how well it went. Oh, and of course, to report it to the ghost guy.

'Happy. Happy,' grins Sophie.

'Bella,' I announce, 'get ready for another chat with your buddy, Ernie. This time he'll talk . . . or else . . .'

THIRTY-EIGHT
Farewells to All. True Feelings Unspoken

Day Five

Manny and Dolly-Ann stand at the doorway of the trailer, after a very early morning group breakfast of cold cereal, saying their goodbyes to their somewhat guests, Hy and Ida. Multiple conversations and thoughts are going on at the same time:

'Bye, Hy, it was so nice seeing you again.' Dolly-Ann gives him a good manners kind of kiss on the cheek. She sighs. They had one last chance last night. Not really. With Ida, she made three. Dolly-Ann would have liked to go to bed with Hy, but truth be told, he's just an old man. And, she reasons, if she'd married him instead of Johnny, they'd be divorced by now anyway. Dolly-Ann thinks of herself as a tragic heroine in her own life story.

'Ditto,' from me,' says Hy, having learned something from this experience. He had no longer been tempted to cheat last night. He is reminded of the title of a book he read long ago. *You Can't Go Home Again.* Thomas Wolfe. Yeah, he can't go back to the past. But his future with his wife is hopefully still intact.

Manny says to Hy, 'Sorry, guy, that I was so tough on you. Only kidding.' Manny thinks, he'd still like to mangle him into the shape of a pretzel. He hides his clenched fists.

Hy with false bravado, 'No big deal. Truce, okay? We were just a couple of foolish kids back then.' Hy would like to smash that idiot's face in. If he wasn't such a coward. Truth be told; the dork could still hurt him. Besides, he just wants out of this awful place. In one piece.

Ida to Dolly-Ann, 'Probably won't see you again, but so nice meeting you.'

Ida, who determined at midnight that it was too late to return home, decided to stay over. She'd informed Julio. He said he'd pick her up in the morning. He lived close by, not a problem for him. So she was invited to stay the night.

What a hoot! Last night in a sleeping bag on the kitchen section of that old floor in the trailer a couple of doors down. She giggles to herself; she was to become chaperone over Hy and Dolly-Ann. But, surprise, there he was, happily sleeping the sleep of the innocent.

Dolly-Ann to Ida, 'So nice meeting you, too.'

Hy and Ida leave. But not together. Hy, in his mind, emotionally preparing for the denting of his precious Mazda and pretending a concussion. Ida climbing into Julio's truck. Glad to be rid of the bunch of them.

Julio thinking when he tells his family about these *gente loca,* how they will laugh.

THIRTY-NINE
Bearding the Lion in his Den

We arrive later in the morning, sleep-deprived, hoping to get this business over with. The Hemingway ghost promised us an answer in return for his cigars and cape. In and out fast, I hope. I'd caught Evvie up with my incredible phone call with Jack. She is in àgreement. We settle this fantasy-adventure today.

The Wassingers are thrilled to see us yet again. And they thank us again for going to the mansion last night. Would we like a tour of their garden first, before going upstairs? So many new buds are blooming. They'd like to show us the tulips, asters, mums and sunflowers. Here they go again, in delaying mode.

'But are the Calla lilies in bloom?' I ask, parodying the famous Katherine Hepburn line in a movie that few young people are old enough to remember. Of course Evvie, my movie buff, knows exactly that the 1937 excellent movie, based on the stage play, was called *Stage Door*. And done again as a radio play in 1939.

We've come to see the wizard. (The wonderful Wizard of Oz.) And only that.

We do not wish any pre-discussions of world affairs, or special room exhibits or antique displays or flowers; or anything else they come up with to slow us down.

Why the hindrance? Since they desperately need us to solve the crime? Because we are a puzzle to them. They cannot 'read' us. They worry about our behavior. And our disrespect. And our cynicism. But they have to put up with us. We're all they have. They hope to bribe us into kindness to their ghost. They're lucky, at least they have Bella.

By now they should be used to townspeople jeering them about their imaginary resident. But they are the only ones who see and hear the late Mr Hemingway. What does that make them? Nutcases? Bella, also?

With a promise of best behavior, we head up the stairs, with the befuddled Wassingers clambering right behind us, chattering, muttering, how glad we're on their team again.

Louie. 'Warning. It's been a difficult day.' Uh oh, now what?

Sadie. 'He's always cantankerous when his ex-wives visit. They're all here. His last wife, too.'

Time to play our part in their game. I ask sweetly, 'What do the ex-wives want?'

Louie. 'The usual, more alimony.'

Sadie. 'That second wife, Pauline. She always wants more money to add on expensive things to the mansion. That swimming pool must have cost a fortune. Drives him crazy. Papa swears she bankrupted him. Mary is different; she doesn't want anything.'

Evvie is nodding, following my act. Sophie is surprised. Bella is delighted.

Evvie comments, tongue-in-cheek, 'Such a pity. Do the ex-wives visit often?'

Louie. 'Usually the end of the month, when they're broke.'

Of course they do. Welcome to the booby hatch.

We continue to huff and puff our way up to the roof. Same scene; gated little area with chairs and little table. No one there to see, but our three visionaries quickly gather at the picket fence. Same drink, however the new cigar box. And a bright red cape folded neatly on one of the chairs.

Bella. 'Good morning sir, Papa.'

'Humph.' Bella reports from our ghost.

Evvie groans, annoyed at this immediate nonsense. It will take forever to get where we're going.

Sophie worries because Bella is starry-eyed; will she need to be committed?

I say to the adoring trio, 'You will tell us everything Papa says.'

All three believers nod their heads. Recitations begin.

Bella, on the job, quoting Papa. 'Are you dolts back again?' To us, she asks, 'What's a dolt?'

Sadie to Louie, 'Isn't it exhilarating? The dolts are on our side.'

'Something nice Mr Hemingway would like to say to us?' I say, in my most business-like tone.

Sadie reports, 'He said "Grrr".'

I pray for patience. 'Surely he can do better than that.' I scan the table. 'Brand-new cigars. Beautiful cape. Hint. Hint. Wonder where they came from?'

Silence. All eyes on where we assume the dead big shot is standing. We take our cues from the trio of sycophants.

Finally. Louie says in a low subservient tone, 'He says thanks. He also wants to tell you he once fought bulls in Spain in that cape; isn't that wonderful?'

Sophie says sarcastically, 'Whoopie!'

Evvie, trying to keep a straight face, points directly at where Papa should be. 'You said you have proof. We want it now, without the insults.'

Sadie tugs at Evvie's arm and whispers, 'He just left his chair. He's walking around.'

'Oops,' says Evvie, rotating her eyes from side to side.

Louie, 'Yes, Papa, I'll tell them.' To us, 'Papa will reveal all, but there is another price.'

I take him on, tough, 'No. No. No. We already paid your price. One price to a customer.'

'Yeah, what Gladdy says,' agrees Sophie, hands on hips, her idea of looking strong.

Bella cringes; torn between her friends and her ghost.

I negotiate with the empty air, 'You got what you want, let's hear the proof you promised. If you really have any.'

Bella giggles. 'He's saying bad words again. You're annoying him. You shouldn't doubt him. He doesn't like it.'

Louie recites proudly, 'The proof is in the pudding, the pudding is in the boat. The boat is in the key. The key is in the sunshine.'

Evvie writes it all down.

Sadie, with a chuckle, 'He's reciting poetry. No, first he's singing. "I'm in the mood for love". Isn't that sweet?' For a moment, she sings along, 'Love me or leave me . . .' She stops, embarrassed. 'I guess Papa is in a loving mood.'

Bella says, 'Papa is quoting himself, "If two people love each other, there can be no happy end".'

Evvie claps. 'Clever, but cynical.' She is thinking, Hemingway at his corniest.

Louie is energized. 'Another line from one of his books, "I am so in love with you, that there isn't anything else".'

Bella, having a wonderful time is also quoting, 'Why, darling, I don't live at all when I'm not with you.' She blushes.

Suddenly the three advocates stiffen. Their master has turned angry. Louie recites, timorously, 'Out, out all of you. Out Martha, Out Pauline. Out Hadley. Yes, even you, Mary. Out the lot of you!'

Silence as Louie, Sadie and Bella watch a parade of whatever it is they see, crossing the roof.

Evvie asks sarcastically, 'Are the wives leaving?'

Sadie says, 'Yes, they're running. And in high heels, too.'

I start for the staircase. 'I guess we better go, also.'

Louie is right behind me. Eagerly, 'Please don't go.'

'Bye bye,' Sophie says walking away. 'We've had enough.'

As we reach the stairway, Bella calls out, 'He says one more thing. "Robert was killed by love. Dolts!".'

We can't get out of that house fast enough.

FORTY

Hy and Ida Head Back Home

They drive for a while, neither Ida speaks, nor Julio either. Finally Julio is curious. 'You are not driving home with Mr Binder?'

Ida, huffy, 'No, I am not. And just how did you get involved in my case?'

'What is a case?'

'Never mind. Suddenly yesterday you and Mr Manny Bloom got cozy?'

'What is cozy?'

Ida is frustrated. 'Forget it.' She smiles, thinking, this guy solved the case for her and she'll get the credit.

Julio smiles thinking, this lady has much strangeness. It was so easy to fix Manny's problem.

Julio pulls up in front of Ida's building. She notices that Hy must have arrived. She smiles at the new dent in his front fender. She wishes she was a fly on the Binder wall to see how the amnesia story works out.

She pays Julio and thanks him for a job well done. '*Hasta la Vista,*' she says proud of her new knowledge of the language.

'Until we meet again,' Julio says, master of his new language.

In her apartment, the first thing Ida does is kick off her heels. Then turns on her air-conditioner. She goes into her bedroom, carrying the famous raincoat. Opens her closet and folds the raincoat lovingly, and places it in the bottom rear of the closet, where it lives hidden. She can never tell Gladdy or the girls. They don't believe in weirdo things.

She faces the poster on her door. 'Job well done, Frank. We're quite a team.' She prides herself on having learned his first name way back in the series. Few viewers knew that. She salutes the poster of her hero, Lt Columbo. Then closes the door.

Hy hopes no one noticed his arrival. He's glad it's still so early. Thank goodness, traffic was light on the freeway. Don't want any of the yentas spotting him, sneaking back. Though, sure of his Lola, she wouldn't have let anybody find out he was gone. What irony, depending on the likes of Ida to keep his secret safe.

But then again, there's that nosy Tessie to worry about. She seems to gossip about everybody's business. He hurries into his building.

Fingers crossed. He opens his door, hoping he doesn't wake Lola.

The apartment is silent except for the sound of the air-conditioning and Lola's petite snoring. He tiptoes into their bedroom and looks affectionately down at his sleeping wife; on her side of the bed as usual. Her back is to him. Hy admires her for a moment. Such a beauty.

He quickly drops his clothes to the floor. And remembering Manny's exploits, he giggles. Maybe he should raid the fridge first. Nah! He'll cut right to the chase.

He slides his naked body into the bed and gently wraps his arm around his sweetheart wife. Ready for the action he missed in Miami.

In seconds Lola wakes up, screaming. 'Help! Rape! Help!'

He shushes her, trying to reach for her mouth to cover it. 'It's me! Don't yell, it's me!' She thrashes him, pummeling him with her fists over and over.

Lola leaps out of the bed; turns and stares at him; furious, then puzzled, then happy all in turn. 'Hy? You? Thank God, you're alive!' Then, 'What's that – sand in my bed? Where the hell have you been?'

Hy dramatically touches his 'hurt' forehead and begins his amnesia story.

FORTY-ONE
Back at the Inn. Clues Rock

We are gathered in Evvie's and my bedroom. Skipping B&B breakfast.

Sophie sums up. 'Big waste of time. He got his cigars and *shmata*. And all we got was a lot of nonsense.'

Bella, defensive, 'Don't call it a rag. His bullfight cape is an antique!'

Amazing, we're talking about Papa, as if there really is this apparition that tells us he (it) was a witness to a murder. But what the heck, here we are.

Sophie comments, 'So, where's our proof? A trade is a trade. He promised.'

Evvie waves her notebook. 'Somewhere in this gibberish. Amid the love poems.'

I get it! I really do. 'He told us what we need to know, but he's making us work for it. Evvie, read the part about the pudding.'

Evvie finds it in her notebook, and reads, 'The proof is in the pudding, the pudding is in the boat, the boat is in the key. The key is in the sunshine.'

The girls look dumbfounded. Sophie, 'That's the clue?'

Evvie bounces up on her bed. 'Now I get it, too.'

I say, 'Take away the pudding; that's him showing off, and read the words without it.'

Evvie is excited. She reads, 'The proof is in the boat, the boat in the key. The key is in the sunshine. Sunshine Key! Remember I read about that key in my tour book. So, the boat didn't sink, as the police believe. And there is something in that boat that proves—'

I finish it, 'That he was killed by love.'

Bella confused, 'How can you be killed by love?'

Evvie answers. 'You can if you are a lawyer by name – Albert Love. Of Strand, Smythe and Love.'

Wow! Silence, chewing, digesting and thinking.

Bella shocked, 'A lawyer killed him?'

'Gee whiz!' says Sophie, impressed. 'That was a really good clue.'

I add, 'That's why he kept quoting lines about love. Over and over, quoting those boring lines, singing those songs.'

'So all we need is to get to Sunshine Key and locate the boat and find the evidence.' Evvie shrugs well aware of how impossible this would be.

Sophie, 'So what do we do now?'

I add ironically, 'We need a boat, to find a boat.'

Evvie adds, 'What we really need is an exorcist.'

FORTY-TWO

An Important Discussion with Smart Teresa

After a quick impromptu brunch, we head back to find Teresa. At first we thought to go to Robert's fishing friends; but they remember it was always Robert's boat they used. Somehow I feel more comfortable asking Teresa for help. She's savvy and has information about everything in this city and the people in it. We need her advice; we want information that we won't be able to get anywhere else. We knock at her office door, and luckily she's in there.

It's a small room, yet continuing the charm of the rest of the inn. Immaculate, as I would expect. Her small desk is neat. There are numerous commendations on the walls, congratulating the inn for winning first class in hotel awards year after year. Family photos share the walls. She obviously has many smiling relatives. There's even a photo of Jin in his *Cage* costume.

It will be a tricky conversation because Teresa is sane and wouldn't believe in ghosts either. And we cannot think of mentioning such an aberration to that sensible woman. Even though we have what might be explosive information.

She welcomes us, surprised that we've chosen her office in which to meet. Customers usually don't do that.

But I apologize, explaining we need privacy and her advice. She says she'll be glad to help. So we fill her in, carefully. After a while, she sums up our discussion. 'Let me get this straight. You need to borrow a boat to find the boat that Robert had been in when he died.'

'Yes,' I say cautiously. 'We have a tip there is something important on that boat that would prove Robert's death wasn't accidental.' I sound wacky even to myself.

'A tip,' she says, doubtfully. 'And where does this tip come from?'

I was afraid she'd ask that. 'From the Wassinger house.'

Teresa peers in each of our faces and reads us correctly. The less said the better about this.

'It could look like we're just taking a boat ride on a nice sunny day,' comments Bella, to my amazement. I was terrified she'd blow the whole thing and spill the beans. But she's a loyal, although dim, team player.

We don't make any mention of who we believe is a killer. We don't want to stretch the credulity further.

Evvie adds, 'And if we just happen to discover a missing fishing boat at Sunshine Key, we think that could be helpful.'

Big sigh from Teresa. 'You win the award for most out of the ordinary, most motivated visitors this inn has ever had. Or the most gullible. Four old ladies hot on the trail of a killer. Amazing.' She can hardly hide her disbelief.

I say, 'But we have a problem. We can't take out a boat by ourselves, since none of us know anything about boats, not that we could handle one . . .'

Teresa stops me with a raised hand. 'Be at the Old Town dock at two p.m. sharp, wearing what you think absurd people wear at a costume party on a ferry.'

We are effusive with our thanks. We have to hurry upstairs and change our clothes. She winks at me. Notice, there was not one word about ghosts mentioned.

FORTY-THREE
An Absurd Group of Boat People

At two p.m. we're at the dock and already loading what is a beautiful large white ferry boat. The name on its side reads *Rainbow Community* and the deck is festooned with flags and balloons in many colors. Evvie and I recognize that the name has to do with gay people, but no point explaining it to Bella and Sophie. That will take up too much time.

Teresa's nephew, Jin, is there to meet us and be our guide and helper, obviously thanks to a phone call from his aunt. We almost don't recognize him in his flashy outfit, a startlingly white pantsuit, bell-bottoms with glittery multi-colored stripes. Is he wearing make-up? Yes, he is, and his hair is set in a *bouffant* style, sprinkled with gold dust. We try not to gape. We attempt to seem sophisticated.

He informs us that this is a celebratory, private party for their successful musical, *La Cage aux Folles*, the show he mentioned at the inn. Seeing the surprise on the girls' faces, he explains this is what he wears in the play; he is one of *La Cagelles*, a member of the chorus line.

As we climb up onto the ferry we are dazzled by all the vividly costumed cast members and guests already on board. Wild colors, wild plaids and checks, silk and satins, weird, strange, never-seen-before hairdos. Tons of make-up. Anything goes. Teresa wasn't kidding – this is absurd boat wear.

And who might win the award for most absurd outfit is our own clothes-maven, Sophie. She who *shlepped* along her hot pink taffeta Empire gown and tiara, with matching pumps and purse, which she is proudly wearing.

Sophie is self-righteous. 'I told you so, that this gown would come in handy.'

Evvie nods, smiling, 'You fit right in.'

The rest of us wear conventional leisure clothes.

Jin tells us to help ourselves to food and drink, and he'll find us when we reach Sunshine Key. He's worked it out with the captain to take us there, not to worry.

'But won't it spoil the party?' Evvie asks.

'By then, everyone will be sloshed and won't care about anything but their next drink.'

'Have fun,' he says and waves as he leaves us on our own.

The girls are dumbfounded, staring at the costumes, hairstyles and make-up. They gasp at the feathers and spangles.

Bella points to a big person. 'Is that a tall boy dressed as a tall girl?' she asks.

Sophie thinks. 'It's just a tall girl with too much make-up.'

Bella, 'I say boy.'

Sophie, 'Girl. Kinda homely.'

Bella, 'A very pretty boy. I like the feathers.'

Evvie, 'Give it a rest. They're gay.'

Bella nods, 'Yes, they do look very happy.'

Evvie grins, 'Not gonna touch that with a ten-foot pole. I'm going to get one of those amazing *tall* drinks.' She abandons us.

The ferry leaves the dock. The music level climbs higher. Probably the music score from their play. Couples dance wherever they find legroom. Girls dancing with girls, boys with girls, boys with boys, and so on.

I snack on wonderful canapés I find on long tables covered with multi-colored tablecloths. Bella and Sophie, terrified of eating something alive, reach for cheese slices.

We watch the dancing for a while. It's interesting to say the least; the dancers are exhilarating and inventive.

Two guys pass us, sipping. 'What are you drinking?'

His buddy (or girlfriend) says, 'An Ingrid Bergman.'

'Nice. I'm gonna stick to my Meemaw old fashioned.'

We stare. What, those are drinks?

Evvie joins us holding up a card. 'Look, here are some choices of drinks we can have. Free!' She reads, 'Pisco Sour, Berry Bellini, Strawberry Swamp Water Octane. Mango Mimosa. And much more. I'm drinking some kind of Slurpee. I don't know what's in it, but I'm feeling no pain.'

We pass. 'I'm sticking to my iced tea,' says Bella.

'Is it regular iced tea or that Long Island iced tea? One of them is potent liquor.' Evvie is the new bar know-it-all.

Bella quickly discards her drink. She doesn't want to find out. 'There you are.' Jin catches up to us. 'Come on to Captain Barnaby's bridge. We're going to keep an eye out for Robert's boat. We're nearing Sunshine Key. The boat might be hugging the shore somewhere. Or lodged on a rock.'

On the bridge, we lean over the rail, five sets of eyes, plus the captain's crew, with binoculars, searching in all directions. How nice of them to help us. For a while it seems like we're on a pointless mission. We see nothing. Water, water everywhere. The boat must have sunk by now. And if so, so are we.

We can still barely hear the music from inside, but out here, other than waves slapping the ferry's side, there is silence.

And more silence. I am afraid we face failure, but the kind captain doesn't quit. The ferry moves slowly along the shore. More waiting.

A shout and a waving sailor pointing; one of the crew. And we see it. A crippled torn-apart boat, rolling with the waves on a deserted beach.

Captain Barnaby pulls us up close and drops anchor near the shore.

We see what's left inside of Robert's boat: trash, a soaked life jacket floating, tangled fishing gear, in other words, a mess.

Dear Jin. He's slipping on hip-high rubber boots. He wouldn't think of any of us older ladies trying to climb into that wobbling piece of boat. He will clamber in and look for whatever he can find. Silly us. We never thought past finding the boat, let alone climbing into it. Not at our ages.

Some members of the *Cage* party come out of the ballroom, questioning. Why are we stopping and why here? This doesn't look like Key Largo.

I tell them we are looking for a clue to a mystery and suddenly, we have a crowd of happy show-people onlookers, buzzing with curiosity, holding drinks, waving rainbow-colored flags.

For a few moments, Jin digs around, looks up at us, shaking his head. But he doesn't give up.

Moments later, he holds something up. Aha. 'It's the plug.'

Sophie, holding on to her tiara, asks, 'So, what about it?'

He explains. 'The plug is never pulled out of a boat, unless necessary. Once the plug is out, the boat fills with water, and sinks, but this one must have caught on to something and didn't totally sink. Lucky.' Jin says, modestly, 'I do a bit of sailing myself.'

I ask, 'Would a plug fall out by itself?'

'Not likely. I would guess someone pulled it out on purpose.'

'The purpose?'

'To sink the boat, no other reason.' Jin tries to talk low because others are listening. 'Robert would never have pulled it out.'

'Someone else did?'

He nods meaningfully.

But I am deflated. 'Is this the clue? I expected more.'

Evvie worried, 'That could make the cops suspect suicide.'

'Agreed.' Jin is now rooting around the mucky bottom. 'I think I've found something else.' Excited, 'It's his iPhone! A miracle. The battery looks dead, though.'

'What good is a wet, dead phone?' Sophie is disappointed.

Jin says, 'An iPhone with camera capabilities. Remember the selfie, he sent?'

Sophie, 'With the big fish, ready to jump on top of him.'

Bella. 'I'm still waiting for someone to tell me what a selfie is.'

Evvie. 'Keep waiting.'

Jin climbs out of the leaking boat and attaches his own iPhone charger to Robert's device. A few seconds later the phone switches on. 'Another miracle,' Jin says. 'There's no pin code to log on. Here's another photo he took of himself!' He is getting more and more excited. 'Fantastic! A photo, one he didn't know he photographed.' He stares at it, realizing, 'And didn't get a chance to send.'

'We are so lucky that we have Jin,' I say. 'Even if we had been able to get into the boat and found the phone, we would not have known it also worked as a camera. When we get home, we're going to have to catch up with the tech world.'

Jin, eyes flashing with awe, says, 'Look ladies, look at the second photo he took but didn't get to send!' And, one by one, we see Albert Love leaning over Robert's shoulder and stabbing him in the stomach as the loosened fishing rod with its attached marlin drops away into the ocean.

Jin sends the second selfie to his own iPhone, then turns to the broken boat and takes further shots of the now-found boat and its contents to add to our proof.

There is a stunned silence for a few minutes, as both my girls and I, and the crew and watchers, let that amazing find sink in. Murder. It was murder!

The murder witnessed by our ghost, Hemingway! Omigod!

Jin smiles, satisfied. 'Now we have definite proof. Robert was killed by lawyer Love.'

I am astonished.

The word is passed around the entire ship. These odd old ladies just uncovered a slaying; done to a man they know by a man they also know. iPhones are clicking wildly, cast members photographing us. Tomorrow we'll be famous on Facebook, heaven help us. We'll be celebrities.

Captain Barnaby congratulates us. 'Shall I turn my ship around and head for home?'

I start to say, 'I wouldn't want to spoil . . .'

I am interrupted by a rousing shout from the energized onlookers. 'Yes! Let's go back and seize the killer! We're not going to let him get away with this!' The theater party is forgotten. Cast members revert back to being citizens of their fair city. Justice will triumph!

We are stunned. Only Papa knew. Only a ghost knew! If we hadn't followed the information given by a fantastical specter, a death would not have been avenged.

Bella smiles, the heroine of this happening.

Sophie hugs her. 'You did it, sweetheart, you saved the day!'

Evvie and I stare at one another, speechless. Wait 'til I tell Jack! Who woulda thunk?

FORTY-FOUR

Respected. About Time.
Revenge is Sweet

This time we don't bother to make an appointment. We walk straight into police headquarters, heads held high. Photos in my clutched hand. Demanding to see Sergeant Barbara Ella, ignoring her last name.

She comes rushing out, emitting steam. 'You crazy ladies again! How dare you waste my time again? Why don't you go back to Kissammee, or wherever you belong?'

Bella whispers. 'Kissammee. Where's that?'

Evvie whispers back, 'In Osceola County.'

Bella again, 'Where's that?'

'Sshh,' hisses Sophie, 'you've been there.'

Bella, 'I forget.'

'Fort Lauderdale, lady.' I correct her. 'Try to get it straight,' I am furious, sarcastic. 'Jin LeYung sent us.'

'Jin sent *you*? What have you and my cousin have to do with one another?'

Evvie, curious. 'Jin is *your* cousin? You don't look related.'

Hands on hips, Barbara is trying to push us out the door. We don't budge. 'It's a small town. Lot of people are related. Don't just stand there. Explain, then leave.'

'We don't move an inch until you look at this.' I shove into her hands Jin's phone with the photo of Albert Love killing Robert with what looks like a marlin's jaw! From a fish they once caught! Proof positive. 'Death by selfie? Remember?'

She turns various shades of red, then purple, then deathly pale. 'Where did you get this?'

'Out of Robert Strand's missing fishing boat.' Oh, such glee we feel. Nothing's more satisfactory than being right.

She's flummoxed, stuttering, unsure of what to ask next. 'How could you get it out of his boat? How did you know about a boat? A boat that sank.'

We show her Jin's boat photos as well. 'The boat did not sink. Makes you cops look bad, don't it. Did you even bother to search?' I imagine they did, with no luck. Not very nice of me; I am enjoying rubbing it in. And the girls are pleased by my performance. 'Your cousin Jin climbed into Robert's abandoned boat and found the iPhone and the second selfie.' I'm suddenly a confident tech expert, spouting as if I was born to this knowledge.

Those condescending cops surround us. Barbara Ella, hands shaking, passes the photos around. And again, amazement.

'Would you ladies like to sit down,' says one cop, deferential suddenly.

'Coffee, maybe,' from another, the next new fan.

For a moment I think of our Hy Binder back home who got revenge on us for treating him unkindly. I wonder if the girls are making the same connection as we get revenge. I also wonder how Ida is doing with her case. Where could Hy have disappeared to?

I put the police out of their misery. 'We had a tip from an unknown caller (a little fabrication here) that there was a big clue to be found in that boat. Jin took us on a party cruise ferry and we found it.'

'Just like that?' One of the cops.

Evvie can't resist. 'Only took brilliant investigating skills. Just like *that*.'

My girls applaud.

Sergeant Barbara Ella is all a twitter. 'We must get on this at once.'

'Not to be concerned, *Barby Doll*. Right this minute there are dozens of rather charmingly costumed recruiters on the city streets taking care of bringing in Mr Love and his accomplice, Mr Smythe.'

Sergeant Barbara Ella looks as if she might faint. If she does, she better take her gun off her belt first. It might go off and shoot her. Maybe right now, she wouldn't mind.

I giggle at the thought.

FORTY-FIVE

The Very, Very, Very Colorful Recruits

Sergeant Barbara Ella, near hysteria, is on the phone. She is trying to reach Jin who hasn't answered. 'Pick up! Pick up,' she howls.

We are seated, enjoying the ice-cream cones Officer Bud went out to get us. They tell us their names. Bud and Gregg, finally friendly.

'What should we do?' Gregg asks Barbara.

She answers curtly. 'Nothing, not until I find out what Jin is up to.'

A half hour goes by. We would leave, but this is too much fun watching Barbara pace and squirm. Delicious as our cones. I'm dropping the Sergeant and Ella names by now, along with our respect.

Finally, Jin answers. Barbara screeches at him. 'What the hell are you doing?' The phone is on speaker so we get to hear it.

Jin answers mildly, 'Just trying to help out. The kids are doing a nice job.'

'What kids?' She can't pull her voice down.

'The kids in the show.'

'Kids? You mean those half-baked untalented old farts are running around town trying to make arrests?' Uh oh, I think, not a smart way to put it.

Jin stays relaxed. 'Are Gladdy and her associates still there?' Finally respectful. How sweet it is. How deserved. I shouldn't gloat. It's not nice. Hah! I will gloat. Days like this don't come around that often.

'Yes,' she hisses. 'Those people!'

'Hi girls,' Jin shouts loud enough to be heard. 'Did you fill Barb in? How about that selfie!?'

Barb stays mad. 'What are you doing out there!?'

'Well, first we had to make sure our lawyers couldn't escape, so Uly Tolson, he plays Monsieur Renaud, he's a charmer, and that darling boy who plays, Albin, so adorable—'

Barbara interrupts. 'Spare me the reviews. What are they doing?'

'Done, darling cousin. Already a *fait accompli*. Done. Let the air out of the killers' tires, so they had to try to escape on foot.'

'Oh, God.' Barb is fanning herself with one of the photos.

Gregg says, 'Whatever happened to innocent until proven guilty?'

Bud grins. 'Gone, when it's proof by selfie.'

'Where are they now?' Barb begs to know.

Jin gives us the play-by-play. 'Well, they split up and it's been quite a problem to unravel where they went. Smythe was spotted trying to hurry a cab to head for the airport. But there was so much traffic, the cab couldn't get through.'

'What traffic? What are you talking about?' I wish Barby would stop yelling.

'Well, it's pretty funny. The entire cast on our boat trip got involved, 'bout forty to fifty cast and backstage people, and their families are racing down alternate streets, running in the gutters; cars have to pull over. It's a scream.'

'What's a scream?' Her voice getting hoarse.

'Well, Smythe takes one look at big Moe. He's six-seven. Our set builder. Great with a plunge router. He opens the cab door and Smythe crawls meekly out, sobbing into his hankie. Do straight men still use hankies?'

With hardly taking a breath, he goes on. 'Then some of the people in the streets recognize the cast and they decide it's fun to join in to whatever it is they are doing, so that adds about twenty to thirty more or so, then . . .'

He cackles. 'You hadda be there to believe it. One guy yells out, "Watcha doing, Jin? Wrong month for the Gay Pride parade". And I think its Philby who yells back, he's the one raises and lowers our curtains, "We can have a parade whenever we want". So this guy on the sidewalk says, "So count me in," and he joins them in the middle of the street with two of his buddies. Then it becomes a free-for-all for lots of the LGBTs out there. And then the mob breaks into the song from *Cage*: "I Am What I Am". What great publicity. We'll be sold out tomorrow. Isn't that cool? So we're talking one hell of a parade.'

Barbara is a shivering mass of jelly. She blubbers. 'He wants to be a cop. My cousin Jin wants to be a cop and I encouraged him.'

Bud takes over the phone. Gregg tries to comfort Barbara, who continues blathering, 'I'll be fired. I'll be fired. I know I'll be fired.'

Bud asks Jin, 'Where's Mr Smythe now?'

'Back in his office waiting for one of you to come pick him up. He's either writing a note to his wife or writing a confession. Or maybe a suicide note.'

Bud again, 'And Mr Love?'

'That's trickier. We lost him on Duval.'

Gregg leans towards us to explain. 'That's the busiest street in all of Key West. A million tourists.' Grim, 'Watching your parade.'

Bud says to Jin, 'May I suggest, we send some policemen over to help you search?'

Jin must be smiling. 'Sure, if you want. Gee, it must be so much fun being a cop.'

Bud is droll. 'A barrel of laughs, kid. It'll be fun to have you aboard some day, so keep up the good work.'

I wonder if Bud meant it or was that sarcasm?

Our job is done and the police are on it, and we're exhausted from gloating; time for us to leave.

Nobody notices us walk out.

Poor, sobbing Barby. She doesn't seem to be cut out for police work.

FORTY-SIX

A Gathering of Suspects. The End

B reakfast, the next day. It's heartwarming to us; what a sweet send-off Teresa gives on our behalf. We are heroes who solved a terrible crime. Bad guys in jail. Wassinger house saved. With a big write-up in the local newspaper with that hilarious photo of a *Cage* actor, naked above the waist revealing the hairiest chest ever, and below, a pink tutu with matching pink ballet slippers, carrying a huge birdcage with a real canary in it. In his other hand some sort of antique killing weapon, maybe a truncheon. Brandishing it as he runs after lawyer Albert Love down Duval Street.

We are surrounded by our new buddies. Jin, of course. The Wassingers, naturally. Robert's four fishing buddies, Tony, Clipper, Donny and Vito. Maybe they've come just for the free breakfast. Some of the cast and workers on *La Cage aux Folles,* definitely here for the free breakfast.

We saw the play last night and enjoyed it, though Bella kept bothering us with questions every minute. Why are those people mad at those other people? Why is one older couple not happy about the young couple getting married? Why is the bridegroom worried about the bride-to-be's family meeting his family? Is their maid really naked under his apron? Or is that 'her' a 'his' apron? What is that club where they're all dancing, looking weird in those glittery costumes? And singing odd songs? Why is there another wife? Who's really the mother? Why are the police running on the stage after them? On and on.

We whisper, 'Shhh, we'll tell you later, on the trip home' But we won't.

While we finish our breakfast, and sipping more coffee, my girls and I are asked some thoughtful questions:

Clipper asks, 'Why do you think those lawyers, Love and Smythe, didn't hire a hitman to do their dirty deed? They could afford it.'

Evvie answers, 'But they couldn't afford to take the chance. Too dangerous. Leaves them open to blackmail.'

Tony says, 'Love is a shrewd guy. How come he didn't take the iPhone out of the boat? They knew there was one, because of the first selfie.'

I answer, 'Just guessing. A number of possibilities. He had to do it all fast; jump on the boat, kill Robert before Robert saw him. Worried, in case any other boat came by and saw him. Forgot the phone due to nervousness? Or had he already unplugged the boat and water was leaking in; and he had to get out quickly? He looked for the phone and couldn't find it? Didn't think it was important? He had no idea there would be a last photo? Probably he needed to rush back in time to make sure of his alibi.'

Vito, sarcastic. 'Yeah, "alibi" was waiting in some motel. I'm guessing with his ding-a-ling dumb receptionist.'

Jin, 'Fact is, I had to dig all around the mess at the bottom before I found the phone stuck in a wedge of wood. I got lucky. I bet he just couldn't find it.'

Evvie, 'That's probably why he pulled the plug. To make certain the boat would sink and never be found. There's a well known certainty about criminals. They make mistakes.'

Donny, 'That one was a doozie. Glad he blew it.'

Teresa, angry, 'It was arrogance. They were both so arrogant; they felt confident they could get away with it.'

'I got another question,' says Tony. 'What about those texts we got from Robby not to go fishing with him?'

Evvie answers this one. 'No doubt Love probably got hold of Robert's phone the day before and he did the texting, pretending to be his doomed partner.'

Jin jumped in, 'It would have been easy as Robert didn't use a password or pin code, so anyone could have picked up the phone and sent messages.'

'Hold on!' This from Clipper. The fishing buddies have been paying close attention. 'What about the first selfie? It showed the marlin bearing down on him.'

I smile, because I know the answer. 'The killers must have been thrilled when that photo turned up. They killed him with the jaw of the marlin they'd caught earlier; their "proof" that it was a marlin. Having Robert about to catch a marlin was a break the killers never expected. Proof positive that that marlin was the culprit. What a great lucky coincidence. But we found out, Mr Pebbles, the coroner, suspected there was a real killer.'

Louie and Sadie throw us a kiss. 'But it didn't fool you girls. You saved us,' Louie says gratefully.

'A toast,' Teresa says, raising her coffee cup. 'To Gladdy Gold and her amazing girls. They are terrific private eyes.' The guests clap hands. And cups are raised on high.

Respect at last.

FORTY-SEVEN
Girls Travel Home Again. Jiggity Jig

We say goodbye, with much hugging from one and all, and pack up the old Chevvy wagon. Full of goodies from Teresa; she has learned how much my girls enjoy eating on the road. And off we head back for home.

We're only a mile or two down the highway when Sophie goes directly into complaint mode. I was waiting for it to happen. My girls are so predictable. 'We never saw anything in Key West. Not a museum. Not the Truman winter home. No night-time cruises. No steel drums. No fireworks. Nothing.'

Bella objects. 'We did see Papa's mansion with all the cats.'

Evvie can't resist. 'Yeah. After midnight, with a flashlight; and Sophie thought they were rats.' We laugh.

Bella, 'Not even one slice of key lime pie.'

Sophie, 'No eating in seafood restaurants.'

Evvie, 'No sunsets at that famous Mallory Square.' She grins. 'But we did get to take a ferry boat ride and get to see a play in a theater.'

Bella, sulky, 'That doesn't count. That was work.'

I jump in. 'All right already. Stop complaining. We came to do a job and we did it.'

Evvie, 'Even if we didn't get paid.'

Mumbles about that; not that we really care. What we care for is success and we had that. A happy successful ending.

'Louie and Sadie did hug us,' Bella offers. 'They were grateful.'

Evvie scoffs. 'There was that.'

Quiet for a while. There's the same elephant in the car, I wonder how long it will take to be brought out.

About five miles later.

Surprisingly, Evvie is first to fold. Low voice, embarrassed, 'Okay. I admit I saw him.'

Sophie, pauses, then shrugs. 'I thought I was the only one. I saw him, too.'

Heaven help us; I admit, 'I think I did, too.'

Bella. 'What are you all talking about? Who did you see?'

I say it. 'He was standing across the street from our B&B.'

Evvie, 'Laughing at us.'

Sophie, 'A real hunk.'

Evvie, 'Egotistical SOB.'

Bella pokes Sophie, then Evvie, 'Who? Who?'

Evvie admits, 'Papa . . .' As if she doesn't know. 'Hemingway . . .'

Me, 'In that dashing red bullfight cape . . .'

Sophie, 'Smoking a Cuban cigar.'

Bella's eyes pop wide open. 'You saw him, you really saw him!'

Evvie, 'He even waved.'

Bella starts laughing and hiccupping and can't stop. 'I thought I was crazy.'

We really saw a ghost?

Nah!

Some more silence. Evvie, always the logician, 'If he could get around, like out in the ocean where Strand's boat was, and yesterday across the street from us, why couldn't he have moved to some other building to live in?'

If there ever was an outrageous conversation, this was it.

Bella decides to answer this question that was constantly puzzling us. 'Because he liked it at the Wassingers. They were nice to him. And besides, they could see him and could talk to him. And furthermore, who else would believe he existed?'

Asked and answered.

I reach for an envelope out of my purse, next to my seat. 'It's a note from Mrs Wassinger. I saw Sadie sneak it into my purse while we were eating breakfast. Evvie, please read it.'

Evvie opens the envelope. She reads,

> *Dear sweet Gladdy and your darling girls.*
>
> *Thank you so much for helping us. Now that you were able to use Papa's clues to solve the case, Papa was free to finally leave this mortal coil. He is on his way up to the pearly gates (at least I hope Peter or Gabriel lets him in; he did have a rather checkered career). We no longer care about the house. We are putting it up for sale and with the money, retiring to Paris. Thanks again. Your devoted friends, Sadie and Louie.*

'Un-be-lievable!' says Sophie.

'All that work for nothing,' says Evvie.

'No check for us in that envelope, I suppose.' Sophie is sulking.

Quiet for a while, thinking, the solved case released Ernest from being earthbound? Who knows? What about our seeing the ghost? Maybe we all saw nothing and thought we saw something. A group optical illusion?

'Okay,' I say, 'when we get home, not one single word about having a ghost for a client.'

Bella, 'But I did . . .'

A swipe at her from Sophie. 'You did not!'

Me speaking again, 'Swear, swear none of you will never, ever, ever mention it. And especially not to Ida. You know how she gets about creepy things.'

Everyone swears.

Bella, 'Not as a ghost story?'

Three voices screech, 'NEVER!'

Quiet for a few minutes, then Sophie, 'I'm thinking about revenge. What we'll do to Hy Binder for putting us on that you hoo tube . . .'

More deep thinking, then:

Sophie, 'You know those teeny, tiny alligators they sell to tourists? We buy one and drop it in his toilet.'

Evvie, 'Spray paint his precious Mazda with skunk juice.'

Bella, 'Steal his ugly bathing trunks off their balcony and cut holes in them.'

Raucous laughter.

And for the rest of the trip, that is the only discussion.

FORTY-EIGHT

A Happy Ending to our Story

B uddha has been quoted as saying 'Three things cannot be hidden: the sun, the moon and the truth.'

But with the return of all groups as well as singles: Gladdy and the girls; Ida; Hy; Jack, Joe and Sol, will put a lie to that statement.

Gladdy and the girls. As told to Ida: 'We had a wonderful experience in Key West. We solved a murder by using our wits and also by good tips from a stranger.' Truth: their ghost will never, never be revealed.

Ida as told to Gladdy and the girls: 'Well, I looked for Hy; never did find him.' Truth: yes, she did. Her raincoat remains hidden literally and figuratively.

Hy and Lola. Lola bought the amnesia story. Because she wanted to believe her husband wouldn't lie to her. Truth: Dolly-Ann and Manny.

Hy to Gladdy and the girls. With Ida standing by: Hy shows up with roses and candy, apologizing for his behavior at the pool. He's taken the photo off the Internet. Ida laughs, he did it because he's guilt-ridden. Apology accepted. Hugs all around. Truth: he owes Ida forever for not betraying him. And her odd raincoat remains a secret.

The guys to Gladdy and Evvie: Jack and Joe extol the joys of the safari and photographing wild animals. A perfect, safe trip. Truth: one fearful night when they forgot to stay downwind of the baboons, the apes ran wild and were truly dangerous. A narrow escape never to be mentioned.

But wait. There's Tessie greeting her dear hubby, Sol, just climbing off the airport bus. 'You want to kiss me? Tell the truth. Did you eat any cockroaches? What are you not telling me? If you did, don't you dare put your mouth near mine!'

'I swear, I didn't,' sobs Sol. Truth: he did.

Home, Sweet Home.

> The human heart has hidden treasures.
> In secret kept, in silence sealed;
> The thoughts, the hopes, the dreams, the pleasures,
> Whose charms were broken if revealed.

Charlotte Bronte

POSTSCRIPT

There exists a notable international Flash Fiction contest. The concept; write the shortest short story you can imagine using only six words. Ernest Hemingway, in his short story collection, *In Our Time*, might have been the first to publish one that became famous. 'For sale. Baby shoes. Never worn.'

However, attribution has been argued through the years. Other possible forerunners were The Algonquin Round Table. *Terse Tales of the Town*, in 1906. A long list of others, going as far back as *Aesop's Fables*.

But I choose to pay *un homage* to Mr Hemingway, by having each of my novel's chapter headings a flash fiction six-word story.